PRAISE FOR THE

I Knew Yo...

"Readers will fall head-over-heels in love with Nate and Faith. Lane's latest is filled with a huge dose of Southern Texas charm."

—*RT Book Reviews*

"First-rate writing and memorable characters prove that sometimes things are worth the trouble as demonstrated by Ms. Lane."

—*Jenerated Reviews*

"A fun, endearing, yet heartbreaking read that kept me eagerly turning pages just waiting to see how everything works out for Faith and Nate."

—*Romance Junkies*

"For those who love a Texan man and some good flirtation, I recommend *I Knew You Were Trouble*."

—*Harlequin Junkie*

Cowboy Take Me Away

"A sexy, charming Southern read."

—*RT Book Reviews*

"Soraya Lane keeps the story going and exciting to the very end."

—*Reader to Reader Review*

"If you like steamy cowboy romances, you'll love this book."

—*Bitten By Love Reviews*

Also by Soraya Lane

I Knew You Were Trouble
Cowboy Take Me Away
The Devil Wears Spurs

Cowboy Stole My Heart

Soraya Lane

St. Martin's Paperbacks

For all my wonderful readers out there—thank you for being on this journey with me.

This is a work of fiction. All of the characters, organizations, and events portrayed in this novel are either products of the author's imagination or are used fictitiously.

COWBOY STOLE MY HEART

Copyright © 2018 by Soraya Lane.

All rights reserved.

For information address St. Martin's Press, 175 Fifth Avenue, New York, NY 10010.

ISBN: 978-1-250-13101-0

Our books may be purchased in bulk for promotional, educational, or business use. Please contact your local bookseller or the Macmillan Corporate and Premium Sales Department at 1-800-221-7945, ext. 5442, or by e-mail at MacmillanSpecialMarkets@macmillan.com.

Printed in the United States of America

St. Martin's Paperbacks edition / January 2018

St. Martin's Paperbacks are published by St. Martin's Press, 175 Fifth Avenue, New York, NY 10010.

10 9 8 7 6 5 4 3 2 1

Chapter 1

SAM MENDES pushed through the crowd, holding his hand high in the air as he waved to the fans he'd spent the last hour talking to. No, make that *three hours*. He'd been booked for a two-hour event, and then he'd spent the rest of the time patiently listening to people tell him about their horses and ask him the same questions he'd been answering almost daily for the past year.

"Sam!"

He cringed and forced himself to turn, dialing a smile. He'd been so close to reaching his car . . .

"I'm Lila," a pretty brunette said, holding out her hand. "You're a hard man to get close to, for all the wrong reasons."

He laughed. "I'm not sure I understand." Was she trying to hit on him?

"I'm from Star PR," she explained. "I watched you get mobbed back there, and if you had someone with you, a publicist for instance, we get to be the bad guy and tell everyone you need to get going." Lila laughed. "It means you'd get home faster, and your fans wouldn't think any less of you."

He nodded. "And here I was thinking you were going to ask me out for a drink."

She passed him a card, her smile fixed, her eyes warm. She was friendly but professional. "Seriously, if you ever want assistance, call me. You're at the stage in your career when you should be thinking about building a team to work with."

Sam nodded and turned around, pushing the card into his pocket, doubtful that he'd ever get around to calling her. He was more interested in scaling back on his commitments, not growing them. His rental car was waiting nearby, and he strode across the concrete to get there. He'd been traveling for a month now, a different event every few days to promote his new book and show horse owners exactly how to put his advice into practice, and he was more than ready to get home. He missed his ranch, his dog, and his horses. Hell, he missed just working on his own with horses, quietly out the back of the King family ranch where he'd first started to realize he had a knack for dealing with equines that any sane person would have given up on.

He ran his fingers through his hair, brushing out the dust that was still lodged there from working in the arena and having horses cantering around him. Sam checked his watch. If he wanted to make his flight he was going to have to drive fast, and there was no way he wanted to hang around the airport waiting for the next flight back to Texas if he missed this one.

He settled into the driver's seat, punched in the GPS so he didn't take a wrong turn on the way there, and plugged his phone in to charge. It'd been turned off since earlier in the day, and he switched it on, seeing he had new messages. He hit voicemail and started to drive, the monotone voice telling him he had three to listen to.

"Hi, Sam, it's Phil again. We're looking at booking another multicity book tour and we need to know if you're interested and when you're available. Call me back."

Sam shook his head. They were like vultures. As soon as his books and training clips had started to do well, everyone had suddenly wanted a piece of him, and although the attention and money had been exciting to start with, he'd soon realized that quietly working long days under the sun was what he liked doing best. He wanted to be working horses, not talking about how to do it. It wasn't that he wasn't grateful; hell, he'd only been able to buy his own ranch because of all the success, but he needed a break. He wanted to plant his boots in the dirt and work with the animals he loved for a while, wearing his favorite jeans and an old shirt, the sun in his eyes, and his only company the horse he was working or the dog trailing around after him.

He hit delete and the next message started to play.

"Hey, Sam, it's me. Just checking you're okay, but I guess now you're famous you don't have to check in with your little sister and your nieces anymore, huh?" He grinned as he listened to Faith. He'd definitely been a crappy brother lately. He'd call her once he'd checked in for his flight. "I drove past and put milk and juice in your fridge, and there's bread and some other stuff on the counter. See you soon."

When he hit delete this time he was still smiling. He needed to spend some time with his sister and those damn gorgeous little twin girls of hers.

"Mr. Mendes, it's Walter Ford here from River Ranch." Sam sat up a little straighter, listening to the man's deep, southern drawl and recognizing the name. "I know you're a busy man, but Nate King speaks highly of you, and I'd like to make you an offer. We need someone here to do some work with our horses, someone with your kind of expertise. There's a stallion here that, frankly, only a man like you should be dealing with. Money's not an object, and I'll have an offer letter waiting for you. But I need to hear from you by tomorrow evening, otherwise I'll find someone else for the job."

Sam pushed play to listen to the message a second time. Walter Ford wanted him to swing past for a visit? He would ordinarily have said no, he didn't do much work on individual ranches anymore for private clients, unless Nate or Chase King needed a hand with an unruly colt or filly, and that was more of a favor, but this had piqued his interest. As an adult he'd never crossed paths with the Ford tycoon, but as a kid? Hell, he'd never forget the day he was playing at the King family ranch, home to his best friend Nate, and Sam's unofficial second home growing up. Walter had pulled up in his big Bentley, the shiny black car catching Sam's eye the moment he'd seen it. Ford had stepped out, with a little girl, but she'd run off to see the ponies and Sam had hung around to gape at the car. He doubted Walter Ford had even noticed he existed back then.

Now the man in question had called him personally, and it made him grin. A couple years earlier, he'd never have imagined a man like Ford dialing his number and needing anything from him. Hell, a few months ago he'd have flatly said no to the job, because he'd been too damn busy building his brand and touring the country sharing his horsemanship techniques. But right now, he wanted to get back to working with horses rather than *talking* about working them, and he was curious about this stallion. Maybe it was the kind of job he needed to take to get some of his passion back.

He'd stop by on his way from the airport, it was only an hour from his ranch and was hardly out of his way. It'd be stupid not to see what Ford had to offer him.

Mia Ford sat with her feet dipped in the pool and stared into the water. She wriggled her toes and watched the perfect blue water ripple in a tiny whirlpool around her, pink toenails like smudges of color as she moved her feet.

The sun was warm on her shoulders and she shut her eyes for a moment, blocking her thoughts, pushing everything away and trying to enjoy the simple feel of the warmth of the day and the light breeze pulsing past her.

She sighed and opened her eyes, replaying her latest disagreement with her father through her mind again. He didn't approve of her most recent equine purchase, and she was terrified he was going to sell her stallion out from underneath her.

She'd fought tooth and nail to buy the horse, refusing to take no for an answer and determined to outbid whoever else was trying to buy him, but she wasn't stupid. Without her father's money she'd never have had the chance to own him, and she hated being indebted to him over something that meant so much to her. Especially when he was still so vocal about his disappointment in her choosing a career she loved over one in a big city law firm since she'd returned home from Europe.

"Hey, Mia."

She turned, smiling when she saw one of her brothers standing behind her, hands shoved into his pockets, cap pulled low over his brow.

"Hey yourself," she said to Tanner, pulling her legs out of the water and standing up.

"Thought I'd better swing by before I left."

She nodded, embracing her brother and laughing when he squeezed her too hard and lifted her clean off her feet. He was tall, well over six feet, and he dwarfed her as she stood in front of him.

"How long are you away for this time?" she asked.

Tanner shrugged, running a hand through his too-long hair when it brushed his eyes. "A month I think. Depends how well I do."

Mia grinned at him. He *always* did well. He'd fast become the state's top bull rider, and she was fairly certain he'd be in the running for being the best in the country if he kept going the way he was. She worried about him a lot, but telling her brother to give up bull riding would be like him telling her to give up horses, so she never bothered to tell him how dangerous it was or how badly she wished he'd choose a different career. Since she'd come home it had been nice spending time with him, and all she cared about was that he was happy.

"Good luck," she said. "Knock 'em dead, and don't come back until you have another big fancy title belt to show me."

Tanner laughed at her and held his hand up in a wave, shielding bright blue eyes from the sun. "I heard the old man talking earlier about someone coming to help out with the horses. He mention it to you?"

Mia slowly shook her head, panic rising. Why would he do that? Why did her father always have to try to micromanage everything in his life, including his daughter? She sucked back a breath.

"Who is it?" she asked.

"That horse whisperer guy, Sam Mendes," Tanner told her. "Something about having him come by the ranch to discuss working here for a bit. I think Dad's convinced that damn stallion's going to kill you, if he doesn't get someone to help with him."

A shiver ran through Mia that had nothing to do with her bare wet legs. *Sam Mendes* was coming to their ranch? She might not have been back home for long, but she'd have to be living under a rock not to know who the famous horse trainer was. "Thanks for the heads up."

She waved to Tanner and then headed back inside her house. She'd built her own place, well away from the main ranch house, and it was the complete opposite of the big house she'd grown up in. Her place was small and ultra-modern, with a flat angled roof and glass engulfing every side. She had views of the ranch from every room, as well as out to her pool, and there was nothing about it she didn't love. Whereas her family home had been filled with period pieces and exquisite, expensive antiques that her father loved, her furniture was minimalist to match her white walls and high ceilings. The house was perfectly matched to her, and some days she found it hard to leave.

Mia changed into tight cream riding breeches and a T-shirt, grabbed her phone, and stopped to give her cat a scratch under the chin. "See you later, little man." She dropped a kiss to his fluffy black head, smiling at his big yawn, eyes still half shut as he put up with her petting. She'd rescued him from an old barn on their ranch only months earlier, and already he was basking in the luxuries of being a house cat.

She ran down the path that led from her home to the stables, looking forward to seeing her horses before finding her father and demanding to know what he'd done, and why exactly he thought she needed the help of Sam

Mendes. It wasn't that she was opposed to spending time with the gorgeous horseman, but she'd have preferred a heads up first.

She slowed to a walk and took her phone from her pocket, searching his name and pulling up his photo on Google. She hardly needed reminding of what he looked like, but it was a good excuse. She remembered him from the time she'd spent at the King family ranch as a girl. He was five, maybe seven years older than Mia, and she'd watched with awe as he'd ridden around the place bareback, always going at a hell of a speed. As a young woman, she'd been one of hundreds of adoring fans at one of his local events when he'd first started out, but their paths had never crossed.

She sighed and put her phone back in her pocket. Working with him one-on-one would be amazing, a dream come true for her professionally, so long as he understood how important the stallion was to her. Her horses were her life, and she wasn't about to let anyone come on to her ranch and tell her that horse was a lost cause. Horse whisperer or not.

Chapter 2

SAM pulled up outside the Ford ranch house and turned off his ignition. He rubbed his chin, the stubble prickly, and he wished he'd gone home first and made the trip out the next day. It'd been a long day and the flight from California had been delayed by an hour.

He stretched when he got out, pushing his door shut and taking a look around. The house was as impressive as he'd imagined it would be, with garages to both sides and a huge oak door that he was making his way towards. The house was big, even by Texas ranch standards, and from the looks of the trees and hedges surrounding the entrance and leading around to a big garden, the Fords had full-time help.

He raised his fist to knock, imagining living in a place as impressive, as he rapped on the solid timber. His house wasn't exactly modest, but he doubted anything in the state rivaled Walter Ford's home.

"You must be Sam."

He lowered his hand and turned. A pretty blonde was standing a few paces away, her hair up in a high ponytail

and dressed in riding attire. The tight breeches fit her like
a glove, and her dusty black riding boots told him she'd
probably already been out riding for the day. She was girl-
next-door gorgeous and then some. Her blue-green eyes
were warm as she stared at him.

"That's me. I'm looking for Walter," he said.

"I'm Mia," she said, stepping forward and holding out
a hand. "Walter's my father."

Sam nodded. So this was probably the little girl he remembered from years ago, except she was all grown up
now; she'd obviously graduated from borrowing ponies
and had horses of her own. He hadn't expected her to be
so cute, not to mention the fact that she actually looked like
she'd been getting her hands dirty instead of relying on
grooms.

"Your father left a message for me. He made it sound
kind of urgent that I come out and take a look at a stallion, as well as working some of the other horses you have
here."

Mia's smile was friendly, hand raised to shield her
eyes from the sun as she watched him. He noticed that her
eyes matched the color of the bluest ocean, her smile reaching all the way to make them sparkle. She was as pretty
as a college cheerleader, but with a maturity in her gaze that
told him she probably wouldn't appreciate the comparison.

"My father thinks everything he wants requires urgent
attention. He doesn't like waiting," she explained dryly.
"I'd really appreciate your help with the stallion, but I'm
not so sure I need help with the rest."

He nodded. "So he's not here to meet with me?"

"He's about as interested in horses as he is in . . ." she
smiled and held out an envelope to him that had his name
scrawled across the top. "I can't even think of anything to

compare it to. He tolerates them because I love them, but he'd prefer to get rid of any animal that isn't at the top of their game and start over. He's more interested in what he calls the *money makers*, so in his eyes only top grade ranch horses are required here."

Sam took the envelope and slid his thumb beneath, gliding it open, curious about Mia and what she had to say. "And you? What do you think?" Walter Ford was serious-kind-of-money wealthy, and Sam knew that men like him had to be ruthless to be so successful. It didn't surprise him that the old man wasn't the sentimental type, but his daughter was obviously cut from a different cloth.

"I think that all animals' lives matter, and I sure as hell don't think you give up on a horse just because they're not behaving perfectly after humans have ruined them. But then what would I know, huh?"

Sam smiled, guessing he'd have disliked her old man anyway, if he'd been there to meet him. He'd straddled two worlds all his life; one as a poor kid trying to look after his sister and protect her against their dad, and the other as the best friend of super-wealthy Nate King, which meant he'd been surrounded by his friend's wealth since he was little. It had opened his eyes and given him perspective, but he never felt comfortable in the world of the rich and famous. He preferred to keep his boots firmly fixed on the ground, no matter how much money he happened to be earning.

He glanced at the letter and realized it was a formal retainer offer. *Two grand a day for however long he needed to be at the ranch, but an expected one month minimum duration.* His eyebrows lifted at the generous sum. It was probably open for negotiation, too, but he wasn't motivated by money on this job. He'd make his decision once he'd seen the animal that needed his help.

Sam glanced at Mia. She was standing still, expectantly, probably waiting for him to say something. He smiled as he gazed past her for a moment at the big, dominating oak trees that flanked the long drive in to the property, wondering if he should have just driven straight back out the way he'd come. He looked back at her.

"He thinks I'll need a month here," Sam said, clearing his throat. "What do you think?"

She shrugged. "I think he doesn't know a thing about how long you'll be needed. I'm the one in charge of my horses, and we can discuss your plan once you've seen what you need to do. Follow me."

Sam did follow her, but he wasn't about to blindly let her tell him what he was doing, or who was in charge. He wasn't used to taking orders when it came to his work, and he wasn't about to start saying "*yes, ma'am*" to her, either. She was hard to read; was she happy he was here to help or not?

"I think we need to establish some ground rules here," Sam said, walking alongside her and noticing how golden the skin on her arms was, as if she spent most of her life outside under the sun. She was pretty in an expensive kind of way, her hair the perfect shade of blonde, her skin flawless and her riding attire impeccable. He doubted she was the horsewoman she liked to think she was. No doubt her father had indulged her, and she didn't do anything other than look pretty and cash in her trust fund checks, but he'd wait and see before making a judgment call. "If I take on this job, and that's a big *if*, then I have to be the one in charge of the horses and what work they need. We work my way or no way, otherwise there's no point in me being here. I don't take orders and I don't get told what to do."

She stopped walking, one hand on her hip as she stared at him. "Sam, my father might have made the call to you, but these are *my* horses. He wouldn't even know one of their names, and I spend every day of my life working with them. If you can't work with me, then you can't work here." He guessed she wasn't one to mince her words. "I'm a big fan of your work, but I need us to be on the same page."

He ran his fingers through his hair, desperate for a shower and ready to walk straight back to his car and get the hell away. Why had he decided to call by anyway? He didn't need the work, and he definitely didn't need to take shit from a woman trying to throw her weight around and tell him how to do his job. It was the one thing he was good at, and he wasn't about to start taking orders.

"How about we take a look at what you've got here, and then we talk, okay?" he suggested, not about to argue with little miss princess and see her get all worked up. He could take a look, politely leave, then leave a message declining Ford's offer. Who the hell did she think she was? "If the stallion's a problem, and it seems like he is, then you probably aren't handling him right. But if you want someone like me to work with him, then you need to step back and not interfere with the process."

Mia looked defiant, hand on her hip still. She might be petite but she was tall—even in her flat riding boots she made a strong impression standing there, chin raised as she stared at him, aqua eyes not missing anything. She might be annoying the hell out of him, but she looked damn gorgeous doing it.

"I was looking forward to working with you, but it sounds like you're not used to having anyone else in your team."

"I don't work in a team. I never have," he replied with a shrug, pushing his fingers through his hair. "I have a method that works, and I don't change it."

She made a noise that sounded like a snort and he tried not to laugh. "You're kidding me, right?"

If she hadn't been so right, he'd have laughed at her, the way she threw that at him. But it was true. He wasn't a team player and he never had been, unless his team involved a four-legged creature instead of another human being. But he didn't need to be a team player to do the work he did.

"Look, I think we've gotten off on the wrong foot," he said. "How about we take a look at the stallion and you can tell me a bit about him." She was beautiful and fiery and he appreciated that in a woman, but this was work, not pleasure and he wanted to set the ground rules.

"Yeah, let's do that," Mia replied, sounding relieved. "The way I see it, there's no point in you working a horse here without me learning from you, so I can put the same practices into place. That's all."

Sam didn't reply, he just walked alongside her and quietly chuckled to himself about a cute, leggy blonde trying to give him a scolding about not being a team player. He'd take a look at her horses, politely give her an excuse about why he wasn't right for the job, then head straight home and never come back. He didn't need her telling him what to do, and he sure as hell didn't need to be a riding coach for Walter Ford's daughter, not even for two thousand dollars a day.

She obviously loved horses and wanted to learn, but Sam wasn't interested in being anyone's babysitter.

Mia glanced at Sam as they walked, amazed at what an asshole he was. How had she crushed on him for so long and not realized what a jerk he would be in real life? Or maybe he wasn't, maybe he was just a guy used to doing his job a certain way and she'd rubbed him the wrong way. Or he was so damn handsome he was used to woman dropping at his feet. But she'd gone from furious with her father for enlisting his services to excited about learning from a man that so many in the horse world were calling a genius. Only it was quickly becoming apparent that he wasn't used to working with anyone other than himself and whatever horse he was focused on.

Or maybe, just like everyone else in her life, he didn't take her seriously. To almost anyone she met, she was the pretty, rich blonde who spent her time playing with horses instead of working a real job, and she hated that. She'd thought Sam would take her seriously, that they'd bond over their mutual love of equines, that she'd be able to talk to him about her horses and learn from him, but it looked like he was no different than anyone else.

"How many horses do you have here?" Sam asked.

She wished he wasn't so damn handsome. His eyes were as brown as the darkest shade of chocolate, his skin so tanned she wondered if he'd ever spent a day inside in his life, and his hair was just a bit too long the way it brushed his ears and dipped close to his eyes when he put his head down. She hadn't been able to ignore how lean he was either, or how at odds that was with the breadth of his shoulders and his height. He was all sinewy muscle under that plaid shirt, she was sure of it, only her fantasies of finding out for herself how he looked without his clothes on were fading. She doubted they'd get that far if they were already at odds within minutes of meeting.

Mia slowed as they reached the stables, smiling at the beautiful horses looking out over the half doors, obviously curious about who was coming to visit.

"I have four of my own, plus the stallion that my father told you about. I keep all mine here, stabled overnight and out during the day unless I'm working them."

He walked closer and so did she, grinning when her favorite mare, Indi, nickered out to her. She was always the most vocal of the group, and Mia never tired of her call. When she'd been working in Europe, it was Indi she'd taken with her to compete. She liked to win, hell, she only competed to win, and Indi was worth her weight in gold.

"You work with the ranch horses too?"

She nodded. "I oversee them all, but we don't keep them up here. I had this purposely built for my horses, with the arena and other facilities I needed. We keep the rest of them turned out closer to the main ranching facilities." Mia gestured to the right, where the main barn was located, the roof just visible. "Our foreman runs the show over there, but I like to check on their health and make sure they're getting well looked after. They're definitely under my watch."

"Impressive place you have here," Sam said, stopping outside Indi's stall and stroking her cheek. Mia couldn't help but notice how relaxed her sometimes highly-strung mare was as Sam touched her, and she wondered if the horse whisperer tag might actually have merit. Although she already knew from watching him at his shows that he was talented, unless half of the horses he worked with had already been trained and it was all an illusion for the crowd and cameras.

"So do you want to see them all or just the stallion?" she asked, watching him, trying to read his expression that had seemed, until now, completely impassive.

"Do you need help with the others?" he asked.

"How much do you know about show jumping?" she

asked wryly. She was used to having top trainers, and she was open to learning anything and everything about her favorite four-legged creatures, but she doubted even Sam Mendes could help with her jump training.

"Ah, and here I was thinking you were a Western rider." His smile hit his eyes, making them soften, and she wished it didn't make her heart skip a bit. It made it a lot harder to hate him. "So you're a show jumper or an aspiring one?"

"Let's be honest, Mr. Mendes. You thought I was a rich girl with a string of expensive horses that I play around with every day instead of working a real job. Trust me, I'm thick skinned, and to be honest I'm kind of used to it by now."

This time she didn't find his chuckle and smile so endearing. "Maybe I thought that." He grinned. "Hell, I'd be lying if I said I didn't still think that."

She glared at him, but she did appreciate his honesty. "Well, you'd be wrong. And no, thank you, I don't need any help with any of these horses right now. And no, I wouldn't classify myself as *aspiring*." She'd been *aspiring* as a teen; now she was a full-fledged show jump rider who made money from riding the show jumping circuit and goddamn winning.

Mia could have slapped his hand away from Indi's nose. She didn't even want the man touching her horse, let alone thinking he could act all superior to her. She'd just finished a successful season in Europe competing against some of the best riders in the world, and she took her reputation as a professional rider as seriously as successful people took their careers, so she wasn't about to let him make her feel inferior. One thing she was not was a pathetic little rich girl living off a trust fund and not working hard.

"He's down here," she grumbled, pushing past Sam and

taking the lead. She shouldn't have expected Sam to know, hell, he probably knew nothing about show jumping, and she'd always been careful to stay under the radar, but being treated like a complete amateur had rubbed her the wrong way.

"You want to grab a halter or something for him?" Sam asked, his voice husky, lower than it had been before.

"I wouldn't bother," she said. "No one can get near that damn horse right now, so the best you'll get today is a look at him, unless you're God himself."

Sam raised an eyebrow but didn't say anything, and she guessed the arrogant horseman probably thought that he'd be able to get near him if he wanted to. She almost hoped the horse would teach him a lesson.

"I doubt even someone as good as you is going to get so much as a rope near this one," she said defiantly as they approached.

Sam leaned on the wooden railings of the fence and stared at the stallion. He was gorgeous. He was the kind of horse that he loved looking at, and given the way he'd rolled his eyes and snorted at them the moment they'd come close to him, he was the kind of horse Sam instinctively knew he wanted to work with. His coat was a rich, mahogany brown, and it gleamed in the sun although covered in a light layer of dust. The white blaze down the front of his face was like a paint splash that extended all the way to the tip of his nose.

This was the type of horse he loved, and this was how he'd started out in the business. He took on horses that no one else could train, and he slowly worked them until he gained their trust, and in time changed their entire temperament toward the people trying to handle them.

"He's a damn fine stallion," he said to Mia, noticing that she was leaning on the fence too, her elbows pressed against the timber.

He hitched his heel on the rail and turned his body to face her, wishing he'd brought his hat as he squinted into the sun.

"You know, I think we need to start over," he said.

She kept staring straight ahead, but he saw the kick of a faint smile. "You think?"

He laughed, knowing he'd probably sounded like a jerk. But he wanted the job now, and up until a few minutes ago, he'd thought he'd be fleeing the scene as soon as he could.

"This stallion, he needs my help."

This time she did turn to face him, folding her arms across her chest. "You're so arrogant that one look at him and you know you're the right person to step in and help him?"

He'd offended her earlier and now she had her back up. He deserved it, but he wasn't exactly sure how to handle the situation. He tried smiling. "Look, there's only one thing in this life that I'm any good at, and it's helping horses that have a crappy outlook on life. I can tell just looking at him that he's too much for you to handle. Look at the arrogant son of a bitch, the way he's holding himself and looking at us."

Her stare became ice cold. "Really? You can tell that just from looking at me, can you? And you have the nerve to say the *horse* is the asshole?"

Sam knew he wasn't helping things, and he had no idea how to dig himself out of the hole he'd dug. "Look, I want to help," he said simply. "You're right, I have no idea what kind of rider or horsewoman you are, but what I do know is that there is a big damn horse, and he either has no respect for people or he's been traumatized. Maybe a little of both." He frowned, considering the horse again before looking back at Mia. "But he's too big to behave like that, and one day soon he'll end up hurting someone, and I'm guessing that someone will be you."

Mia turned away from him again then, something passing over her, something he couldn't put his finger on. At the end of the day, he'd walk away and forget about the stallion if he had to, but something about the horse's eye, the way he'd backed up the moment they'd come near, his defiant stance, spoke to him. Reminded him why he did what he did. He didn't like giving up on horses that needed his help, and he didn't want to give up on this one now that he'd seen him. It wouldn't be so easy to tell Ford no, not now.

"You can't work with me, but you can watch me," he said, knowing he had to offer Mia something.

"Should I be thanking you for your generosity?" she asked, looking less than impressed.

"No, but if you want me to work him, then I need space, and I need to be able to do it my way."

"You don't work alone when you're doing your exhibitions," she pointed out. "I thought you liked teaching people, or is that just part of the act to get us all to come to your shows?"

Sam grinned. So she'd been to one of his shows. "No, but people don't bring me true problem horses to those events. They bring me horses with quirks, horses they already love, and it doesn't take me a lot to iron out those kinks. Or the young horses they bring me to start working with, they're well-loved animals that respond quickly to my training."

She was quiet and he watched her, intrigued when she brushed a tear from her cheek, eyes never leaving the stallion.

"I love him," she muttered quietly, "so don't go thinking he's unloved."

Sam went to say something then shut his mouth. He had no idea what he'd walked into, what kind of issues this horse had or why Mia was so loyal to the animal, but he guessed he'd slowly find out. *If she let him.*

"How long has he been here?" Sam asked, climbing over the railing, his back to Mia now.

"Two months," she said. "He's unpredictable, so don't take your eyes off him."

"Why him? Why did you buy him?"

She didn't answer and he decided not to repeat the question.

"I should have bought Tex and had him put to sleep the day he arrived," she said, her voice so low that he only just heard it. "But I didn't, and I can't."

Sam didn't need to know any more. The stallion could tell him the rest.

He watched this Tex move, entranced by the noble, arrogant way he held his head and lifted his hooves. When he stopped he snorted, pawing at the ground, his hoof thumping against the hard-packed dirt as he stared Sam down. And then he charged at him. Out of nowhere, with no warning, he aggressively galloped towards him.

"Whoa!" Sam commanded, standing his ground, staring the horse in the eye and moving towards him. He wasn't about to start with the stallion thinking he had the upper hand, but it did strike him that perhaps his first move should have been a quick leap over the fence.

Sam moved smoothly out of his way, careful with each

footfall, not blinking as he watched the stallion. He was in his space, and the horse wanted him out, that much was clear. His dark coat gleamed in the sunshine, his four perfect white stockings stretching up his legs to the knee, white blaze high as he defiantly held his head up.

He stayed out of his way, still staring at him, but not ready to challenge the stallion head-on yet. He would respect his space and figure out how to get through to him another day, right now he just didn't want the horse to think he'd scared him.

"He is an asshole," Mia muttered, looking worried as Sam hauled himself down from the fence. "I shouldn't have argued with you about that before."

"The problem isn't that he's an asshole, it's what made him think that he should hate the world. Horses aren't born mean," he said, brushing his hands down his jeans.

"I know."

He stared at her. "So either you tell me why he's hardwired this way, or I figure it out myself, but either way I'm signing that contract and I'll see you here on Monday morning."

She looked surprised. "You're actually going to take the job?"

"Unless you're interviewing other candidates?"

She scowled at him, clearly not appreciating the joke.

"I'll see you two days from now, then," she said.

Sam didn't wait for her to walk him out. Instead he held up his hand in a wave and headed back for his car on his own. He'd take the letter home with him, sign it, then make his way back after the weekend. Right now he needed to get home, take a hot shower, then fall into bed.

He smiled, thinking about the look on Mia's face. She was beautiful and headstrong, and he liked that in a woman. Except he hadn't been in the market for almost a year and he wasn't about to be now. He wouldn't have made a play for Walter Ford's daughter anyway. Besides the fact that he didn't do relationships, he didn't mix business with pleasure, and he doubted she'd be the kind interested in casual sex.

He laughed as he drove down the drive and headed for home. He also doubted that she'd ever be remotely interested in him. Mia had been glaring at him like she'd rather murder him than sleep with him, but damn, that perfect pout of hers and the arrogant way she'd flicked her ponytail over her shoulder . . . Sam gritted his teeth. He didn't need any complications in his life right now, and no matter how much other people in his life would like him to forget the past and move on, he wasn't ready. Not when it came to women.

Chapter 3

"YOU need to stop laughing at me!"

Mia glared at her friend, refusing to laugh along with her. They were sitting outside, enjoying the warm air now that the sun had gone down and dusk was settling around them. The pool twinkled as light reflected on it, the darkened fields of the ranch slowly disappearing as night blanketed the sky. Mia reached for the half empty bottle of wine and offered Kat more before pouring her own glass.

"He can't be that bad. You're just exaggerating because he stepped on your toes." Kat ran her hands through long dark hair, scooping it up and twisting it away from her neck.

Mia shook her head. "No, he did more than step on my toes. He made me feel worthless."

"Honey, there are hundreds of women out there who'd like Sam Mendes to make them feel *worthless*."

Kat burst into giggles again, laughing at her own joke, and Mia fought the urge to strangle her. Her friend hadn't seen how goddamn cocky the man had been, but then she couldn't exactly disagree. *She'd* been one of those women until today, harboring a crush on the hot Texas bachelor.

"Just because he's handsome doesn't mean I have to like him."

"So you've noticed? How *handsome* he is, I mean."

"Why am I friends with you?" Mia glared at her, not about to admit how much she'd thought about him since the one time she'd watched him in the past, before she'd met him. Those dark eyes and honey-laced drawl at his exhibitions had been enough to make her fall for him back then, but not now. "Honestly, I'm not sharing my wine or my pool with you again if you keep sticking up for him." She wished Kat was wrong, but she was so, so right. She sighed. It had only been a couple of months since she'd returned from overseas, and it was nice to just sit and be with a friend, someone she'd known all her life and who knew her well enough to tease. Even if she was driving her crazy right now. The two closest people to her in her life were Kat and her sister, but with Angelina working up a storm as an attorney in California, it wasn't like they had much time to talk, let alone hang out in person.

"Come on, I'm only teasing. And besides, if he gets through to the horse, then isn't this as much about Kimberley as anyone?"

Kat was right. Mia took a slow, tiny sip of her drink as she stared at the pool shimmering under the lights. She missed Kimberley so much. They'd always promised one another that they'd never let their favorite horse be sold if anything ever happened to them. Only neither of them had ever truly expected anything terrible to happen, and yet here she was with her own favorite horse, Indi, safely stabled for the night, and her best friend Kimberley's stallion behaving like a madman out in the field.

"I miss her so much," Mia confessed, not bothering to fight the tears that began to pool in her eyes as they talked about the friend they'd lost.

"I know, so do I."

They sat in silence a while, the mood between them oddly somber where earlier it had been playful. The three had been best friends since elementary school, and Kimberley's death had been hard.

"So you think I need to give him a chance, is that what you're saying?" Mia asked.

"I don't know why you were so prickly in the first place," Kat said. "Sorry, but it's true."

Mia loved Kat because she was always brutally honest with her. She was a straight shooter and she didn't sugar-coat her words.

"Even if he shuts me out and won't let me deal with my own horse?"

"If it helps the horse, then yeah. Don't you want help getting through to him?"

Mia thought about it for a moment. "Fine, I'll stay out of his way and keep my mouth shut."

Kat gave her a wicked grin. "You know," she said, drawing the words out slowly, "it has been a *long* time since you dated."

"Oh my god, are you kidding me?" Mia pushed her, wondering if she should push harder and shove her in the pool. "I do *not* want to discuss my love life right now." Especially in the same breath as talking about Sam. She wasn't going to let herself think about him like that, not ever again. "Besides, you have no idea who I've been sleeping with. I could have some hot cowboy in my bed waiting for me right now. Maybe I've told him to stay quiet while you're here?"

Kat laughed. "Yeah, but you *so* don't. Maybe you should lighten up a little and bat those pretty little lashes at the horseman next time he's here."

Mia could have killed her, but instead she took a big sip of wine and got up to put some music on, padding across the concrete. She had homemade pizza in the oven, another bottle of sauvignon blanc chilling in the fridge, and her pretty fairy lights were twinkling all around the outside of the house and down to the pool. It was a beautiful night and she wasn't about to ruin it by getting all grumpy about Sam arriving on Monday morning.

No matter what Kat had just said, she wasn't going to let him take over the one thing she was good at. She'd been in charge of all the horses on this property since her eighteenth birthday, when she'd proven herself to her father and both her brothers, Tanner and Cody, that she knew what she was doing. As far as she was concerned, it was going to stay that way, even if it did mean having to beg Sam to let her learn from him and be part of whatever training he had in mind.

Tex was a handful, he always had been, but when he'd been Kimberley's horse, he hadn't hated every single human he laid eyes on. It wouldn't be so bad if she didn't blame herself for the angry, unpredictable beast he'd turned into.

"I shouldn't have laughed at you," Kat said, surprising her. Mia hadn't realized she'd gotten up, or that she was standing so close.

"Don't be silly. I can handle it." Mia walked inside and checked the pizza. She decided it was ready and took it out, pleased with her culinary efforts for the evening.

"You know, if this guy can't get through to Tex, then no one would blame you for . . ."

"I'm not giving up on that horse, Kat. Not now, not ever." She owed it to Kimberley to look after him, and she would find a way to get through to the difficult horse even if it took her years. "When I received that phone call when I was away, that he'd finally been found, it felt like a reason to come home. I want to give him a real chance."

"Well, let's get another bottle of wine, stop talking horses, and eat that pizza. I'm starving."

Mia grabbed her friend and gave her a big hug, holding her tight. "Thank you."

"For what?" Kat mumbled against her.

"For not giving up on me even when I'm a pain in the ass."

They both laughed and Mia finally let her go. Things had been rough for a long while now, but she'd always had Kat to make her laugh and get her through the hard times, and she wouldn't have survived without her friend by her side.

"Just promise me that if he hits on you, you won't go all mean girl on him again."

"Kat!" Mia yelled, sliding the pizza expertly onto a plate before she followed her friend out the door.

Kat was holding the bottle of wine she'd retrieved from the fridge and sporting a smile so innocent it was ridiculous.

"I'm just saying. He's a handsome guy and you're a gorgeous girl. Sometimes . . ."

"I know how the world works, Kat. I don't need the birds and the bees talk, okay?" She grinned. "Right now I think he hates me, but I promise, if he deals with Tex *then* tries to rip my clothes off and take me to his bed, I won't say no."

Kat giggled, and Mia felt like they were teenagers talking about a crush all over again.

"See, it wasn't that hard to admit he was hot, was it?"

Mia groaned. "Seriously, tell me why you're my friend again?"

Sam had his arm slung around his dog as he turned into the River Ranch driveway for the second time. The big, dominant trees waving their limbs above the extravagantly wide driveway still caught his eye, and he admired the pristine timber fences and perfectly mown grass. It was one hell of an entrance.

Earlier in the day, when he'd been sitting out on his porch watching the sun come up, sipping his coffee before going down to the horses to feed out, he'd wondered what the hell he'd agreed to. But something about the stallion had stuck with him, something he couldn't shrug away, and there'd been a look in Mia Ford's eyes that told him the horse was special. He'd probably been a jerk to her, but he'd met her type a hundred times over, except for the getting her hands dirty part, although he hadn't actually seen her do that yet. It wasn't that he was jealous of the money she'd grown up with—his best friend had his boots firmly planted on the ground, and his family was worth a fortune—but then his friend had forged his own way in the world. He doubted Mia had ever gone a week without using daddy's credit card.

"We're here," Sam muttered to his pooch, raising his eyebrows as he looked at Blue. They'd been glued at the hip since he'd arrived back, and his dog had taken the seat beside him and ridden shotgun the entire way. "How the hell am I so damn good at training horses, but I can't ever get you trained to sit in the back?"

He scratched Blue's head and then signaled for the dog to wait in the vehicle. He received a whine in response, but the dog did lie down, head on his paws, looking woefully unimpressed.

"I won't be long. Let me see if you're allowed out first, huh?"

Sam crossed the gravel forecourt outside the stable complex and looked around for Mia. She'd said the horses were her domain, but he didn't see her. He walked over to the stables and smiled when three sets of noses poked out over the wooden half-doors, checking out the stranger. It was one thing he loved about horses, how innately curious they were, and how settled they always seemed to be in his company for some strange reason. Around the stables was immaculate, freshly swept and free of anything out of place. He wondered if Mia kept the place herself, or whether she was just a fussy boss to a poor ranch worker.

He spoke softly to the horses under his breath as he passed and kept walking, out the back, towards where he'd met the stallion the day before. And then he saw her.

Sam moved a little closer to the arena, not wanting to disturb her, but it was obvious it was Mia. Her blonde hair was in a long plait that hung in a straight line down her back, a black velvet helmet shielding her face from him. She was as elegant in the saddle as she was on the ground, and he admired her straight posture and steady hands. He smiled. It was time to see her in action.

He leaned on the fence as she cantered around, moving fast around the arena. Her horse was stunning, and he recognized it as the mare she'd been giving attention to the other day. The horse was unusual looking, with a pure white mane and tail and a warm, rich brown coat. Aside from a tiny star on her forehead, she had no other markings that he could see.

Mia had a course of show jumps set up around the

arena, and he was impressed at the height of them. He'd never jumped himself, other than the odd fallen log or fence in his way when he'd been younger and working on ranches, but he knew good style when he saw it.

The horse was compact and much smaller than many of the show jumpers he'd seen before, but her ears pricked and her speed accelerated the moment Mia pointed her toward the jump. He watched as they soared over it, not missing a beat and heading toward the next. He liked the way she rode, was impressed with how soft she was with her hands, not yanking the horse around the course but working with her, using her legs as aides, her straight back showing how confident she was. But he could see they'd started to travel too fast, and the mare had knocked the last two rails of the bigger fences.

Sam ducked through the low timber fence and moved closer to the center of the big arena, never taking his eyes off the duo. The mare glanced at him, but she was loving her work. He could tell that she was a natural and loved jumping as much as her rider seemed to. He wondered who'd planned the arena and surroundings out—it was slightly elevated and it gave an impressive view of the sprawling ranch, endless acres of fields dotted with trees as far as the eyes could see.

"You're letting her get away on you," Sam called out, focused on Mia now. "I love that you're gentle, but you need to be more firm with her when she pulls like that. Sit up tall and force her to go deeper into the fence before taking off."

He didn't know if Mia heard him because she never acknowledged him, but he saw that she did ride more aggressively into the next fence and they soared over it. Sam grimaced when they went too fast into the next one though and took a rail. He walked over to collect it and place it back on top, impressed with how perfectly the striped poles had been painted, all red and white like candy canes.

Mia had slowed now, her canter turning into a trot, and he watched as she let the reins slide through her fingers until she was only holding the buckle, before transitioning into a walk. He'd expected a smile, but she looked fierce, and not in a good way.

"She's a beautiful horse," Sam called out, wanting to break the ice. He'd been tired and ready to get home the first time he'd met her, and this time he was hoping things wouldn't be so tense between them.

"I didn't realize you were a show jumping coach," she said dryly, riding over to him and halting beside him. She dropped her reins and dismounted, landing beside him with a soft thud.

"I'm not," he admitted. "But sometime it's a hell of a lot easier to see the problems on the ground than it is when you're the one in the saddle."

"Is that right?" she asked, still looking frosty. "Because until you showed up we hadn't taken a pole, and I'm not exactly an amateur."

He shrugged, wondering if he was supposed to know of her show jumping reputation. The truth was, he only followed rodeo and Western riding, which meant he knew very little about her area of interest. "I was only trying to help. The truth is that you'll never get her clearing fences any higher unless you tweak the way you're riding her."

Mia glared at him. "Are you serious? We've jumped bigger than this before and won." She paused, but he could tell she wanted to say something else. "In fact, we *regularly* win over bigger fences than this. I ride to beat the competition and that's exactly what we do."

He hadn't meant to annoy her, but somehow she looked more pissed than she had when she'd first met him.

"I'm guessing you compete then?" he asked, taking the reins over the horse's head and holding them for her. She snatched them off him, holding her own horse, and he stepped back to give her some space. "Have you been . . ."

"Yes, I compete. I thought that was obvious," she said. "And Indi is my best horse. She might be little but she has a big heart and she never lets me down. We've actually just returned from a season in Europe and I have a career as a show jump rider, Sam, so if you're wondering why you're managing to annoy me so much treating me like a beginner, that's why. I compete all show jumping season, and when I'm not competing I'm here training."

Sam nodded. "Got it." He should have done some research about his new boss.

"Any other expert comments?" she asked dryly.

"My suggestion was about tweaking the way you ride her, not changing anything dramatic," Sam said, impressed now that he knew she was obviously good, and serious, about her riding. "She has a lot of guts, but you're relying on that instead of riding her into the jumps. I bet you ride her differently than you do your others, and I don't have to know anything about show jumping to help you ride your horse better. My job is to improve the relationship between horse and human, period."

She looked at him, her anger seeming to slide away and be replaced with something less fiery. "Maybe I do. I'm not sure."

"My guess is that you *ride* them more instead of just trusting them, and with this horse? It's a fine line between you telling her what to do, without interfering with her natural ability."

She stared at him, and he wondered what the hell she was about to say, she had such a serious look on her face.

"Maybe you can watch me ride again later then," she said, clucking to Indi as she started to walk off. "So long as you don't try to tell me how to ride a goddamn jump again."

Sam followed alongside her, falling into an easy pace and trying not to laugh. "I don't make a habit of apologizing, but I think I judged you too harshly the other day. You're a damn good rider, so don't go taking my tips as criticism." He was fast realizing he'd underestimated her actual riding talent, and her personality.

Mia stopped walking and he glanced at her. The horse halted beside her.

"Too quick to judge a book by its cover, right?" she asked, looking smug, or maybe she was just surprised by his words and felt the need to say something smart to avoid showing her embarrassment. He didn't care either way.

"I give praise where it's due, that's all. You did good out there, and yeah, maybe I was a bit hasty in my judgment."

She nodded. "You'd think I'd be used to it by now, but I'm not."

"We all get judged, it's part of life."

She sighed, audibly, and he stood back so she could walk Indi into her stall and take her gear off.

"Can you imagine working your ass off all your life to prove yourself, and then all you hear is negative crap about how you'd never have gotten where you were without help from your father?"

He shrugged. "No, but I do know what it's like to be judged because of who your daddy is. Mine was an alcoholic asshole who failed miserably to look after us when our mama ran away. It's fair to say he did a really crappy job of it, and I'm damn lucky I didn't end up tarred by the same brush." Sam paused, wondering if he should say more and deciding not to. His father was gone now, but he still felt the need to work extra hard to prove that he was nothing like the man who'd raised him.

"Ah, so maybe we do have something in common."

He liked the sound of her laughter, and how much softer her voice had become. "Tell me, it can't be all that bad. Living here, having all this. Is it worth being pissed at the world for judging you on this one?"

Mia looked at him over the half-door of the stable, her blue-green eyes meeting his. "Yeah, it is. Because, aside from my first horse and that stallion you've come to work, I've bought all my show jumpers myself, from my own prize money, and I paid my own damn flights to Europe and worked hard to keep myself over there. I fund my own team of horses, I always have, and I don't even have a groom so I never have to ask anyone for money. I work as hard as anyone out there on the show jumping circuit, but it doesn't seem to count for anything. Sometimes I wonder why I've always been so stubborn, since people's opinions of me have never changed. Maybe I should just cash in my trust fund checks?"

Sam was quickly starting to comprehend how wrong he'd been about little miss rich girl in more ways than one, and he liked this side of her. Sure, she was mouthy and quick to judge, but then so had he been, and he appreciated a straight shooter. Maybe they'd both judged one another all wrong.

"No, that's not right," he said. "Because you know, and it's you who matters."

He listened to her sigh and then looked in, curious about what she was doing. He watched as she brushed her horse down, using a soft body brush over the mare's sleek dark coat, bending low to follow the grooves of her legs. Sam followed her movements then glanced up, noticed the soft curve of her butt in her skin-tight breeches.

"So what's our plan with the stallion today?" Mia asked, and Sam stepped back, folding his arms and leaning against the outside wall.

"Well, *my* plan is to not have a plan," he said. "I feel my way as I go, and I have no idea how long it'll take to crack this one."

Mia had let herself out of the stable, and she looked distracted, her eyebrows drawn together as she stared past him.

"What's that noise?"

He listened to the howling before grinning. "Oh, that's my dog. Blue," he said. "I'd say he's not so happy that I left him in the truck."

"You were worried I wouldn't let you have your dog out? On a ranch?" she laughed. "Funny, you don't strike me as the type to ask first."

"What does that mean?" he asked, arms folded as he watched her.

"It means that you're probably used to doing what you like and asking questions *after.*"

"You're now an expert in human behavior?" he asked, trying not to laugh at her.

"Hey, sometimes it's easy to see faults from standing down here than up there," she said, repeating his own words back to him and putting the brush in her hand back in the box before walking off.

He'd give her that one. She was fiery all right, and he was starting to think the job here might be more interesting than he'd thought.

"Where are you going?" he asked.

"To get your poor dog out of there before he dies from lack of oxygen."

Sam didn't bother to tell her that he'd left both windows down for air to get through, because he was fairly certain she was trying to rub him up the wrong way just for the hell of it. And she was doing a damn fine job of it, only he was also certain that she'd have no idea how much he was enjoying it. It'd been a long time since anyone had been outright rude to him or spoken their mind. It was one of the things that frustrated him the most right now about his career. He didn't want to be surrounded by *yes* people so often, people who liked to stroke egos and make others feel more important than they were. He liked real, and he liked sassy, and there was one particular little cowgirl who was trying very hard to get on his nerves, and was doing the exact opposite right now.

He glared at his dog when he saw him leaning into Mia, gazing up at her as if she was the love of his life. She was making such a fuss of him the dog was as good as mesmerized. Sam whistled and saw Blue's ears prick, but he didn't move, loving the attention too much to bother listening to his master.

"Damn traitor," Sam muttered, half laughing and deciding to head down to the stallion on his own.

He had to admit, being petted by Mia wouldn't exactly be torture, but he still expected more loyalty from the dog. He'd rescued him from the side of the road, chained up, skinny as a bag of bones and with the biggest brown eyes Sam had ever seen. He'd been working a new job and driven past the dog maybe half a dozen times, and on the day he finished up on the ranch, a two-hour drive from his home, he'd pulled over, broken the malnourished dog free, and taken him with him. And the pooch had been by his side almost every day since.

A wet nose touched his hand and Sam looked down, wanting to growl at the dog for his disloyalty but giving him a pat on the head instead. He had his tongue lolling out, big grin on his face like he was the happiest damn dog in the world.

"Hey, wait up!" Mia called out.

"Not my fault you're too slow to keep up," he shot back.

"Oh, I'm sorry, I was only trying to rescue *your* dog!"

Sam chuckled. "And I'm here to do a job. Keep up if you can."

He strode ahead, not slowing for her, and when he stopped outside the stallion's pasture he turned and noticed Mia, red-faced and breathing hard from running after him. He smiled when she blew a stray piece of hair from her face, the escaped tendrils wisping around her cheeks.

"What are you going to do first?" Mia asked.

"First?" Sam repeated, elbows to the timber, leaning low and meeting her gaze when he looked sideways at her. "*First* you're going to tell me what the hell happened to this stallion, and how in god's name you ended up with him."

Chapter 4

MIA gulped. She'd played that day over and over in her mind so often, but actually talking about it was something else entirely. She smiled at Sam, trying not to let her feelings show, putting on the brave face she'd perfected over the years. She almost hoped their foreman, Stretch, would come over and interrupt them, or one of the other ranch hands, but when she did a quick glance around, there was no one. Even her father would have been preferable to having this particular discussion with Sam.

"See how you go with him today. We can talk more once you've spent time with him," she said.

Sam frowned, his eyes still trained on her even though she was looking straight ahead at the horse now.

"It's a simple question, Mia," he said, in a slow voice as if he were speaking to a child. "How did he end up here? What's happened to him?"

She gritted her teeth, steeled her jaw, not ready to talk to a man she hardly knew about what had happened to the stallion grazing in the field nearby. Tex hadn't bothered to acknowledge them yet, but she knew he would soon, and when he did it wouldn't be pretty.

"You don't think much of me, do you?" she asked in a low voice. "Why can't I have just decided to buy a temperamental stallion to train as a show jumper?"

Sam laughed, but his face sobered instantly when he saw the serious look on hers as she turned to face him. Her eyes were glistening, she knew it, but she sure as hell wasn't about to cry. Instead she turned to look out left, staring hard at a mob of Black Angus cattle and slowly trying to count them—anything to take her mind off what she was hiding from Sam.

"I can't not like you, I hardly know you," he said. "So I don't think lowly of you, that's silly to say."

"No, you made a judgment call on me the moment you met me, and that call hasn't changed," she argued, turning back to him and hating that she was being so defensive. She couldn't help it—when it came to Tex and the past, it just hurt too damn bad to go back. "Just work the horse, would you?"

He stood straighter then, and she did the same, unimpressed by how much smaller than Sam she felt when he was pulled up to his full height. His arms folded across his chest, eyes on her, staring at her and making her stare right back at him, so she didn't feel like she was backing down. She hated bickering with him, but something about him rubbed her the wrong way.

"Fine, when I first came here I picked you as some pathetic socialite who liked to play around with horses." Sam was like a statue before her. "But I saw you ride today and I thought, hell, there's a girl with some goddamn talent. You're good in the saddle, and you rode those big fences boldly."

She swallowed. Hard. She hadn't been fishing for compliments, had just wanted to get everything out in the open rather than simmer over things that hadn't been said.

"You don't need to say that," she said, dragging her eyes from him and scuffing her boots into the dirt. She dropped to pet his dog, stroking his fur and smiling down at him before glancing back up at Sam. "I just need for you to take me seriously. This horse is important to me, and I want you to work your magic on him. Can we just leave it at that?"

He nodded, rubbing his hand across his chin. "Look, I came here thinking I was going to be working alone. I was intrigued about the stallion, and I still am, but just the way he behaved the other day? That tells me he's been through some trauma, and if that involved a rider or abuse or whatever the hell it was, I need to know to keep me and him safe."

She stood and stared out at Tex. "You know," she said after a long pause, "he was named Tex because he had an ego as big as Texas, right from the moment he was a foal. He was never easy."

Sam moved closer to her and they stood side by side, surveying the big horse who was still grazing, as if oblivious to them, head dipped low. But she could see that one of his ears had turned out slightly, that he was listening to them for sure.

"You've known him that long then?" Sam asked.

She nodded. "A long time. Only he wasn't always this much of an asshole."

"Yeah, well, stallions can either turn out like big teddy bears or arrogant sons of bitches. No different than a bull or any other male full of too much testosterone and not enough manners. And they're no different than humans, either. You can't just change a personality, but you can work on changing attitude."

Mia hoped so, for her sake and for Tex's. She knew Sam's reputation, hell, she'd seen him work firsthand, but what if he wasn't the right person to be working Tex? What if he was just a really good showman who'd managed to do well in front of the camera and crowds? She didn't know how much longer she could keep Tex if she couldn't get through to him, and he was too dangerous for her to even attempt to handle. She made a mental note to go visit her father later on—she needed to make sure he wasn't planning anything without talking to her first.

"We only have a month," she told Sam. "Maybe a little longer if I beg, but he put one of the ranchers in the hospital last week, that's why my daddy called you."

Sam didn't react, just spoke in his soft drawl. "What happened?"

"We were trying to move him, and he's become pretty territorial," Mia explained. "He lashed out, after appearing fairly placid to start with, and I got over the fence but Cal didn't. He was kicked in the hip and I only just managed to help him out before he got kicked again. He's in hospital now and my father's footing the bill, so he's less than impressed."

Sam rubbed his chin again and Mia realized he did that whenever he was chewing something over. "You told me you purchase all your own horses," he said. "But not this one?"

She shook her head. "Not this one. I couldn't afford him."

"Why?"

Mia didn't want to admit how much she'd paid for him, or how much it had cost to truck him here, or anything else much about how she'd ended up with him. "He meant something to me. The price was too high, and I begged my father to buy him for me. I know, it makes me sound like a silly little girl with a heart set on a horse she couldn't handle."

"Well, yeah, it does," Sam said. "And you're right about him being too much for you to handle."

"Thanks," she said dryly. "Great way to boost my ego."

His expression was hard to read. "For the record, I don't think you're a woman with bad taste in horses, but this guy? He's too hot for most riders to handle, so don't go taking that as a cheap shot at your ability. I'm just calling the situation as I see it."

Every time she was pissed at him, he managed to make her feel stupid for flying off the rails at him. Of course Tex was too much horse for her, it wasn't exactly rocket science to figure that out. She hoped that would be the end to their stupid back-and-forth arguing; it wasn't like her to be so petty.

"So what do you want to do?" she asked.

"What I want is to move him into a round pen," Sam said, looking around. She watched as he held his hand up, shielding his eyes. "That's it over there?"

She nodded, looking from the pen in the distance and back again. "I don't like our chances."

Sam climbed up onto the railing and stared at Tex. He'd made it clear that he'd seen them now, and he pawed the ground, shaking his head and staring them down.

"How aggressive is he once you're with him?" Sam asked. "For instance, if I had a halter and rope on, would he lead?"

She shook her head. "I think he's past behaving properly. He's pretty wild these days."

Sam sat on the fence, and she considered him, wondering who he was and what he was all about. She got the feeling that he hadn't grown up wealthy at all, he was too grounded, too . . . she didn't know what. But it was a feeling she'd had since she met him, that he wasn't like other guys she'd met. The only thing that didn't fit was how at ease he'd been when he'd first arrived, not at all overawed by her family's ranch, which was unusual for someone who hadn't grown up with money. The massive house and sprawling gardens was usually enough to make a person's jaw drop. She knew that from years of having people fawn over her, thinking she was important, wanting to be with her and part of the lifestyle they seemed to associate with her. Only she wasn't special. Her riding made her special, because it was something she trained hard to be good at, but she knew firsthand that money didn't buy happiness, only privilege.

"What about this," Sam said, moving back down to stand beside her. "We get in there and make a space with temporary fencing. That way I don't have to move him until I have his trust, which is safer for everyone involved, and I can make a makeshift kind of ring."

Mia was the one raising her eyebrows this time. "*We?*" she asked. "I thought you worked solo?"

He chuckled. "Maybe I need to be more open to change. You can watch, but I don't want you in there distracting me or him."

She doubted she was capable of being much of a distraction. Sam hadn't shown the least bit of interest in her, and the horse would be far more intent on killing Sam than bothering with her. She was fairly certain about that.

"Do you think you'll be able to crack him within a month?" she asked, terrified of her father deciding to follow through with his threat and have the horse shot if he was still a menace to society by then.

"I don't know," Sam replied. "I've never worked a horse that I couldn't form a relationship with pretty quickly, and if I'm honest? It's because of him that I'm standing here. I don't do private work like this anymore because I don't need to, but something about him spoke to me. I think I'll learn as much from him as he will from me."

"You talking about the beast?"

Mia spun around at the deep voice. "Geez, Stretch, I just about jumped out of my skin!"

She grinned at their foreman as he tipped his hat at her, his wicked smile cracking her up as it stretched his tanned, weathered face wide. Her father was beside him, and she gave her daddy a smile, too. It wasn't often he bothered to venture down to the horses.

"Just the man I was looking for!" he boomed as he locked eyes on Sam.

Mia traded glances with Stretch as her father hooked his thumbs into his belt loops, his big Stetson firmly on his head as he strode toward Sam. She wondered if he'd feign an interest in her horses for Sam's benefit.

"Good to finally meet you. I'm Walter." She watched as her father shook hands with Sam, only just shorter than the horse whisperer he was greeting. Even she had to admit that her dad was still handsome, and the way he stood, shoulders straight and head always held high, meant no one would ever have guessed he was knocking sixty five.

"Walter, it's nice to put a face to the name."

"Hi, Daddy," Mia said, leaning in to kiss his cheek

when he came closer to her. She loved him to bits, she just hated that he treated her like his little girl so often just because she was the baby of the family. He seemed to forget she was twenty eight.

"What do you think?" Walter asked. "If it was my decision we'd have put him to sleep by now and put us and him out of our misery, but it's hard to say no after everything that happened. Did Mia tell you he killed his last rider?"

She went ice cold, goose pimples tracking across her skin. If she could have dug herself a hole and crawled inside, she'd have done it. She caught Stretch's eye and he raised an eyebrow. The old rancher had known her all her life, and he seemed to gauge her reactions a whole lot better than her father did.

"Daddy, why don't you leave us with the horses?" Mia suggested, clearing her throat. "Sam was just about to get started and . . ."

But Sam wasn't looking at her father now. He was staring, eyes like ice, at her.

"He did what?" Sam asked quietly.

Walter looked between them. "It's hardly a great secret, it was all over the news a few years back. Surely you remember! Mia's been tracking him down ever since, haven't you, Mia?" He laughed. "When this one makes her mind up, there's no stopping her."

Mia swallowed, rocks in her throat, before nodding. "Daddy, I'll come find you later on. How about you let us get on with our work here?"

"I can tell when I'm not wanted, so I'll leave you both to it. We're off to take a look at some new stud bulls that Stretch wants me to write a check for." He reached out his hand and shook Sam's again. "Mia's been looking forward to working with you, Sam. You've got quite the reputation around these parts it seems. Join me for a whiskey later on your way out if you have time."

Mia went through the motions, saying goodbye to her father, watching him go, looking back at Sam. He was still like a statue; immobile and glaring at her. If looks could kill, she'd be long dead. Mia took a deep breath and filled her lungs.

"And you were going to tell me about him killing his last rider *when* exactly?" he asked, his voice deeper than before.

"I didn't want you to . . ." she started before he interrupted her.

"Get the hell out of my sight," he growled. "You want me to work with him and see if there's any coming back from the horse he's become? Then you start telling me the goddamn truth when I ask for it."

Mia nodded. He was right, she should have told him. But it wasn't easy reciting what had happened, not to a stranger.

"Do you still want help constructing the makeshift pen?" she asked.

"No," he ground out. "Will I find what I need in the barn over there?"

"You will. Everything you need is there, and if not, you can radio one of the ranch hands from in there," she told him. "Just tell them you're here working with me, and they'll get you whatever you want."

He stormed off, his dog leaping up and running after him.

"Sam," Mia called out, cringing, wondering if she should have just let him go without saying anything. "I'm sorry. I should have told you."

He was walking backwards now, slowly, face like thunder. "Was he nasty as hell when he killed the rider, or was it an accident? At least tell me that."

She took a deep breath, fisting her hands so hard her nails dug into her palms. "It was an accident. He was nothing like this then."

He nodded. "I'll work with him for today, see how it goes, then I'm coming to find you," he said. "If you don't tell me the truth about this horse then? About what happened to him and whatever the hell is going on with him? Then tomorrow is it. No amount of money is going to entice me to work this horse without knowing the full story, for his sake and mine."

Mia let him go then, didn't bother responding. She needed some time alone to clear her head, to figure out how she was going to talk about something that had traumatized her so badly she'd wondered how she'd survive and taken the life of her best friend. She watched as Sam became smaller in her vision, his broad shoulders fading away as he strode off. She wished she'd been nicer to him, but then he hadn't exactly been charming himself.

Some things weren't supposed to be relived, but Sam was right. He couldn't work Tex without knowing everything, and she couldn't expect him to.

What she needed was to go for a long, relaxing ride around the ranch to gather her thoughts. *Without* Sam. And then figure out how to tell him he story that needed to be told. She needed to breathe in the pure, fresh country air, feel the strength of her horse beneath her and get lost in the endless acres of grass that stretched on for miles. Or maybe she needed to roll her sleeves up and get dirty, helping out the ranch hands with whatever tasks they were working on. Nothing took her mind off things like doing something physical, that was for sure.

Or maybe she just needed to call Kat. She bit down on her lower lip and then pulled her phone out of her back pocket.

Kat answered on the first ring.

"You fired him already, didn't you?" Kat began, her voice muffled. It sounded like she was eating.

"Ha-ha no, but he might walk out of here and never come back at the end of the day," Mia admitted, feeling better just hearing Kat's voice.

"Sorry, don't mean to chew in your ear but I've just come out of surgery and I have consultations starting in fifteen."

Mia nodded. "It's fine. I just . . ."

"What is it?" Kat asked.

"I'm going to have to tell him about everything. About Kimberley and what happened and I just, well," she blew out a deep, shaky breath. "It's so hard talking about it, you know?"

She could almost hear Kat nodding. "Yeah, I know. But you've kept a lot bottled up inside. It might feel good getting it all out." She paused and Mia waited. "Look, he's there to help you and he's there to help Tex. Just be honest with him, okay?"

Mia gripped the phone tighter. "Okay. You're right, it's just hard."

Dogs barked in the background and Mia felt bad for calling Kat at work. Her friend worked long hours as a veterinarian, and she would never usually call her during work hours.

"You'll be fine, but I have to go," Kat said. "Call me later."

Mia said goodbye and hung up, heading back to the stables. She'd saddle one of the horses up, go for a nice ride, and then head back to her house. If Sam wanted to talk, then her only option was to answer him. Honestly this time. Because if she didn't then she was certain he'd leave River Ranch and never, ever come back.

Chapter 5

SAM was still angry as hell as he strode around and up the path to the front door of the ranch house. He took off his hat and knocked, loudly. He was about to raise his fist and give the door a damn good thump when it swung open.

"Can I help you?"

He dropped the frown when he found himself face to face with a woman he guessed was the maid. He was angry with Mia, not the whole world, and this poor woman definitely didn't deserve to be on the receiving end of his scowl or his temper.

"I'm looking for Mia," he said, glancing past her and into a hallway full of expensive looking antiques and paintings. The wooden floor was gleaming—it was polished to within an inch of its life.

"Mia doesn't live here. She has her own house, over past the stables." The woman smiled and stepped out, pointing. "You'll need to walk around there. It'll only take you a few minutes."

He nodded and stepped back. "Thanks."

Sam turned and headed back the way he'd come. He

hadn't expected that she would have her own place on the property, not with a house as big and impressive as that to be living in. But then she'd mentioned being at odds with her father over the horses, so maybe she liked her own space. He knew that feeling well. Or maybe she was just a grown-ass woman who wanted her own house.

He kept walking, stopping once he reached the stables and looked around. He took a few more steps, then realized the low slung roof in the distance wasn't another farm structure. Once he was closer he saw the start of a timber path and followed it, walking along the faded cedar towards a small yet contemporary dwelling, surrounded by modern grasses and shrubs, and facing a rectangular lap pool. It was completely at odds with the more traditional style main house, but he liked it, especially the glass wrapping around each side of the house. He liked seeing his own property from every room of his place, and he was guessing that was why she'd built it this way, so she had 360-degree views of the fields, the trees and the animals dotted around the place.

"Knock knock," he called out when he saw the big doors open around the side. The house faced the pool, and he was tempted to strip down and jump straight in after working up such a sweat with Tex.

"Come in!"

When he heard Mia call out, he wandered around, intrigued by her house. If he wasn't so angry with her he'd have taken more time to appreciate the architecture—it made his big old ranch house look positively ancient in comparison.

"Nice place," he said when he saw her sitting on a cream sofa, bare feet curled up beneath her, coffee mug in hand.

Even her furniture was at odds with the traditional feel of the rest of the ranch, but he liked that she had her own style. Mia looked pale, eyes bloodshot, and he wondered if she'd been crying.

He felt like an idiot then for being so damn mad with her, because whatever had happened with that horse was more than just an accident; it was written all over her face. Sam sat down on a chair beside the sofa, glancing out at the crystal-blue water of the pool once again. It really was an incredible place. Her sofas were modern but still looked comfy, with throws at one end and plenty of cushions, and she had neat little piles of books stacked everywhere along with fresh flowers.

"We need to talk," he said reluctantly. "If you don't tell me the truth about that stallion, then I'm going to leave today and I'm not coming back. You're not giving me any other choice, Mia."

"Just like that?" she asked, leaning forward and setting her mug down.

"Yeah, Mia, just like that," he said softly, his anger slowly dispersing. He didn't have the right to be angry with her, she didn't owe him anything, but he did have the right to walk away if she didn't let him in. "I've spent the last few hours trying to get that horse to trust me, but something's happened to him, something so deep that he might be impossible to get through to," he admitted. "I don't want to walk away from an animal that needs help, but I need to know his past so we can move forward. It'll help me know what buttons not to press, and it'll keep me safe. And him." He shrugged. "I'm only asking what's fair."

Mia nodded. "Do you want a coffee?" she asked.

He ground his jaw. Had she not heard what he'd just

said? "No, I don't want coffee," he muttered. "I need your goddamn help, and instead of being honest with me, you're offering me a hot drink?"

He watched as Mia settled back, drawing her knees up to her chin, eyes wide like she was a little girl about to tell a scary story. Sam leaned forward, wanting to hear what she had to say, wanting to know how a horse as magnificent as Tex had been scarred for life. Not to mention what had Mia all tied up in knots.

"Kimberley was my best friend," Mia said, her voice low and soft, nothing like the firecracker who'd stood her ground so firmly only a few hours earlier. "You'll probably remember the accident, like my dad said it was all over the news. She'd won more show jumping titles than I could possibly count, and I was jealous as hell of her in the best kind of way possible. Every time we went out, she'd beat me, but she was good for me. She made me determined every damn day to win, to push myself harder, to start beating her."

"Tex belonged to this friend of yours, didn't he?" Sam asked, feeling like an asshole for being so damn mean earlier now he'd heard part of the story. Mia was hurting and she'd been through as much as the stallion. Only she was better at hiding it than an animal with no control over keeping his emotions in check.

"Tex was her baby," Mia explained, brushing under her eyes with the back of her knuckles. Her eyes met his then, and he didn't break the contact. Vulnerable, emotional women weren't usually the type to get under his skin, but Mia's story was making him feel like the biggest jerk in the world. He felt an unfamiliar urge to want to protect her, to rise up and sit closer to her, to comfort her. He wondered how often she let her guard down like this and doubted it was very often.

"He was always difficult, but what gave him the edge when they were competing was how gritty he was. He'd get around a course at a hell of a speed and never knock a rail, and then he'd carry on like a madman after, rearing and trying to bolt on her, so pleased with himself. It was almost like he knew there was no one out there better than him."

Sam smiled, imagining how stunning the big horse would have been in his glory days. "So how did he go from that to what he is now?"

"He loved Kimberley and she adored him right back. She knew how to make him work, and she was firm with him when he acted out. They formed a partnership that lasted about three years, and then they were invited to do a charity display."

Sam saw the pain on Mia's face as she spoke of what had happened. He doubted this was something she relived often.

"I remember now," he said solemnly. "I remember hearing about it from one of my clients, how the rider and horse both had a terrible accident." Sam recalled it, how devastating it had been, the reports about her fall. But the news reports had only mentioned what had happened to the rider, not the horse.

"She was showing off, jumping a flat deck vehicle with hay bales stacked on top. It was a hell of a jump to tackle, but she was confident as hell and she'd nailed it when they'd practiced earlier."

Sam nodded, a lump in his throat as he imagined the scene, playing through his head now as if he'd been there on the day. He might have heard about it before, but not like this.

"They cantered around the ring and she jumped it. The crowd went wild and Tex was crazy. He knew he was the champion and she must have decided to jump it one more time." Mia sighed. "Once was never enough for her, it was why she was so good, that way she loved to show off."

"They didn't make the next one, did they? He clipped the deck on his way over?"

She nodded. "They went into it so fast. Tex was galloping, both of them were overconfident, and she didn't slow him enough. He took off all wrong, and it was too big and too solid for them to make it." Mia was speaking fast but quietly, and he leaned forward to listen, feeling her pain. "He had a hell of a fall himself. He somersaulted over as she went flying. They both made it over, just not together."

"She broke her neck?" Sam asked gently.

"She landed on her head. I saw it with my own eyes. I'll never forget the moment she landed, like it was slow motion as she awkwardly hit the ground. But it was Tex flipping that killed her. He connected with her as she fell, and the impact on her neck killed her instantly."

Sam reached for Mia's hand, grazing her fingers and then clasping them. He might not be a team player and he knew he was a jerk sometimes when it came to his work, but he had a goddamn heart, and he could tell when someone else's was breaking.

"I'm sorry," he said, and he knew he was apologizing for more than just her loss.

"He suffered a big blow that day, physically and emotionally," Mia said. "I took him when the medics were working on her, and we got him back to the truck and the vets checked him over. He was badly lame, but he seems to have recovered from those injuries."

"What happened to him after that?" Sam asked. "Where did he go?"

"Her family sold off all her horses, him included, and they refused to let me take any of them at any price. They wanted them gone. Tex went to a new show jumper who couldn't handle how hot he was, then some so-called horse whisperer who claimed he could sort him out. That was the last time I saw him, messed up and crazy, before he was sent to a stud." She went silent for a moment, staring out the window, and Sam realized he was still holding her hand then. He reluctantly pulled back, breaking the contact with her warm, soft skin. "I found him there, in a tiny yard that was full of mud and shit. He was knee deep in it. It was disgusting, and it was like he'd actually gone mad there, locked up and with no one giving a damn about him. It was the saddest thing I've ever seen." Her breath shuddered out. "I went overseas to ride, but I never forgot about him and they finally accepted my offer to buy him after all these years."

"He's been through hell and back then," Sam said, thinking about the stallion and knowing that everything was in the horse's head then. He'd been screwed up by humans, that was for sure.

"He went from being so loved, the center of his rider's universe, to being treated like crap. I fought for him, I tried so hard to buy him for so long, but now I'm wondering if it's too late to save him."

"I'll be honest with you, Mia. It's not going to be easy." Part of him thought this particular horse might be damn near impossible to turn into a safe riding horse for Mia, but he decided to keep that to himself for now.

She smiled at him, and for the first time he felt like he was seeing the real her and not the person she wanted the world to see.

"I promised her, Sam. I promised her I'd always look after Tex, and she promised me she'd always look after Indi." He saw her tears then, glistening from her eyes as she stared at him. "I let her down once, but I'm not giving up on him without a fighting chance now."

Sam sat back, considered her, looked at the beautiful woman seated across from him and realized how stupid he'd been not to see past the money and beauty from the moment he'd met her. She was real and strong and determined, and it was blatantly obvious now.

"I'll try my best, but I'm not making false promises," he said, shooting straight. "I don't like to over promise, but I'll try my best to over deliver on this one."

"I have your word?" she asked, her voice low.

He leaned in and held out his hand, smiling when she clasped it. "You have my word," he promised. "So long as you pour me a beer and let me dive into that pool before I head home. In case you didn't know, I've had one hell of a day. My new boss is a goddamn slave driver!"

She laughed at him and shook his hand, her cheeks pink now, the color seeping back into her skin as she stood and stared down at him. Damn she was pretty. He'd expected something so different, yet sitting here she was just a cute girl with her hair in a ponytail, still wearing her riding gear and not caring that her shirt was dirty.

"Fine. I'll get you a beer, but if I find out you've left that poor dog in your truck instead of bringing him down here . . ."

Sam grinned. "Yes, ma'am," he said. "Seems I've, ah, forgotten something though, I'll be back in a minute."

Sam tried not to laugh as he walked off to get Blue. Mia wasn't so bad after all. It'd been a long time since he'd been able to relax and just enjoy a woman's company, and if she hadn't been his boss? Maybe they'd have gotten along better from the start.

He glanced back, saw her standing there by the pool and dragged his eyes away. He wasn't going there. Sam forced himself to keep walking, breaking into a jog as he headed back for his dog. Mia was off limits. She was his boss, she was . . . *beautiful*. But beautiful wasn't enough for him, because his fiancée had been beautiful too, but it hadn't stopped her from breaking his heart and making him vow never to be vulnerable when it came to women ever again.

Chapter 6

SAM had actually been looking forward to arriving at River Ranch since he'd woken, although he was tiring of the one-hour commute from his place. Walter's personal assistant had left him a message the day before extending an invitation to stay, but lately he'd spent enough time travelling away from home and not sleeping in his own bed. For now, he'd put up with the drive.

His phone rang and he pressed answer on his hands-free. It was Nate.

"Hey, how's it going?" he asked.

"So tired," Nate replied. "Seriously, you have no idea what it's like having kids. I mean, why does nobody tell you how goddamn exhausting tiny humans can be? Not that I'd have ever believed it anyway."

Sam laughed. When Nate had married his sister, it had just about ruined their friendship, until he'd eventually realized that his sister was crazy for the guy and he would have to get over it and learn to embrace it. Now, he felt sorry for his friend. His sister kept him on his toes, and now he had twin daughters to wrangle on a daily basis.

"Want to come give me a hand with the stallion I'm working? He'd do a damn fine job of taking your mind off changing diapers."

"Wish I could," Nate replied, "but I'm on a plane to New York in an hour. My eyes are hanging out of my head, but at least I'll be able to sleep in flight."

"You leaving for long?" Sam asked, frowning as he thought about his sister being left alone with the two kids. They weren't a year old yet and they'd been a handful from the moment they arrived. "I can swing past and check in on Faith if you need me to."

"I'm only gone for thirty-something hours. They might drive me crazy but I can't leave my girls for longer than a day or two."

"So no chance of catching up for a beer any time soon?" Sam asked. He missed seeing Nate. Hell, he missed doing a lot of things since life had changed so dramatically. Right now all he wanted was to hang out with Nate and his brothers, talk shit and drink beer, and then spend a month or two working his own horses and relaxing at his own ranch. Only he had to remind himself that he wouldn't even *have* a ranch if he hadn't worked his ass off and toured the country.

"How about the night I get back? I'll have my car at the airport, so I can swing past your place on my way through."

Sam grinned. "I'll say yes, but I have a feeling you'll forget all about me and speed on past to get home by then." He knew how it was, and he wasn't exactly going to begrudge Nate time with his family. They'd both been bachelors long enough before Nate had settled down.

Nate laughed down the line. "You got me," he said. "Love my girls, but I need that beer with you. I'll see you tomorrow night."

Sam ended the call and smiled to himself. Nate had been completely whipped by his sister, and even though he'd personally stopped believing in love, he knew his sister and Nate had the real thing going on. And if Nate ever let her down, he'd forget they'd been best friends since pre-K and beat the shit out of him.

Sam pulled up and opened the door, waiting for Blue to jump out. He could have left his dog at home, but after all the months of seeing way too little of his canine friend, he'd decided to let him tag along. He had good people working for him, and they took great care of his animals while he was gone, but his dog was like a family member, and he kept him close whenever he could.

"Come on," Sam said to him, ruffling his head then shutting the door. His ex had taken a lot from him, but at least she hadn't tried to take his dog.

"Morning," Sam called out as he passed one of the ranch hands. "Mia around?"

"In the arena," he replied, hefting a bale of hay and nodding his head. "Good luck with the horse."

Sam laughed. "I think I need more than luck," he muttered.

"We're all placing bets on you walking off the job before the end of the week. That stallion thinks he's the king of the ranch and then some."

They both chuckled, and Sam raised his hand in a wave and kept walking, pleased Mia was busy training. That meant he could avoid her and start working with Tex before she had a chance to insist on joining him. As much as he felt for her over what had happened, he still preferred to work alone and he didn't want to change his methods just because she had a serious emotional attachment to the horse.

He didn't bother collecting a rope and halter, instead stopping by the barn to grab an armful of hay. He'd left Tex in the makeshift round pen overnight, and he wanted to reward his trust with some extra food.

Blue trotted faithfully at his side, but he ordered him to lie down well away from Tex. The stallion had serious issues about his own space, and he didn't want his dog getting anywhere near the beast.

"Morning, Tex," he called out, not making eye contact with him. Sam took a small amount of hay in with him. The horse hadn't been fed since he'd left the night before, so he knew he'd be hungry.

He put the hay down and backed off, senses on high alert even though he didn't look directly at the stallion. Tex cautiously approached the hay and snorted at it, as if he were inspecting it to make sure it wasn't poisoned. Sam went back through the makeshift fence and leaned against the timber rails beyond it.

The horse was cautious, but he was eating, and Sam was hoping that it would help him with his trust issues to be the one who fed him each day. Once he'd finished and there wasn't any hay left to distract him, Sam went back in. He still didn't make direct eye contact. Instead he stood, looking away for a moment, and let the horse size him up. Once he'd done that for a bit, ready to react if the situation changed, he looked at Tex and started to walk towards him. The horse snorted, pawing at the ground for a moment, before starting to move away. What he was doing wasn't anything special, it was simply him motivating Tex's natural instincts. Horses were flight animals, and right now Sam was behaving like the predator. He moved him around the pen, forcing him to keep moving. Eventually he stopped and stood still. He could hear Tex breathing when he turned away, his back to the horse. This could go horribly wrong, but he had to try it. Others would have, hell, Mia had probably tried something similar, but the whole process could be ruined so easily by not following through with the precise steps required; he doubted anyone in the last year or more had trusted the unpredictable stallion enough to turn their back on him and completely let their guard down.

Sam felt vulnerable, but he pushed the feeling away, breathing deep. It was important not to look at the horse, not even a peek to see what he was doing. In the past he'd spent hours sitting on an up-turned feed bucket, waiting for a horse to approach him. He did that a lot with the mustangs that he worked with, gradually getting their trust by ignoring them and letting them inspect him on their own terms, but they were different. They were wild horses, curious by nature, who had no fear of humans and a completely different outlook on life. Tex disliked and distrusted humans, and Sam needed to start over with him, re-teach him and remind him that humans hadn't always been so cruel to him.

He hadn't ever been scared of horses, and as unpredictable as Tex was, he wasn't scared of him, either. Stallions could be notoriously difficult to work with, but he wasn't going to change the way he worked unless he had to.

Sam breathed deep again, calm and happy to let the horse figure him out. Growing up he'd had it rough, so he'd been plenty scared before, he just hadn't ever seen horses as being something to fear. He treated animals with respect and never pushed them, and he always got a lot back from them. He'd become used to trusting his instincts, and something in his gut told him that for all the overt anger Tex displayed, he wasn't going to charge him and kill him while he was standing there. Although he also knew how easily he could be proved wrong.

He felt the horse move closer. Still he didn't turn. He wouldn't turn until Tex approached him, touching him or waiting expectantly within a foot of him, otherwise it would be over. He needed the horse to see him as a safe place.

He'd been standing for some time, waiting and biding his time, when he heard a soft snort behind him. Sam smiled and kept his back turned, only tilting when he felt the horse close. He wasn't as close as he'd have liked, but he was close enough.

"Good boy," Sam murmured, knowing the horse would be listening. "That's a boy. It's just you and me here."

He slowly pivoted then, keeping his eyes downcast. He stood still, waiting for Tex to stretch his neck out. He did, eventually, but he was timid.

Sam slowly, slowly raised his hand, holding it out and letting him sniff it. Once he'd done that, he walked back a couple of paces and then turned to exit the pen. He wasn't going to push him any further for the day.

That's when he heard the clapping.

"Impressive," Mia said, sitting on the grass with his dog. Blue had his head in her lap. "I'm annoyed that you snuck around here and didn't invite me to watch, but damn impressive either way."

Sam grinned at her, hoping she wasn't too pissed at him. He got the balance of the hay he'd brought and ducked back through to leave it for Tex.

"Here you go, buddy," he said, eyes lowered still so as not to challenge him. He left the hay there and exited again, only to find Mia waiting, arms folded over her chest as she stared at him.

"Sorry, I didn't want any other distractions on my first proper session with him," he said.

Mia raised one perfect brow as she glared at him. Her expression was hard to read, but it was like a cool breath of wind had blown through.

"I've been here for at least fifteen minutes. He was so busy watching you he didn't even care."

Sam shrugged. "I'd say that's lucky then," he replied. "But then maybe it was me who would have been distracted, had I known you were sitting there watching."

He leveled his gaze on Mia, secretly pleased when she faltered. She was full of so much spark and although he admired it, he wasn't used to having to justify what he was doing and why.

"Is it that hard for you to let me be part of this?"

He groaned. "Kind of, yeah. I'm a creature of habit, and I'm the kind of creature who likes being alone."

"So no lucky wife then, huh?"

Subtle. Very damn subtle. He ignored the question. "I'd be lying if I didn't admit to making my way down here without you seeing on purpose," he said, not about to discuss his personal life with Mia.

"Maybe I should thank my lucky stars I didn't get another critique on my riding this morning," she quipped.

He laughed. "Bet you rode her into the jumps differently today though." When her cheeks colored but she didn't reply, he grinned. "And I bet you had the ride of your goddamn life on her."

Mia burst out laughing. He hadn't been expecting that. She twirled her long blonde ponytail and shook her head. "God, I hate you," she muttered. "But yeah, I did, and she responded just like you said."

He cupped his hand to his ear, leaning forward. "Sorry, did I miss something? I think this is the part where you thank me for my incredible tips."

Mia didn't look impressed. "No, this is the part where I realize that you're worth the exorbitant sum we're paying you. I'm just pleased I don't have to fire you."

Sam whistled his dog over and patted his head. He crouched down, looking up at Mia as she stood there, full of attitude and overconfident. He had a feeling that she was actually full of bluster, that she projected a confidence that she didn't truly feel, and that it was her instant defense mechanism. He'd spent a lot of his life reading horses, but he got a feeling from people too, and he doubted he was wrong about her.

"If you're not going to say thanks, the least you could do is make me a coffee."

"Hungry too?" she asked, pausing to look at the horse before starting to walk off.

Blue jumped to attention and ran after her, and Sam silently cursed the dog for taking such a liking to her as he jogged to catch up. He fell into step beside her, adjusting his pace to hers.

"Most of our workers bring their own coffee and lunch," she said dryly, glancing across at him, her eyes dancing with what he was fairly sure was humor. "But then again, you're not exactly our usual kind of worker, are you?"

"No, ma'am," he said, saluting her. "But in exchange for a coffee and a turkey sandwich, I'll let you hang out with me and Tex for the afternoon."

He saw her smile, knew she was trying not to laugh. He had no idea why, but he suddenly would have done anything to see her smile or hear her laugh again. And he wasn't about to tell her that he'd already finished up with the stallion for the day. He was damn hungry, and he wanted that sandwich.

Mia watched Sam as he guzzled a bottle of water. After he'd left the night before, she'd downloaded Sam's book and started to read up about him a bit more, brushing up on his techniques. Instead of resenting him still, she was curious again. One minute he seemed kind of standoffish, and the next he was charming as hell. She didn't know what to make of him, but the familiar flutters she'd always felt when she'd thought about him *before meeting him* were starting to return.

The clips on his website and on YouTube didn't do enough to show how impressive he truly was working a horse. Even watching one of his shows live was nothing like being one on one and seeing him work. For all her fuss about being annoyed with him for working alone, she had to admit that he was a genius. He'd been able to read Tex in a way she doubted any other human being could have.

Around her, he was guarded and hard to figure out, but the way he was around a horse was the essence of calm and control. Watching him was something incredible, being part of his work . . . She wished she didn't admire him so much, but she did. And she knew that from now on she needed to respect what he was telling her rather than getting her back up over being told what to do. The man knew horses, and she'd be an idiot if she didn't try to learn everything from him that she could.

Not that she was about to tell him that and make his ego any bigger than it already was though. Hell, there were Pinterest boards and a Facebook fan page dedicated to him, so she doubted he needed any more females fawning over him. She also guessed he was single, he'd sure as hell seemed to be flirting with her today, and there had been very little written about his personal life online. He obviously liked to keep to himself and not openly share anything that went on behind the scenes.

Not interested, she whispered silently to herself. She had to keep reminding herself that she was not interested in the man, no matter how damn gorgeous and talented he was. She wasn't about to become some pathetic groupie.

When Sam put down the bottle of water she'd brought over for him, she passed him a sandwich she'd made earlier and settled down beside him to eat hers, trying hard not to look at him. She was careful to put some distance between them, not liking the way he threw her off balance. She'd always been wary of men, used to them having ulterior motives for wanting to get to know her or date her, but with Sam she didn't know what to think. He treated her like a regular person, hardly put her on a pedestal just because of who she was or how much money her family was worth, and she found it . . . unnerving. For so long she'd been desperate to be treated that way, but she'd become used to the exact opposite. The only other person she was herself around was Kat, and talking with Sam wasn't anything like hanging out with her siblings, that was for sure.

"So are you the only family member living on the ranch, other than your dad?" Sam asked, his question taking her by surprise.

"I'm the only one who has a permanent base here," she said, picking at the crust of her sandwich. "My brother Tanner rides rodeo, and he comes and goes if he's passing by, but my other brother's a banker in New York, and my sister is an attorney in California." Mia leaned her head back and took a tiny bite, chewing it quickly then swallowing. "Tan and I spent our childhoods riding and hanging out on the ranch, and Cody and Angelina spent as little time outside and around animals as possible. They're more interested in my family's investments, and I'm more interested in ranching."

Sam laughed. "It's funny how four kids can be brought up the exact same way, and have such different interests."

"Trust me, my dad would have liked us all to have big city careers," Mia said dryly. "He didn't exactly hide his disappointment when I turned down college in favor of making a living from riding, but at least Tanner had fought the same battle before me. It made it a little easier to say no to him."

"There ain't nothing wrong with wanting to breathe fresh air every day instead of air conditioning, that's for sure," Sam said. "Good on you for doing what you love. Deep down he probably respects the fact that you're your own woman with your own passions."

Mia shrugged. She hoped so, but she didn't do what she did for her daddy's approval, she did it for herself.

"So what are we doing with Tex this afternoon?" she asked, leaning against the barn wall where they were having lunch. She had her legs out in front of her, basking in the sun. It wasn't too hot and she was enjoying the heat on her bare arms, even if she did have to squint against the glare.

"Yeah, I may have misled you about that."

Mia chewed and swallowed her mouthful. "I'm sorry, what?"

She sat in silence, waiting as Sam wolfed down the half of sandwich he was holding. He'd attacked it like he'd never eaten before. She was used to watching her brothers devour more food than a human being should ever be able to consume, but watching Sam was different. He was sexy as hell, and she found it hard not to stare at him now that they were close. He had a shadow of stubble on his jaw, his dark hair was tousled, and his shirtsleeves were rolled up past his elbow showing off tanned, muscled forearms. When he turned to her and flashed her a smile, she knew that Kat was right. She did think he was gorgeous and it had been way too long since she'd been with a man.

"I mean," he said, looking guilty as hell, "that I might have misled you just to get you to give me lunch."

"You *what*?" How could he be so gorgeous but so damn infuriating!

"I don't want to push him, he did good today. So I'll leave it at that until tomorrow. Other than to give him some more hay before I leave."

"Sam! I'm not the hired help, you know. I don't exist to bring you coffee and sandwiches for no good reason."

She was pissed now. He was treating her like . . .

"*The hired help*?" he chuckled. "No, that would be me. Technically you're the boss, sweetheart."

She glared at him, losing interest in her lunch. "Well, as your boss, I'm telling you that I expect more from you today."

"Oh really? Well, I say that boss or not, you don't get to tell me what I can and can't do with the horse."

Heat flooded her cheeks, burning her skin and vivifying her anger. Who the hell did he think he was?

"So you're done for the day?" she asked, trying to keep her voice steady.

"No," he said, eyeing up her sandwich. "You done with that? They were damn good."

"Have it," she said, hastily passing it to him, yanking

her hand back when his fingers touched his. She angrily watched him eat it. "So what is it you propose to do for the rest of the day?"

He kept her waiting, taking his time to finish eating. "I propose that you saddle up a horse and get riding. Your father's employing me to work here, so I may as well give you some pointers."

"Pointers?" She dug her nails hard into her palms as she fought the urge to explode.

"Look, everyone needs coaching. It'll be fun."

Fun my ass, she thought. But she sucked up her anger, refusing to let him see how easily he'd managed to rattle her. She was a professional horsewoman, not some beginner, but he was technically right. Everyone needed coaching, and if he could give her an edge on her competition, then she'd be a fool not to listen to him and see what advice he had.

"Okay, fine," she agreed. "I've already ridden Indi today, but I have a young gelding I was going to ride this afternoon."

He laughed, and she wondered why he could rile her so easily.

"What?" she asked, drawing her knees up and feeling oddly vulnerable around him.

"Nothing. It's just that you're not used to anyone telling you what to do, are you?"

"I don't know what you mean." she replied, meeting his gaze, looking into eyes so dark they reminded her of her favorite dark chocolate.

"You're Mia goddamn Ford. Everyone looks up to you and everyone your entire life has probably been slightly in awe of you," he said simply. "You're used to being treated differently."

She let his words wash over her, watching him, listening. "That's not true," she said, but the moment she said it, she knew she was lying. Maybe she had grown used to being treated differently.

"Look, I get it. You're supposed to be my boss while I'm here. Well, you know what? I'm not any good being told what to do and having someone micro-managing me, just like you're not used to being told you're anything less than perfect."

His words were blunt, but they were accurate. She didn't even know what to say to him in reply.

"I'm a serious loner, and you're a princess. We're not exactly a team made in heaven, but I'm here and I'm curious about your riding, so what the hell are we waiting for?"

She laughed. She had thought she'd be more likely to cry than laugh, but the moment he looked at her and grinned, she couldn't help it. There was more than a chance he was going to drive her absolutely insane while he was here.

"You're *fucking* crazy," she muttered.

"*Oooh*, did the princess just land an F-bomb?" he teased.

"Yeah, she did. And call me a goddamn princess again and I'll punch you in the nose and break it."

He shook his head, howling with laughter now. "*Break* my nose? Sweetheart, you couldn't throw a punch that'd break my finger."

"Oh yeah?" she sputtered. "It just so happens that I have two big brothers who beat the crap out of me when I was a kid. I learned quick to punch back hard, so don't be so quick to judge me."

They were both smiling when they pushed up to their feet, and Mia realized she hadn't felt so good in a long time. Sam might be arrogant and a bit of a jerk, but he was honest, at least, and she appreciated that.

"Truce," Sam said, holding out his hand.

Mia nodded and clasped it, smiling when his fingers wrapped around hers, engulfing her small hand in his. "Truce," she agreed, thinking about giving him a quick jab to the nose to prove her point, then deciding against it.

"You know, I had you pegged as a pretty little rich girl who hardly knew the back end of a horse from the front, with no intention of ever working hard or getting her hands dirty," he said.

"Guess you were wrong then," she replied.

"Yeah, about everything except the pretty part."

Sam held her hand a beat too long, and when she pulled away and met his gaze, she wished she hadn't. Because the heat there was enough to make her want to back off, fast, and the confident, sexy look on his face told her that he could eat her alive if he wanted to.

Chapter 7

WHY the hell had he said that? He didn't react, the only change in him was the tick in his jaw that he knew was flickering like crazy. Mia wasn't a girl in a bar, she was his boss and he was here to do a job. So what if she looked like a goddamn supermodel?

She was flushed. It was unmistakable, just the pinkest of tinges coloring her cheeks, and she knew that he'd noticed. He listened to her clear her throat, smiling when she gave him a confused kind of look. He shouldn't have said it, but he hadn't exactly been lying, which meant he wasn't about to try to extract himself out of it. If he did, he knew he'd only dig the hole deeper for himself anyway.

"Ah, shall we go saddle up?" Mia asked, her voice husky.

He shouldn't have flirted with her. "Sure thing."

Sam bent to collect the wrapper from the sandwich he'd eaten, balling it up, the water bottle swinging from his other hand. Mia glanced at him, and he gave her a quick smile back, not wanting to encourage her but not wanting to be a dick, either.

"Thanks," Mia said, turning back to him and taking him by surprise.

"For what?" he asked.

"For saying I'm pretty," she said. "It's been a long time since I received a compliment, so thanks."

He nodded. "You're welcome." He should have told her more, should have said she was damn beautiful, because she was, but he left it there. She hadn't been fishing for compliments, and he wasn't used to dishing them out.

He followed her past the stables, the horses all poking their noses out of their expensive houses. He'd been in some beautiful establishments, but the Ford ranch with all its luxury equine facilities was truly something else. He wondered if Mia had designed the place or whether it had already been here, but something told him that her daddy had built it especially for her. The entire ranch was immaculate and he couldn't wait to take a proper look around the grounds and find out more about their operations. He gathered the ranch was successful, but clearly it was her father's other business interests that had elevated his wealth.

"Have you always ridden?" he called out to Mia, standing beside a sweet-looking bay horse and letting him nuzzle his shirt.

"Yeah. Well, since I could convince my mom to let me ride."

"Your mom?" he asked, curious since she hadn't spoken about her before. He'd gotten the impression it was just her dad at the main house.

"Yeah, my mom. She loved horses, but she was cautious about letting us ride too young."

"Hey, at least yours gave a damn. My mom up and left."

Mia frowned. "I'm sorry to hear that."

"So your mom, does she . . ." Sam wondered why he'd

never heard about a Mrs. Ford before. He didn't exactly move in the elite circles of folk like the Fords, but still . . .

"My mom passed away," Mia said quickly. "I was only a teenager, so it was pretty rough, but she was a wealthy woman before she met my dad, and when she knew she didn't have long to live, she built me this." Mia held out her hands to gesture around. "I lost my mom, but I ended up with the best stables money could buy."

"I'm sorry," Sam said, seeing the pain on her face, the glint in her eyes the moment she'd spoken about her mother.

"Hey, she was a great mom. It's just that I'd give all this up, every single thing, if it meant I could have her back, you know?"

"Yeah, I know," he said. "Believe me, I get it." And he did. His mom hadn't died, she'd left. His dad had stuck around, but he'd been an asshole, and when he'd died after a short illness a year ago, he hadn't even shed a tear. He'd have traded both of his parents a hundred times over to get just one parent who gave a damn about him.

"Enough about me, sorry. I don't usually tell anyone that, I just . . ." She threw her hands up. "Why do I keep telling you so much? I'm used to keeping to myself and training without hardly seeing another soul during the day, and now that you're here I'm pouring my soul out to you."

"That's the problem when you're a loner," Sam told her, chuckling and stroking the horse beside him.

"Maybe I am a loner," she mused, making him laugh. "Hell, maybe that's why you kept rubbing me the wrong way so quickly."

Sam shrugged. "Takes a loner to know one. Now go saddle up. I need to leave at a decent hour so I don't have to feed my own horses in the dark again."

Mia disappeared and he talked to the horses, wandering down the line to look at all of them. He'd only seen her ride the one, her favorite mare, but he had a feeling she was full of surprises, and her horses all looked impressive.

When she didn't reappear, Sam went looking for her, wondering what the hell was taking so long.

"Hey, do you need a hand back there?" he called out.

He squinted in the half-light, dark compared to the full-sun glare outside when he ducked through the doorway and into the tack room.

"Oh, shit, sorry, just give me a sec."

He stopped. Sam stood in the middle of the small room, saddles and bridles covering every inch of wall space, and Mia pressed into one corner, her tears impossible to hide.

"Hey," Sam murmured, striding over to her. Hell, he hadn't expected her to be crying. He'd thought she might need a hand carrying some gear out, but . . . he didn't know what to do.

"I'm fine, please," she said, holding one hand up to her face, the other stretched out in front of her as if trying to push him away before he was even close.

"You're not okay," he said, knowing how gruff he sounded but unable to help it. "Come here."

She shook her head. "Please, I'm fine," she managed, voice cracking.

"Your mom, huh?" he asked, knowing that there was no way in hell he'd managed to say anything to upset her this much. She was still grieving, he could see that from a mile off.

She nodded, dropping one hand, the other still covering her face. "Yeah," she whispered. "It's just I haven't talked about her for a long time. She's been gone twelve years so I shouldn't be reacting like this."

"Come here," Sam said, not taking no for an answer this time as he opened his arms and pulled her in.

He held her, tight, letting her cry. She sobbed once, loudly, a noise that made his heart lurch for her, feeling her pain, before she went silent and relaxed in his arms. It had been almost a year since he'd held a woman like this; comforted a woman and held her and felt something for her. He stiffened. Only that woman had played him, ripped his heart out when he'd have done anything for her. *Anything.*

"I'm sorry," he said. "I'd tell you it'll get easier, but I doubt it will."

He didn't sugarcoat things, even this type of thing, but he did feel for her. She'd tried to talk about her mom all nonchalant to him, laughing about her beautiful stables, when in reality it had torn her in half and left her crying all on her own. She'd lost her mom and her best friend as well; no wonder she'd been prickly when he'd tried to muscle in and take over with the one thing she did have—her horses.

Mia pushed back and he wished she hadn't. He'd liked the warmth of her against him, the tickle of her long hair catching in his stubble as he'd inhaled her shampoo or whatever it was on her that smelled so damn delicious.

"Sorry," she murmured, her hands to his chest as she stepped back. "I don't ever let anyone see me cry."

He believed it. She didn't strike him as the type to let anyone see her vulnerabilities.

Sam glanced down at her, at her hands against his chest, at the way she was looking up at him, her eyes wide. Her mouth parted, tear-stained cheeks making her look so vulnerable that it tugged at something inside of him he'd thought was long buried.

"You've got nothing to apologize for," he muttered, slowly raising a hand and brushing his thumb gently across her cheeks to blur the tears away.

Mia stayed still, her palms still planted against him, head tilted. He looked at her mouth, fought the urge to rub his thumb across her soft pink lips. Instead he dropped his hand, skimming past her long blonde hair on the way past.

Sam bent a little, eyes on her mouth, imagining what her lips would taste like. He wanted to kiss her so damn bad, wanted to push her up against the wall behind her and kiss the hell out of her. But he didn't.

He'd sworn off women for a reason, and sexy or not, he wasn't about to take advantage of his *boss* up against a wall. Even crying she was beautiful, but he wasn't going there. He *couldn't* go there.

Dammit!

Her eyes were dancing, her lips were parted, her hands were slowly dropping away from his chest. But instead of closing the distance between them, instead of hungrily tasting her lips against his, he took her hands, stepping back and squeezing them.

"You take all the time you need," he said instead, hearing the husky note of his own voice. "I'll be out here."

He walked out, ducking back through the door and out into the bright sunlight again. *Goddamn it!* What the hell had he just done? He'd always prided himself on being able to keep his shit together, and he'd let himself get way too close to Mia.

He stalked off, pleased to be alone while she pulled herself together. When he'd found Kelly in bed with another guy, he'd vowed never, ever to let himself get close to a woman again. He'd loved her, damn, had he loved her, and she'd gone behind his back and fucked another guy in their bed when he'd been out at work. Add to that the fact he'd had to pay her big time because they'd been living together for over three years and their home was considered relationship property, and it had been enough for him to never let any woman get close again.

Now he only did one-night stands or casual flings. He met women when he was away traveling, when he could make it clear that he was only in town for a night or two. There were no strings attached, there were no expectations. He wasn't an asshole, he didn't use women, but he made it clear that it was only ever going to be a fun night between the sheets.

But Mia was different. Mia was girlfriend material. Mia was from Texas, she was beautiful and she was . . . *the kind of girl he didn't need to get close to or lead on.*

Sam went for a walk to cool off. He'd screwed up, but he wasn't going to let it happen again. Mia was off limits. Mia was his boss. He just needed to keep telling himself that.

His dog appeared out of nowhere and Sam realized he'd forgotten all about him.

"Hey, Bluey," he said, giving him a big pat when he loped over. "Come with me, bud."

He had everything he needed in his life. He had his ranch, his dog, his horses, good people working on his ranch and his own work. He didn't need anything else, and he needed to remember it next time he got up close with the gorgeous Mia Ford.

Mia was wondering if she'd gone crazy. Had Sam almost kissed her? She lugged her saddle, bridle and brushes out to the stables and looked around for him. He wasn't anywhere to be seen, but she knew he wouldn't be far. Which meant she had about zero seconds to get her shit together.

She let herself in with Fred, the gelding she'd told Sam about. She needed to get her head back in the game and forget all about what had almost happened. Because it *hadn't* happened, which meant *nothing* had happened. Sam wasn't interested in her, he never would be. Guys like him didn't like girls like her, she had no expectations there. What she had was a crush on him, a little fantasy that wasn't ever going to come true. It had been a moment, and that moment had well and truly passed. But Kat had been so right. She was craving being up close and personal with a man, and having a guy like Sam so close had brought it all back to her.

"Come on, we can do this," she said to the horse in a low voice, brushing him down quickly before saddling him up. She used the soft body brush on his face before putting on his bridle, then double-checked his girth and went out to get her helmet, which she'd forgotten.

"Oh," she said, almost walking smack-bang into Sam. He was standing outside the stable, hands shoved into his pockets.

"Sorry, didn't mean to startle you," he said.

She looked up at him, wanting to avoid his gaze but at the same time desperate to know if what had almost happened before had been a mistake or not. From the hungry way he was looking back at her, she was fairly certain it hadn't been a mistake.

"How long have you been standing here?" she asked, suddenly wondering if he'd been listening to her talk away to the horse in a low voice as she'd prepared him.

"Not long. A few seconds," he said, running his fingers loosely through his hair. "You know, I'd love to get back in the saddle. It's been too long since I've had time to actually ride for pleasure."

She wasn't sure what he was trying to say. "You want to cancel our training session and go for a ride around the ranch instead?" she asked.

He grinned. "Hey, I'm not letting you off that easily. How about I bring one of my own horses tomorrow? You can show me around the place after I've worked Tex."

She couldn't help the smile that quickly spread like wildfire across her lips. "I'd love that. I always try to give my horses a fun riding day once a week, so that'd be perfect for Indi."

He nodded. "It's a date then."

Mia opened her mouth, about to agree, but nothing came out. She knew he hadn't meant it like that, but . . .

"Bad choice of words," he muttered. "But I'm sure you get my drift."

Mia nodded. "I'm going to grab my things and I'll meet you in the arena."

She didn't wait for Sam to answer, just hurried into the tack shed again to grab her helmet, clasp it firmly under her chin, and wiggle her fingers into her leather riding gloves.

She paused, looking out the door at Sam as he walked away. She eyed his jeans, the way his Wrangler's hugged his ass and tapered down over his long legs. His shoulders were wide, but there wasn't an ounce of fat on him, his shirt tucked in and making that abundantly clear. He was the perfect physical specimen of man, but something had stopped him from kissing her before, and she wanted to know what. Because now she'd almost tasted his lips, she'd be thinking about it long after he left this afternoon, she was sure of it.

She retrieved Fred, pulled her stirrups down and mounted, walking out to the arena with her head full of Sam. She didn't know what it was about him, but her mom was usually an off-limits topic with anyone except her siblings or her best friend, Kat. But standing there before, when he'd asked her a simple question, it had all but poured out of her, and for some strange reason it had felt so right.

"We're going to show him exactly what we're made of today," she muttered to the horse she was riding.

Her horse broke into a trot, and she laughed. Maybe her animals could understand her after all.

She flushed thinking about the way Sam had held her, his big arms and even bigger body engulfing her as he'd hugged her and comforted her. He might be a loner, but the way he'd behaved had shown her that deep down he was a big softie, and he hadn't liked seeing her cry. There was a lot more to him than met the eye, and Mia was curious now. She wanted to know all about Sam and what made him tick, what had made him the man he was today, and she wanted to know now.

"He's pretty excited," Sam said, standing in the middle of the vast arena as Mia cantered around. He'd set up four jumps in a row, just as she'd instructed him to do, in a grid for Mia to canter down, and he was waiting for her to come back around.

"Maybe it's because of you," she shot back, her smile infectious when she rose slightly out of the saddle and let her horse go faster.

"Perhaps, or perhaps he just needs settling." Sam

watched her carefully, critiquing her when he could, even though her riding today was almost faultless.

"Shall I do it again?" Mia called out.

"Yes. But this time, try talking to him. You're both doing well, but I think he would settle into his natural rhythm better if you were soothing him more with your voice. Hell, sing to him softly if you have to, but just calm him by letting him listen to you."

"The horse whisperer telling the rider to actually *whisper* to the horse!" she called back.

"Laugh all you like, but there's nothing I would change about your riding or his capabilities."

He saw her smile and knew she liked the compliment.

"Don't go getting a big head, just ride him and talk to him."

She did exactly that, and he had no idea what she told the horse, but he cleared the grid beautifully, his timing perfect, his legs tucked neatly under him, his ears pricked. Even when he landed he didn't try to rush off.

"Perfect!" he called out.

Mia slowed him to a trot then a walk, loosening her reins and letting the horse stretch his neck out. She did a big circle before coming over to him, but her smile was gone, replaced with a deep frown as she stretched her leg out, foot out of the stirrup as she flexed her ankle.

"Shit," she swore, dropping her reins as she went to dismount.

"What?" he asked. "What happened?"

"Ugh, cramp in my calf," she moaned. "It's bad."

"Stop," he ordered as she went to wriggle down. He placed his hands on her leg, pulling her long black leather boot off.

Mia stayed still, leg stretched out as he dropped her boot and started to massage her muscle, pushing his fingers hard into her leg. He rubbed back and forth, knowing exactly what that kind of cramp felt like.

"Better," she murmured as he kept working, not about to stop now that he knew it was helping.

Sam glanced up at her, saw the relief on her face, eyes shut, face tilted up to the sky. He smiled and kept kneading, wishing his fingers were on her bare skin instead of through her riding pants.

"Thanks," she said, flexing again, and he took his hands off her.

"No problem. Great riding out there."

It was hot, the sun unrelenting, and her face was pink and gleaming when she smiled down at him. He noticed the long braid she had hanging down her back had become messy, wisps escaping and sticking to her neck. She looked more gorgeous than ever, and he diverted his eyes, not about to let his mind go there again.

Mia swung her leg over and he glanced at her boot just as she came flying toward the ground. Sam acted fast, grabbing her around the waist, his hands firm to her body as he caught her and stopped her from landing.

"Boot," he muttered as she gasped.

Mia froze in his arms, and he slowly let her go. Her hands landed on his shoulders as she turned, standing on one leg, laughing as she tried to hop to her boot and failed.

"You're completely useless when you're not on a horse," he said with a laugh.

Mia was laughing too, and he kept hold of her as she bent to retrieve the boot, pink-socked foot pointed out at a weird angle as she tried to keep her balance.

"Thanks, you're really great with compliments, you know that?"

Sam held her around the waist as she went to put her boot on, steadying her when she wobbled. He hadn't expected her to forget all about putting her boot on and stare up and him instead.

"What?" he asked, voice low since they were standing so close.

It would have taken only one movement to have Mia's body close up against his, her torso to his, her slender body butted right up to his chest. But instead of moving, he stayed rock still, not getting closer, not letting anything more happen.

"Before. In the tack shed," she murmured, tilting her face up. "You stopped something before it was about to happen."

He sure as hell hadn't expected her to bring that up. But now she had, he could hardly lie and pretend that it hadn't happened. He was plenty of things, but liar wasn't one of them.

"I did."

"Why?" she asked.

Sam groaned. This was not a question he wanted to answer. She raised her mouth, expectantly, and he stared down at her, swallowing hard. This was not going to happen. His heart beat faster, hands warm against her sides.

To hell with it. Some part of his brain disagreed with him, pushed him over the edge and shattered all the willpower he thought he had.

Sam reached out and unclasped her helmet with one hand, taking it carefully off her head. She ran her fingers through her hair, pushing it off her face, and when she was done, when she looked back up at him, he bent low and kissed Mia, one hand still holding her helmet, the other around her, his palm flat to the small of her back. His lips moved softly across hers, their mouths slow, gentle, tasting her and wishing to hell he hadn't gone there. When she let out a little moan, the faintest of noises, it was all the encouragement he needed. Sam dropped her helmet and raised his hand, stroking down her long braid and then settling on her cheek.

He kissed her again, this time less sweet and more urgent. When her tongue touched his, he responded, pushing his lower body against her as he fought to get closer to her, to feel her hard up against him.

It was Mia who broke the kiss, pulling back, palm to his chest as she smiled and then wobbled straight back into him.

"I'm still on one foot," she whispered, laughing when he caught hold of her elbow. "And you're kind of making it hard for me to keep my balance."

Sam laughed too, bending to help her with her footwear. Her hands rested on his shoulders, and he listened to her sigh when he stood up.

"What?" he asked.

"Nothing," she said, looking embarrassed.

Sam touched her shoulder and studied her, wondering what she was thinking, what she expected from him. He should have told her first, before kissing her, that he had nothing to give. Not emotionally, anyway.

"Thank you." Her voice was low as she pushed away and leaned into her horse instead, holding onto the reins and giving him a look he couldn't decipher.

"For the lesson?" he asked.

She shook her head. "Nothing, don't worry. I'd better get this one back to his stable for a brush down."

Sam stood and watched her go. He couldn't figure women out, never had been able to, maybe never would. He just hoped Mia didn't have any expectations where he was concerned after one kiss, no matter how good it had been.

Mia watched Sam's vehicle disappear in a cloud of dust as he headed down the drive for home. She raised her hand, touched her fingers across her lips and smiled thinking about the way she'd felt when he'd kissed her. She should have said something, *anything* other than 'thank you' to the man who'd kissed her and made her feel like a breathing, feeling, sensual woman again, but instead she'd lost all power to speak and had fled the scene. What she should have done was wrap her arms around his neck and kiss the hell out of him again until he'd been the one to pull away.

Her phone buzzed in her pocket and she picked it up. It was Kat.

"Hey," she said, smiling when she heard her friend's cheerful voice.

"How's your day been? Any progress with the Handsome Horseman today?"

"Ha-ha, very funny." Mia wasn't about to breathe a word of what had happened—Kat would never let her live it down if she knew.

"Look, I know you'll want to kill me, but my cousin is arriving in from L.A. in the morning, and I might have promised that we'd double date. Is there any way you could go out for dinner with him tomorrow night?" she laughed. "I'll be there too but . . ."

Mia groaned. She hated when Kat tried to set her up with anyone. "I'm not going on a blind date with your pretend cousin. You know I hate that sort of thing!"

"First of all, he's not a pretend cousin. For the record, he's cute and single and charming, so you'll have a great night with us," Kat said, as if she were talking to a petulant child. "Secondly, I have a dog being flown in for a specialist surgery. He's going to be one of the first dogs in the state that receives the new prosthetic elbow joint that we've been trialing. I've been waiting a long time to find the right large canine candidate, so my cousin will pick you up and I'll come along later with Matt. He's the other vet consulting on the case, so we'll all be kind of new to each other. It'll be great!"

Kat knew all she had to do was play on her animal heartstrings and she'd have her in the bag, but a date? Seriously? Going out with someone she'd never even spoken to or met before was her idea of a disaster.

"Fine, but you need to make it clear that I'm not some desperate single and that I'm doing *you* a favor. This is just a group of people having dinner, not a double date, okay?"

"Of course! I promised him a fun night out, so I just don't want to let him down."

Mia wished she wasn't such a pushover when it came to Kat, but it was what she'd said the other night that was playing on her mind. She didn't get out enough, and she hadn't dated in such a long time. Was it really that hard to meet a decent guy and have some fun along the way?

She chatted to her friend for a while then said goodbye, and her stomach did a little jump when she thought about going out with a man. Only it wasn't Kat's mystery cousin that was making her stomach flip and her heart race; it was

Sam. She doubted she'd ever be able to look at his lips the same way again.

Groaning and pushing all thoughts of Sam away, she walked up to the main house and went around back, kicking off her boots and heading inside.

"Dad?" she called out, knowing he was in there somewhere. "Dad?" she said again, wandering down the long hallway and heading toward his office. He liked to work from home whenever he wasn't traveling, and when she paused outside to knock on the doorframe, he finally called back out to her.

"Come in, just finishing up some paperwork."

Mia smiled and entered, loving the feel of the thick, luxurious carpet beneath her socked feet. The hallway and kitchen were all hardwood floors, but everywhere else the carpet was extravagant and plush. She glanced around his office—her father had his head bent and was scribbling away at something—and she smiled as she always did when she looked at the pictures adoring the walls and dotted among books on his dark oak bookcase that sprawled the length of one wall. There was a big photo of her mom, her head tipped back in laughter and her eyes shut, that always sent a shiver through Mia. And then there were endless photos of her siblings—Angelina on the day she graduated law school, Cody outside his new office building, Tanner riding a bull with one hand thrown back, and Mia standing with Indi, her head resting against her horse's neck.

"I look at every single photo every day," her father said, rising from his desk and coming over to kiss her cheek. "How's it going with the horseman?"

Mia kissed him back and wished she didn't feel so conflicted when it came to her dad. She loved him fiercely but they so often butted heads and clashed over her decisions.

"He's . . . well, interesting," Mia said truthfully. "Not what I expected, but he's good at what he does,"

"Pleased to hear it. Join me for a drink?" Her father crossed the room and poured himself a whisky. She shook her head, but happily sunk down onto the big buttoned leather sofa to sit with him.

"You're sure it's worth spending money on this horse, Mia?"

She nodded, hoping they weren't going to argue again. "Yes, I'm sure."

"There a reason you've come over to see me? Or was it just my good company you wanted to enjoy?"

Mia laughed. Trust him to ask her outright. "I actually just wanted to see you, but now that you've asked . . ." she cleared her throat. "I really appreciate you bringing Sam Mendes here to the ranch, but I need you to run things by me first when it comes to the horses. I thought we agreed that I was in charge of all the horses on the ranch?"

He chuckled and took a long sip of his drink. The straight liquor on ice would have made her stomach heave. "Mia, you're too close to this horse."

She took a deep breath, determined not to say anything she'd regret later.

"I'm actually very proud of you, whether you believe me or not, and I can see how capable you are, but I have an obligation to keep my employees safe, and no ranch hand can be expected to go near that beast. We need to take advice on him, and I was told Sam was the best man for the job."

Mia nodded. He was right—she knew it and he knew it.

"I need your word that this is the last time you'll step in and go over my head though," she said. "I understand why you did it, but just . . ."

"You have my word, Mia. Now come have dinner with me. This old man is sick of dining alone."

She laughed and pushed to her feet. "Fine. But you eat out more than you eat in, and I don't believe for a second you're dining alone when you're out."

Her father gave her a wink, and she rolled her eyes and headed for the kitchen. He might be old, but he was as sharp as a tack.

Chapter 8

WHEN SAM arrived the next day, Mia was a bundle of nerves. Her thighs were aching from the long, grueling training session the day before, but she was looking forward to seeing him. After so long working on her own every day, it was kind of nice, even though she knew he was only here for a handful of weeks.

And then there was the kiss.

When he got out of his vehicle and waved, she waved back, pushing her stupid nerves away and heading over to help him unload his horse. Blue jumped out with him, and she went around the back of the trailer to put the back down as he opened the side door.

"Ready?" she asked, before hauling it down.

"Yip, ready," he replied.

Mia admired the dark bay, glossy rear end of his horse as she waited for him to give her a signal to open the back gate containing the horse. When he did, she opened it, and watched as he slowly backed his horse off.

"Impeccably behaved," she said. She was used to well-behaved horses, but that had been effortless.

"Watch this," he said, glancing at her before stroking his horse on the neck to get his attention.

She liked how gentle he was with them. Gentle but firm, his demeanor with the horses so effortless but clearly putting them so quickly at ease around him. It wasn't something a person could learn, it was just the way he was, and she wondered how many of the people who paid a small fortune to watch him work actually understood that.

He never said a word, just angled his body toward the float and the horse walked on. When he straightened, the horse stopped. And when he turned his body the other way, the horse patiently walked off, like he was a robot adhering to pre-determined commands.

"That's a very cool party trick," she said, in awe of how simple he made it look.

"It's my favorite thing to teach a horse," he said, patting the big gelding as he stood patiently waiting. "This fella came to me with serious issues, including a fear of traveling in a trailer after a bad experience. His old owner couldn't get him near one."

She listened, full of admiration for what he did. Growing up she'd believed she'd had the touch when it came to horses, but after seeing Sam work she knew that very little people actually had it, even if they were instinctively good with animals.

"He's handsome," she said, shielding her eyes from the sun as she looked the horse over. He was muscled and powerful looking, clearly a full American Quarter horse, and she wished Tanner was here to see him—it was the kind of horse her brother loved.

"Your horses," he asked. "I've been meaning to ask you their breeding."

Mia flipped the back of the trailer up and they walked side by side across the entrance to her stables.

"They're obviously Thoroughbred, but what gives them that edge?"

"American Quarter horse," she said smugly, always pleased when she was able to tell people what gave her horses their something special. "My secret weapon is that I've bred most of them myself, from a beautiful half Quarter horse stallion, out of Thoroughbred mares. The Quarter horse gives them the powerful rear ends and lovely temperaments, and the Thoroughbred adds the speed and athleticism."

He raised a brow and made her smile. "Clever girl. I'll have to remember that."

She faltered when his eyes lit upon hers, wondering whether she'd done the right thing the day before. She'd poked the bear, done something that she knew was going to result in a reaction from him, yet she'd done it anyway. She'd wanted him to look at her like that again, wanted to taste his lips and feel his hands on her. And damn it, it had felt good.

"So," she said, wondering whether to say anything and deciding not to. "Where do you want to ride today?"

Sam shrugged. "Show me around. Wherever you want to go, I'm just happy to be getting back in the saddle and I'm looking forward to seeing more of the ranch."

So was she. Only hers wasn't literal. She was ready to get back in the saddle where men were considered and put herself out there, otherwise she was going to look back in a few years' time and wonder why the hell she hadn't made more of the last part of her twenties.

* * *

Sam mounted his horse and waited for Mia to join him, noticing the change in his horse when she approached on her excitable little mare.

"Easy big fella," he murmured. "No need to get your tail all in a twist over an itty-bitty mare." He grinned to himself, feeling one side of his mouth kick out into a grin. Pity he didn't follow his own advice. A cute girl had gotten him all worked up in a sweat, too, and maybe, just maybe, his horse had felt his heart beat pick up.

"We're off?" he asked.

"Let's go," she replied, turning so she was facing the same direction as he was before they rode off side by side.

"You know, you're welcome to stay while you're working here if you want. Either at the main house or with me, in mine."

"I'm fine with the traveling," he said, not wanting to even entertain the idea of staying at her place. He'd lain awake the night before thinking about her, trying to figure his shit out but drawing a blank. "But thanks for the offer." He whistled for Blue, checking to make sure he was following them. "Your father said the same thing."

She didn't look too worried, but then he didn't think she'd offered for any reason other than to be polite. Although he wasn't entirely sure what she was up to, because he'd caught her glancing at him a few times since he'd arrived. Or maybe she'd been admiring his horse. He had no idea.

What he did know was that at some point he had to explain to her that their kiss hadn't meant anything. Well, it had meant something, but it couldn't *lead* to anything. He didn't like leading women on, and he sure as hell didn't want her getting the wrong idea.

"Do you have any ranch hands at your place?" she asked.

"Yeah, I have a full time guy, Bill, he's there every day and he keeps the place running for me when I'm not there. His son comes and helps out if there's extra work, but usually between me and him, we keep on top of everything."

"I wondered," she said, her eyes meeting his, "because you obviously travel a lot. It's hard when you have animals."

He nodded. "Yup, sure is. Even with Bill there I worry about them all. Especially Blue. I hate leaving my dog behind, so if I'm going anywhere within driving distance I'll just take him with me."

They rode along in silence for a bit and Sam admired the ranch from his elevated spot in the saddle.

"I'm pretty fond of Black Angus cattle," Sam told her, gesturing toward a herd. "There's something about those big, muscled shoulders and sleek black coats that makes them so damn good to look at, don't you think?"

She laughed and when he looked at her she was smiling still. "I suppose. I'm more into horse flesh though."

They had a lot of feed on the ranch and Sam knew from glancing that the place cost a lot to keep. Every fence rail was pristine, the facilities new or well maintained. The ranch was stunning and he felt privileged to be taking a look around.

"How did you find your horse?" Mia asked, pulling him from his thoughts. "Is he your favorite?"

"Hell yes," Sam replied. "He's great to ride, with a big-ass, rocking horse canter going on. I found him like I find most of my crew, horses people give up on or bring to me, and I take them on as projects and never get around to selling them."

"So you're good at collecting field ornaments, then?" she asked with a grin.

"Ha, good one." He chuckled. "Haven't heard them called that before, but yeah, I guess you could say that. I've got some old horses that gather dust and do little else, but animals come to my place for a good life, not a hard life. They've usually already had a rough time before they end up with me, but I try to make sure that every day after that is a good one."

"You've kind of got this whole screw-the-world thing going on, except for your animals," she mused, looking more relaxed in his company today than she'd been before. Her shoulders were relaxed, her smile easy, and there was a twinkle in her eyes when she spoke that he really liked. "Like when I first met you. I was so looking forward to meeting you, then you arrive and all I could think was what an arrogant son-of-a-bitch you were."

He laughed so hard that his horse startled. "You've got to be kidding me. I'm the least arrogant guy I know!"

"You must know a lot of assholes then," she said, making him crack up again.

"You're serious?"

"Hell yes! Have you not looked in the mirror lately?" she said, sounding exasperated, which made the whole thing way less funny when he realized she was being deadly serious. "You walked in here all *king of the world*, your way or the highway, and it kind of surprised me. I wasn't expecting that at all."

Sam thought about what she'd said. "And now? Do you still think that?"

"You want me to be honest?" she asked, glancing at him as they rode.

"Yeah, I do."

He listened to her sigh. "Look, I've been around wealthy and successful guys my entire life. I've seen how arrogant they get, how the whole sense of importance gets to their heads. I don't think you're necessarily like them, but parts of the way you act are, I suppose."

All this time he'd thought he'd been different, that he was still just the ordinary guy he'd always been. But his sister had called him out on something a while back, telling him he was being a jerk, and he wasn't about to pretend that two women like his sister and Mia were wrong.

"Well, I'm sorry that I made that first impression on you," he said. "You know, I haven't always lived this life. Hell, three years ago I was just a guy training horses out the back of the King ranch, and then my sister posted some videos of me on You Tube, created a channel for me and made me keep updating it every few days, and then I got an offer to do a tour. It kind of exploded within a couple of months, and I was suddenly touring the country showing my methods for training horses, being offered book deals and doing a crap load of merchandizing." He shrugged. "I really want to keep my feet on the ground, and I didn't think I'd ever let all the hype change me, but maybe I'm wrong."

"Want my advice?"

He glanced at her, feeling like he was seeing her for the first time. She'd grown up with so much, but she was so grounded, so impossibly unpretentious, and it was nice to be around. He had a feeling her mom might have been to thank for that, the way she'd been so emotional when they'd spoken about her and her upbringing. "I don't know if I do."

"Well, I'm going to give it to you anyway," she said with a smile. "You don't have to be a loner to stay true to yourself. I've been on my own for so long, professionally and personally, but I don't think it's healthy to always be fighting for yourself with no one in your corner with you."

Sam didn't respond. He got what she was saying, but he kind of liked being a loner. Or at least he always had done in the past—he sure wasn't minding her company right now.

"Want to go for a canter?" she asked with a wicked smile.

"Hell yes."

She didn't wait around once she'd heard his answer, pushing her little mare into a canter so fast he missed a beat and was almost left behind. His horse fought to go faster, to get ahead, but Mia was glancing behind and he realized this wasn't just a leisurely canter, this was a race, and one she was determined to win.

Sam rode hard, his competitive spirit making it impossible for him not to try to overtake her, but Mia was fast and even though her horse wasn't as big as his, she was putting her all into it. He didn't doubt how good they were when they were competing, or why they were such a great team. The mare was clearly as determined as she was.

They cantered across the field, then up a small incline, before heading down into another endless field. They raced past towering old trees and a herd of cattle, although the big black beasts simply lifted their heads and kept chewing, watching them blur past. Maybe they were used to their daredevil mistress flying past at high speeds.

When Mia eventually slowed they were neck and neck, but Sam pulled back too, seeing that their ride was soon to end with a fence looming in the near distance.

"That was great," he panted, hot from the ride, his horse blowing hard beneath him. "Just what I needed."

"Blows out the cobwebs, doesn't it?" she asked, looking

exhilarated, her cheeks flushed a deep pink, her smile wide. "This girl has a lot of go."

She patted her horse and they kept walking, letting their mounts cool down and catching their breaths themselves.

"That's what I miss most when I'm away working. Being able to ride like that," Sam confessed.

"Are you home for long now?" she asked, and he noticed she'd taken her feet out of the stirrups and was flexing her ankles. He did the same, feeling tight and stiff.

"I have a couple of clinics in Texas coming up actually," he said. "It'll be nice to be working within driving distance of home again. But other than the next couple months, I've decided to keep my schedule clear for the rest of the year." He just hadn't told his agent that yet. "I've been touring back to back for the last couple of years and I'm done."

"I spent some time traveling for my riding, a couple of years on the road, touring to every show jumping competition I could," she said. "It takes its toll, and it's always good to get back to your roots, you know? That's what I found hard in Europe. I mean, it was great competing over there and working with some great trainers, but there's nothing like coming home. I like the landscape here, nothing beats it."

"Agreed."

"Want to take a rest over there? It's my favorite tree on the property and you'll get a beautiful view of the river."

Sam followed her point and nodded. It looked like a pretty spot, and when they were closer he admired the big, wicked gnarled trunk of the oak, its limbs fanning out to provide an umbrella of shade from the sun. Behind it the river that was the ranch's namesake curled around, and Sam admired how pretty the setting was, how peaceful River Ranch was.

They dismounted and tethered their horses, and Sam joined Mia beneath the tree, backs against the base of the trunk, legs out in front of them. He watched as she absently picked at some grass and twirled it between her fingers. Blue came and nudged up against him, leaning in, tongue lolling out the side. It had taken him a while to catch up to them.

"I'm sorry about what happened yesterday," he said, knowing he needed to set the record straight and make his intentions clear. "It shouldn't have happened."

She gave him a quick look before going back to plucking grass again. "It wasn't a big deal. You don't need to mention it."

He wasn't so sure about that. "I'm here to work, and I behaved in a seriously unprofessional manner. I didn't mean to make you uncomfortable."

She shook her head, leaning back and staring at him. "You know, the last thing you managed to do was make me feel uncomfortable. But thanks anyway for the apology."

They sat in silence, the only noise the call of birdsong in the tree above them. He shut his eyes, wondered why he always managed to make such a ridiculous mess when it came to women these days. He'd meant to tell Mia something else entirely, but instead it had come out as one big embarrassing apology.

"It must have been nice growing up here," Sam said, hoping that changing the subject would lighten things up between them again.

"It was," Mia replied. "My sister and I were good friends growing up, even though she hated horses, and my brothers gave us a hard time but they would have beaten the crap out of anyone who hurt me or Ange." She sighed.

"But?" Sam asked. "That sounded very much like there was a *but* coming."

She laughed. "It was fun and we got to spend lots of time outdoors and adventuring, but when mom died, the magic of the place kind of died too. For a while anyway. And then Angelina and Cody went off to college and Tanner started to ride rodeo more seriously and he was away a lot, and then it was just me and dad rattling around in that big old house. It was kind of lonely from then on."

Sam was about to ask her more when she slapped her thigh and caught him off guard.

"Let's go," she announced, holding out her hand to him, already standing in front of him.

It was a nice gesture. Clearly she wasn't able to haul him up, but he clasped his palm to hers anyway and pulled up to his feet. Once he was standing in front of her, he noticed she was forced to tilt her head back to look up at him.

He wondered if she was going to say something, her eyes seemingly so full of questions, but instead she held his hand for another beat before letting go and turning. He wanted to reach for her, to pull her back, to kiss her again and think *to hell with it*. But he didn't. He didn't do complicated, and that had complicated written all over it.

"I thought we'd take a longer route back. Just walk and trot to stretch them out," she said, calling over her shoulder.

Sam cleared his throat, mounted up and nudged his horse forward. And this time he kept his mouth shut.

Mia glanced at her watch, surprised by how quickly the day had flown past. She hadn't eaten anything, neither of them had, since before setting out late morning, and now it was already afternoon. Her stomach rumbled in response.

"There's food in the tack shed," she told Sam as she

landed with a thud on the ground. "I meant to have us back earlier."

"It was worth it," he said with a grunt as he landed on the concrete, too. "But right now I could eat a. . . ."

She laughed. "Horse? Quick, close your ears, Indi!"

He chuckled and she realized how comfortable she'd become in his company. He was a decent guy, kinder than she could have expected given their rocky start, but there was something nice about being around someone so calm and sweet with horses.

"Hey, I thought you might like to watch me with Tex this afternoon," he said as he unsaddled his horse.

Mia couldn't have been more surprised if a gust of wind had blown her over. "You're serious? You're actually *asking* me to watch?"

He gave her a look that made her quit with the sarcasm. "An effort to curb my arrogance. I'm not liking your first impression of me." He looked exasperated, and she kind of liked seeing him look uncomfortable, like he was so well out of his comfort zone. "You know what? It's actually seriously fucking me off how badly we started out."

"I can't," she said, wishing she'd never agreed to going out tonight with Kat but knowing she couldn't cancel at the last minute. Hearing him drop the f-bomb had been kind of cute, because he did look seriously annoyed. "Tomorrow?" she asked.

"I was going to give him the weekend off, but yeah, I suppose I could come by tomorrow."

She took Indi over to hose her down, feeling guilty that she'd only ridden her today and one other horse earlier in the morning. She usually tried to fit in at least three rides a day to make sure all her horses were all fit and well-muscled.

"I'll see you tomorrow then," she said as she passed him the hose and led Indi off. She put her away, ran to fetch her some hay, checked her water supply and then hurried off toward the house. She'd left all the food in the tack shed for Sam, so she grabbed a banana off the counter when she ran through the kitchen, pausing only long enough to eat it and to down a big glass of water. She went to dash into the bathroom but stopped to get a packet of rice crackers from the pantry. At least she could eat them as she hurried to get ready.

As she wolfed down the crackers and turned the shower on, stripping her clothes off, she wished it were Sam she was getting ready for instead of some mystery guy. She stepped into the shower, under the hot stream of water, letting it run over her face and down her body, over her breasts and down her stomach. She reached for the soap and lathered her skin up, still thinking about Sam and wishing to hell she wasn't. She was imagining him storming into the house and finding her in the shower, pressing her up against the tiled wall and kissing the hell out of her this time. His lips would be rougher, his hold firmer, his body . . .

She gulped and opened her eyes, turning around and running her hands through her hair to check it was wet enough for shampooing. *Enough with the thoughts about Sam!* He'd made it more than clear that he only wanted a professional relationship with her, and she was going to respect that. She probably wasn't even remotely his type.

She shampooed and conditioned her long hair, rinsed it then stepped out. Kat's cousin might not be Sam, but he was a single guy taking her out for drinks and dinner. She'd be damned if she wasn't going to get all dolled up and have a hell of a time, because it wasn't like she let her hair down very often, and it was time she did.

Even if, deep down, all she wanted was to pull her hair back up into a ponytail and head straight out that door and down to Tex. An afternoon in the hot, sticky Texas sun watching Sam work the stallion would have meant more to her than all the fancy dinners in the world.

She pushed thoughts of Sam away and wrapped her towel around herself, pinning up her hair. She'd made a promise to Kat, and she wasn't going to flake on her. Which meant she had to get herself ready, go out and have some fun. She deserved it, and if she didn't start going out more now, she'd end up an old lady sitting home alone, surrounded by animals and damn lonely at that.

Chapter 9

MIA was starting to get nervous. She knew it wasn't supposed to be a date, but from the text she'd just received from Kat, she was starting to realize just how much of a setup this was. Kat had messaged claiming she had an urgent surgery to attend to, and Mia called bullshit. She was probably sitting at home with her feet up, sipping a wine and laughing at her genius plan to set her best friend up with her cute cousin. She re-read Kat's last message for the tenth time, cursing her all over again.

Don't do anything I wouldn't do. Oh wait, there's nothing I wouldn't do. Have fun gorgeous xx

She looked at herself again in her full-length mirror, crippling self-doubts starting to crack her otherwise confident façade. She had a pile of rejected clothes on the bed, from cute dresses to sparkly miniskirts, but in the end she'd decided to wear her go-to outfit, what she felt herself in and what she was most confident in. She had on her skinny ankle-length jeans, heels and a cute top. It had the back cut out, which made it sexy, but she still felt like her. She sighed and put on some lip gloss. She was used to having her long, straight hair in a braid when she was working the horses or in a ponytail to keep it out of the way, but she'd decided to use her rollers and make it curl a little, so she had bouncy hair to give her an extra injection of confidence.

Mia heard a knock at the door and a new wave of nerves hit, her stomach flipping at the prospect of the blind date she was about to embark on. Why had she said yes? Why was she even doing this, why . . . ?

"Mia?"

She was reaching for her bag but she froze, ears pricked. Was that *Sam*?

"Mia, you here?"

She tucked her bag under her arm and walked out of her room, pulling the door behind her so no one could see into the tornado of clothes in her wake.

"Sam?" she called back, surprised. "Just a sec."

He was standing at the door to her living room. He'd obviously knocked then walked straight around to her open doors, the same way he'd come in the other day.

"Is something wrong? What happened with Tex?" she asked, hurrying across the hardwood floors, her heels click-clacking.

"I . . ." he started to speak then looked her up and down. She stopped, feeling the heat rising at the way he was looking at her. "Damn, you look gorgeous."

She brushed off his compliment, shaking her head. "I'm just wearing jeans, nothing special. What's happened?"

He gave her a look, a look that travelled up and down her body, the warmth in his gaze making her wildly uncomfortable yet excited at the same time. Hell, everything about him was . . . she swallowed, her mouth dry as cotton candy. Sam was positively smoldering just standing there in his low-slung jeans and boots, dusty and sweaty and sexy as hell. *This* was the guy she wished she was about to spend the next few hours alone with.

"Ah, nothing's wrong. That's not why I'm here," he said, leaning in the doorway, hand reaching to his hair. She watched as he brushed his fingers through it, her own fingers itching to reach out and knead through his thick hair.

She waited, wondering what he was about to say. Had he just come over to see her or . . .

A knock sounded out, around the other side of the house.

"You expecting someone?" he asked.

She nodded. "Yes. I'm, well, I'm going out for the evening. That's why you're seeing me all dressed up instead of in riding clothes for once."

Sam opened his mouth to say something at the same time as a loud, deep voice called out.

"Anyone home?"

Mia looked on in horror as Sam's face turned from open and friendly to coldly hostile.

"Mia?" a handsome man asked, appearing from the side of the house, the same way Sam had just walked.

"You must be Trent," she said, smiling and extending her hand. She walked past Sam and smiled when Trent kissed her cheek. He held out a bunch of flowers, long-stemmed white roses wrapped in a crisp white paper and with a huge ribbon around them.

"For you."

"Thank you," she said, blushing as he let out a whistle.

"Kat never told me how beautiful you were."

"Don't be silly," she said, shaking her head. "But thank you for the roses."

She turned to take them to the kitchen counter and saw

Sam watching her, his eyes narrowed, jaw clenched so hard she could visibly see the strain.

Mia paused and smiled at him. "What were you going to say before?" she asked. "Was everything okay with Tex?"

"Fine," he growled out, his face like stone now. She could feel the cool, cold undertones of his mood as she stood in front of him. "I'll see you another day."

Mia watched him stalk past Trent, not even saying hello even as her date held out his hand to introduce himself. She felt numb and stared after him as he left.

"Someone you work with?" Trent asked.

Mia nodded, pulling herself away from Sam's retreating figure, wishing she wasn't so stuck on thinking about him. She was drawn to Sam in a way she couldn't understand, something about him pulling her in and making her want to know more about him, making her want to kiss him again and see his face soften, to see his eyes crinkle as he smiled down at her. But the Sam she'd just watched storm away from her house didn't show any resemblance whatsoever to that man.

"Ah, he's a horse trainer. We've been working together," she managed. Trent raised a brow, looking surprised. "He's an employee of yours? I'd suggest finding a new horse trainer, maybe one with better manners."

Mia smiled. Weakly. "He's great with the horses," she said, realizing how silly that sounded. "But yeah, he could work on his social skills."

She had no idea what she'd done wrong, or why he'd turned so dark on her, but something told her that whatever had been going on between her and the sexy horseman was well and truly over before it had even started. And even though she was all dressed up and about to have a fun time out with a handsome man, she felt deflated. She'd have traded her heels for boots to follow after Sam in a heartbeat.

"Ready to go?" Trent asked.

Mia nodded. "Give me a sec to close the doors up. I'll meet you around the front."

She methodically closed the doors and windows, before hurrying out to meet her date. Trent was cute in a preppy kind of way, his hair perfectly combed, clean shaven, pants pressed and loafers impeccable. She should have been impressed, but instead all she could think about was a man with eyes the color of drizzled dark chocolate, cheeks covered in stubble, wearing worn jeans that he filled out in all the right places.

"Let's go," she said, smiling at Trent and pretending that she was thrilled to be going out instead of longing to stay at the ranch.

"So are we going to talk about it?"

Sam glared at Nate. "Talk about what?"

"Whatever it is that has you all bent out of sorts?" Nate chuckled and Sam scowled.

"Nothing to talk about," he said, straightening his shoulders, not realizing how hunched over his beer he'd been. "How was New York?"

Nate laughed. "Well, I've been telling you about my trip the past few minutes. You've been too busy staring into that beer of yours like you're gonna kill it instead of listening."

"Sorry," Sam muttered, lifting the glass and draining it. "Want to switch to whiskey?"

"Do you even have to ask?"

He watched as Nate pushed his beer aside and nodded to the bartender. "Two Wild Turkeys. Straight up, double shots."

Sam turned to him, heels hitched on the barstool. "It's good to see you. It's been too long."

"Yeah, it has," Nate agreed. "But seriously, what's up? You look like you're ready to commit murder."

"Ah, it's nothing. Forget it," Sam said, brushing it off and sure as hell not wanting to talk about it to Nate or anyone else. "How's my lovely sister?"

"Worried about her brother," Nate said, nudging Sam's whiskey toward him and holding it up. "Cheers."

Sam clinked his glass to Nate's and took a welcome, small sip. It burned a warm trail down his throat, a fire he'd long ago learned to enjoy. He took another sip before relaxing back against the bar. Thank god for strong liquor.

"So? Come on. What's up? You look like shit."

"Me?" Sam laughed. "You're like a dog with a god-damn bone, you know that? And you're the one with dark circles under your eyes, looking like shit."

It was only a half truth; Nate did look tired, but he'd never looked like shit in his life. Sam, on the other hand, knew he probably *did* look like shit.

"How's the work at the Ford ranch going? You tamed that asshole stallion yet?"

Sam grunted. "Yeah, it's fine."

"Ah, I see," Nate grinned. "The problem is with the Ford ranch. Spill."

"Stop grinning like you've won the fucking lottery." Sam shook his head.

"I'm guessing it's not old man Ford causing you to look all pissed either. It's . . ."

Sam raised a brow at the same time as he raised his glass, taking a bigger gulp this time.

"Holy shit, it's one of the girls, isn't it? What's her name, Mia is it? Is she the show jumper?"

Sam glared at him, his fingers tightening around the glass as he stared at Nate. "Don't you fucking tell me you—"

Nate held up both hands, protesting his innocence. "Nothing ever happened between us, don't worry. But she's beautiful and talented, I know that. In fact—"

"Thank god," Sam muttered, draining the rest of his drink. "Another," he said, waving at the bartender.

"So what the hell did she do to get you all bent out of sorts?"

"Nothing," he said. "Can we change the subject? We didn't come here to talk about Mia Ford."

"Oh, but we did," Nate said, chuckling like he was enjoying every single moment of torturing Sam. "I love your sister, don't get me wrong, and I would *never* be unfaithful to her, but I miss this. You know, talking shit, being your wingman."

Now it was Sam's turn to laugh. "You were *never* my wingman. I was always the wingman." Nate had wooed and slept with just about every single attractive woman this side of Texas, which meant Sam had definitely been the Robin to Nate's Batman.

"Come on, tell Uncle Nate what she did to you. You have trouble getting it up?"

"Jesus Christ, Nate!" Sam swore. "Can we please change the goddamn subject?"

"Well, we could, except that I'm fairly sure that's Mia Ford sipping on champagne over there," Nate said, sounding smug. "And I want to know what the hell she's doing with that preppy-looking dickhead instead of keeping you company?"

Sam groaned, convinced Nate was goading him. There was no way she was here. "I call bullshit."

"You can call whatever the hell you want, but see this?" Nate waved and smiled, leaning against the bar and flashing his killer smile. "That's me waving to Mia. And I know her because she's an old friend of the family's"

Sam turned, almost instantly locking eyes with her. She was standing close to preppy guy, smiling, laughing at something he said, and it made his skin burn, as if a match had been thrown against his skin.

"Motherfucker," he muttered.

"Who me? Or the guy she's on a date with?"

Sam wasn't about to keep staring. He turned around and took a sip of his drink, trying to calm down. He had no idea why he was so pissed, why he couldn't smile and go over and say hello. Mia was his boss, they worked together, he should have been able to keep things professional between them. He was the one telling her their kiss had meant nothing.

"Tell me what happened? I haven't seen you so bent out of shape over a girl since . . ."

"There's nothing to tell," Sam said quickly. "She's a beautiful woman, and if I was looking to meet someone, then I'd be stupid not to ask her out."

"You can't be a monk all your life. So you had your heart broken? So what. It's time to move on."

Sam scowled at Nate. "Move on? Maybe if you ever get betrayed like that, find your woman in bed with another man and get laughed at in your own home, you'd understand."

Nate went to say something, then gave him a weird kind of look, and Sam groaned. Clearly his friend was taking it easy on him, because usually he would have threatened to break his nose for saying something like that about Faith.

"Obviously that was hypothetical. Faith loves you and she'd never do that, but . . ."

"I get your point," Nate said gruffly. Sam knew Nate would never get over losing Faith, to anything happening to their relationship, and he wished he'd used a less personal example. "But seriously, you know what they say about getting back on the horse. You're leaving it way too long."

"I'm not a fucking monk," he snapped. "I just don't want a relationship."

"So don't have a relationship. Be friends with benefits."

When Sam glared at him Nate just shrugged.

"Fine, don't be. But don't let some preppy idiot sweep Mia off her feet if you like her. Hell, you never get like this over women."

"I know," Sam muttered. "She's different. There's something about her."

"Which is why you feel like you can't do casual with her."

"Dammit, she's the kind of girl you'd take home to meet your mom. But I don't have a mom to take her home to, so that's all shades of fucked up even thinking like that," Sam said bitterly.

"She's got under your skin," Nate said, draining his glass. "When a woman truly gets under your skin? Only a fool walks away. Trust me."

Sam stared at him, listened to his words and nodded. There was no point getting angry with Nate, he was only speaking the truth and they both knew it.

"Then call me a fool, but I'm walking away."

"You're not going over to see her?"

Sam shook his head. "No."

"Well, if there's nothing to watch, then I'm off," Nate said, sliding his glass across the bar to the bartender. "I've got a wife and baby girls to get home to, and I've missed them like crazy."

Sam frowned. He could have done with another drink, but at least this way he could still drive home.

"Want to come over for a BBQ on Sunday?" Nate asked. "All the family will be there, it'd be good to see you."

"Yeah, sure thing," Sam said, glancing back at Mia and seeing her in conversation with her date.

He grabbed his keys off the bar, leaving his drink half full still, and followed Nate out. It was better this way. If he'd had any more to drink, he'd have ended up making his way to Mia, and he had no idea what would have happened after that. He clenched his fists, wishing he could smack her smarmy date right in the face, knock his damn teeth out and get Mia the hell out of the bar.

"We okay?" Nate asked, his hand landing heavy on Sam's shoulder. He was staring at him, hard, like he didn't mind using force if he had to if it meant getting his brother-in-law out of the bar safely.

"Yeah, we're good," Sam said, forced to unclench his jaw when he had to speak.

"You sure about that?" Nate asked. "Because from where I'm standing, the veins in your neck are about to explode and your jaw is bulging."

Sam grunted and pushed past Nate. "Just get me out of here."

"Good, right answer. Because your sister would beat the crap out of me herself if I let you get into a bar fight."

"*Sam!*"

He heard Nate groan, loudly, at the same time his name was called.

"Were you leaving without even coming over to say hello?"

Sam released his fingers from the tight grip of his palms. "Yeah. Didn't want to, ah, interrupt you."

"Nate," Nate suddenly said, holding out his hand. "It's been a long time. How are you, Mia?"

"Hey, Nate, it's good to see you," Mia said, clasping his hand and leaning in to kiss his cheek. Sam felt the now-familiar clench of his jaw and tightening across his mouth return. Seeing her touch her lips to Nate's face was about to send him over the edge for no sensible reason.

They stood awkwardly for a moment before Mia spoke again. "Would you like to join us for a drink?"

"No," Sam said, realizing how hastily he'd replied when Nate kicked him. Dammit.

"I'm heading home. I've got two baby girls to see and I've missed them like hell these past couple days." Nate chuckled. "I'm looking forward to cuddling them on their night feed, so I'm off. Good to see you again."

"Oh, how sweet," Mia said, grinning. "Well, it was nice to see you again, too."

Sam nodded, seeing how easily Nate was charming Mia. He definitely deserved a black goddamn eye for flirting with her like that.

"Sam, do you have a minute?" Mia asked, her voice lower now, fingers brushing his arm, her big blue eyes trained on his and making him soften.

"Yeah, sure." Sam waved to Nate. "See you on Sunday. Drive safe."

Nate held up his hand and walked off, giving him a long, hard look first. Sam knew that look was a warning; he clearly didn't want to hear about any shit going down after he'd left.

"Everything okay?" Sam asked, knowing his voice sounded gruff as he stared back down at Mia.

"Everything *was* okay. Until you stormed off this afternoon like I'd done something to offend you. What's wrong?"

He suppressed a groan. Talking about his feelings was *not* something he excelled at. In fact, he had zero interest in discussing anything to do with how he felt about Mia or almost anything else.

"Sam?"

"Look, I wasn't expecting you to be all dolled up and heading out on a date when I came by, that's all. You took me by surprise."

"So we're good now? There's nothing—"

He refused to let her finish, cringing as he held up his hand. "We're good. Of course we're good," he mumbled. "Now you head back to your date, and I'll head off home."

"Sam!"

The look on her face told him he wasn't getting let off the hook so easily. "What Mia? What the hell do you want from me?" he fumed. "Walk your pretty little ass back to your date and get on with your evening."

"Why are you being such an asshole?" she asked, glaring at him, her eyes like saucers and making him feel like shit all over again.

"Because you look fucking beautiful and I hate seeing you out with that preppy prick, okay? *That's* why I'm being an asshole."

Fuck! Now he'd come out and said it, and he wished to hell he could rewind and stop the words coming out his mouth.

"Wow," she whispered, still staring at him.

"Yeah, wow. Can I go now?"

She slowly shook her head, catching her lower lip between her teeth. He was about to point to her date, even glanced across and saw the guy propped up against the bar, staring into his drink. He almost felt sorry for him.

"Mia, I need to go," he said, muttering the words as she leaned into him, her palm against his chest as she moved closer.

He knew what he should have done. He should have pushed her back, gently told her no and walked the hell out of the bar as he intended to do. But he didn't.

"You really think I look beautiful tonight?" she asked, her voice breathy, eyes focused on his mouth as she spoke.

"Hell yeah I do," he murmured back, wondering how a woman as wealthy and stunning as Mia could seem so genuinely surprised at a compliment like that.

She closed the distance then, quickly, like she wasn't sure what to do and had just thought *to hell with it*. Her lips met his fast, and he crushed his mouth to hers as she stepped in against him, her breasts to his chest.

Sam kissed her back; he had no choice. He'd thought about kissing her again ever since the first time, and it felt even better than he remembered. She tasted like the champagne she'd been drinking, her breath sweet against his as he wrapped one arm around her, holding her tight, his hand to the small of her back.

Mia's arm snaked around his neck, warm against his skin as she opened her mouth and touched his tongue with hers, her lips so soft, her body so snug to his. He wanted nothing more than to scoop her up and get the hell out of the bar and somewhere quieter, but he doubted that was an option right now.

"Wow," she whispered against his lips as she finally pulled back. Sam claimed one last kiss, one final brush of his lips against hers before slowly releasing her.

Mia's cheeks were flushed as she looked up at him, and

he heard his own ragged breath as her gaze dropped to his mouth then made its way back to his eyes.

"I'd call more girls beautiful if that's the response I got every time," he teased, unable to help himself.

"I'd better go," she said, looking embarrassed as she glanced back toward the bar. Sam almost felt guilty about what he'd done, but every time he'd glanced at the guy she was with, he'd been on his phone. He doubted he'd even have seen it. "You sure you don't want to come over for a drink?"

He laughed. "Yeah, I think it's best I don't. You know, since you're on a date with another guy and I just kissed the hell out of you."

Mia smiled. "Actually, I'd say it was me kissing the hell out of you, but I'll let that one slide." She laughed. "And he's been way more interested in work than me all night."

She reached for his hand and he caught her palm, holding it for a second and looking into her eyes.

"You really do look beautiful tonight, Mia. Really, stunningly beautiful. And if the guy you're with is more interested in his phone than you? I'd say he's a damn fool."

Her smile lit up her entire face.

"You know, you don't look so bad yourself."

She gave him one last, hard-to-read look before disappearing, and he was left wondering what kind of rocks-for-brains idiot he was for letting her walk away.

The sensible kind, he reasoned with himself. He couldn't get involved with Mia. She was beautiful, intelligent and an accomplished rider. She should have been everything he'd ever wanted. Only she wasn't. Because he couldn't do relationships, not anymore. He'd seen his mother walk out on his dad, and them, and then his own girlfriend, *fiancée,* the woman he'd promised to marry, had gone and ripped his heart out. He couldn't trust again, and that meant he wasn't looking for anything serious, and he knew that Mia wouldn't be the kind of girl to do a no-strings-attached affair.

He squared his shoulders and walked out of the bar. The cooler night air was like a soft punch to the face as he headed for his vehicle.

There was no wedding, brood of children or white picket fence in his future, and not even Mia Ford could tempt him to change his mind about that. He was a horseman, that's what his life was, and he was going to live his career and enjoy his ranch. *Alone.*

He could be the world's coolest uncle, he could have casual flings with beautiful women, and he could enjoy every goddamn minute of his life.

Blue wagged his tail, jumping out of the driver's seat when he opened the door and moving aside for him. Sam dropped his hand to his dog's head and smiled down at him.

"You're the closest thing I'll ever have to a wife, ain't that right, gorgeous?" he muttered to the dog, wishing he could push away the image of Mia standing in front of him, lips plump and pink from being kissed, her eyes so vivid they were like staring at a perfect blue sky.

Blue jumped up and licked his face and Sam laughed. At least he had his dog. It wasn't much of a consolation, but it was something.

Chapter 10

MIA stretched out but kept her eyes shut tight. The sun was bathing her in warmth, and she wasn't ready to kick the covers off and give up her snuggly spot on her bed. She pulled the covers up higher, basking in the delicious moment between asleep and awake, wondering if she should just go back to sleep instead of getting up so early.

Buzz buzz, buzz buzz.

She reached across to her side table for her phone, forced to open an eye when she didn't manage to clasp it. Who would be calling or texting her so early in the morning?

She saw it was indeed a text message, actually three of them. Snuggling back down, heart starting to race in anticipation, she unlocked her phone and scanned the messages.

Had a great night, would love to see you again before I fly out. Any chance of round two? T

Mia groaned. Seriously, Trent wanted to see her again? He'd spent more time texting and replying to emails. She got being busy with work, but it had really started to get on her nerves. He seemed like a nice enough guy, but he wasn't for her.

I was thinking dinner again. Or drinks. Pick you up again?

She sunk deeper into her pillows. Not a chance. She was pleased she'd said yes to going out, but there was no round two. Mia shut her eyes, seeing Sam's face, remembering his lips on hers, how his mouth had tasted, the slightly rough brush of his stubble against her top lip that had made the whole thing feel even sexier. She sighed. Maybe Trent would have been more her type if she hadn't already met the delicious Sam Mendes.

She looked at her phone again. Message number three was from Kat, which meant that none of them was from Sam. She wasn't sure what she'd been expecting, but she had only bothered to reach for the phone so soon after waking because of him.

Mia stayed in bed, pleased she hadn't drunk too much the night before. Three glasses had been plenty, because she hated having to work her horses with a hangover. Hours out in the hot Texas sun, wearing a riding helmet, was enough to give her a headache by the end of the day without adding alcohol into the mix.

She scanned the news, checked her messages again, then had a quick look on Instagram before finally rising and walking out to her kitchen in her PJ's. Mia opened the fridge, got out some fruit and started chopping, before pulling out a bowl and emptying some homemade muesli into it. She finished making her breakfast, topped it with some yoghurt and then curled up on her sofa, staring out at the view as she ate.

When she'd built this house, it had been for her own sanity, and it had remained her own little oasis away from the main part of the ranch. She loved the land, land that had been in her mother's family for generations, even though most people who didn't know their history would think her father had purchased it. He wasn't the only one who'd contributed to their billion-dollar family fortune. It was the connection to her mother that was most special to her, and when she watched the landscape through her huge glass windows, she could imagine her riding past in the distance. Her mother had always worn her long hair out, and she'd loved riding bareback, and Mia was certain that was why she'd always been so balanced in the saddle. She'd started riding with her mother when she was young, holding on tight as they'd gone for big rides over their land, until she'd started to ride her first pony, Bubble, alongside her. Even now, she could jump a fence with as much ease bareback as she could with a saddle on.

She finished eating her muesli but didn't move until a soft knock startled her. No one usually bothered her here, especially not in the morning. Her father respected her space and understood that she liked her privacy, and as well as she could recall, she was certain none of her siblings were home visiting. She hadn't seen Angelina in weeks, since she'd last come home for a quick weekend vacation, and Cody hadn't visited in months. Not that her brothers would bother knocking first, they weren't anywhere near polite enough for that, and Ange would have just called out before letting herself in.

She stood, tugging her loose fitting tank top down and checking her shorts weren't riding up too high. The knock sounded out again, a bit louder this time.

"Coming!" she called out.

It only took her a moment to move through her living space toward the front door, and she saw Sam standing there through the glass. It was the only downside to having a house with so much glass on every exterior wall; visitors could see in and she had nowhere to hide.

"Hey," she said when she opened the door, leaning against the heavy timber, conscious of the fact that he was fully dressed and she was wearing only enough clothing to cover her boobs and butt.

He looked down, clearly taking in her bare legs. She knew her stomach was just showing but she refused the urge to tug her top back down for fear that it might then expose way too much of her breasts. She wasn't exactly used to anyone seeing her in what she slept in.

"Hey," he finally said in reply. It had probably only been seconds, but she felt like she'd been standing there forever with him staring at her.

"You, ah . . ." she fumbled over the words, not sure what she was even trying to say or what she wanted to say. Because all she could look at was his mouth and all she could think about was kissing him again. Mouths fused, bodies pressed tight, inhaling the masculine, delicious smell and feel of the man she couldn't stop thinking about.

Sam didn't say anything, but *everything* about the way he was looking at her changed. He looked predatory, the darkness of his eyes and the gentle upturn of his mouth as he suddenly stormed the distance between them exciting her as much as it terrified her.

It took him four, maybe five strides to close the gap, eyes never leaving hers as he cupped her body against his and walked her back against the wall. Mia gasped, the wall cool against her skin, the softness of his plaid shirt brushing against her skin and making her want to move closer into him instead. But then his knee moved between her legs and she realized the shirt was the only soft thing about him. Sam pinned her back, one hand on her hip, the other grazing her face as he brought his mouth down and kissed her. Hard. This was like last night reigniting all over again, his lips unrelenting, his touch firm. She happily gave in to him, wishing she had the courage to push him back and lead him brazenly by the hand down the hall to her bedroom. But she didn't.

Instead she let him lead, let him take control. She surrendered to his touch, gasping when his fingers brushed the bare skin on her hip, his leg even harder against her as she pushed against him and moved closer, drinking him in, unable to get enough of him.

She was being roughed up in her own house, and loving every second of it.

Mia snuck her hands between them, pushing at him, desperate to feel his skin against her fingers. Their lips were moist, meshed together, moving in time, and she wanted more of him.

"No," he rasped, pulling back the moment she tugged at his shirt.

Mia didn't listen to him, pushing against him again, mouth searching out his, not ready to stop. There was no way he was going to leave her like this, and he wasn't the only one who knew how to take charge.

"Mia," he said softly, hands on her shoulders as he held her back.

Why was he stopping? "No," she disagreed, scooping her arms around his neck and smiling as she stared at his lips and then pulled him down. She didn't exactly have to force him to dip his head; one tug and he was groaning and moving to meet her, his mouth rapidly finding hers again. This time his kisses were slower, matching her pace, teasing her and slowly, softly brushing back and forth.

It felt even sexier than before, her whole body tingling in anticipation as his palms rested on her hips, fingers curled into her skin.

When he finally pulled back again, she was breathless. She gave him a little push, hands sliding down his chest when she finally released them from his neck.

"Well, that was a nice way to start the morning," she whispered.

Sam slowly let go of her, but his eyes never left hers.

"Anyone ever told you how sexy you look dressed like that?"

She grinned, embarrassed but flattered. "Actually, no." She didn't tell him it was because no one had really ever seen what she wore to bed. "Anyone ever told you what soft lips you have?"

He laughed. "Lips of silk, heart of steel."

She didn't for a moment believe the heart of steel part, but she didn't bother correcting him.

"I just came by to let you know I was here."

Mia was still catching her breath, unable to resist smiling at his wry words. "Hmm, I think you managed that."

They stood for a moment, the heat between them almost in need of a fire crew to put it out. She studied him, indulged in really looking at his face, more brazenly probably than she'd ever done before. There was something about him, something about the way he looked at her or spoke to her or treated her. She just didn't know what exactly it was.

"You need to get dressed."

"I don't usually ride in my PJ's, so there was no chance of me coming out like this."

"It's not your riding that I'm worried about," he muttered.

She flushed, enjoying the burst of heat that ignited deep in her belly and rose like a wildfire across her skin. "Why are you really here?" she asked, then laughed at her own question when he gave an innocent shrug before backing up a few paces and leaning against the door jamb. "Oh, *I get it.* You were here early to check that my date hadn't stayed over."

Sam's smile was replaced with a face that was impossibly difficult to read. "Why would I do that?"

She shrugged. "No idea. But he's not, if that's what you're wondering."

"Good," he replied. "Now are we going to work the stallion together or are we going to trade jibes while you minx around in your sexy little sleep outfit?"

Mia's mouth twisted up into a smile even though she fought hard to hide her satisfaction. "Yeah, we're going to work the stallion," she said, moving closer to him. She stood on tip-toes, palms to his chest as she grazed a kiss to his cheek. She stayed still, lips still against his skin, waiting for him to move. A thrill ran through her, a shiver down her spine, when he didn't.

When he finally turned his head to her, she pressed a deep, slow kiss to his lips before moving back. She'd never reacted to a man like this before, and she had no idea what it was about Sam that was driving her crazy. Whatever it was, he was good for her, and she loved the way her body seemed to hum when she was around him, as if his kisses whispered from her mouth all the way down her body, skimming across her skin and making her feel more alive than she'd ever felt before.

"See you soon," she murmured, leaving him standing there as she walked away and into her bedroom.

Part of her wished he would follow her, that he'd storm

after her and throw her over his shoulder, like a caveman conquering the woman he'd been lusting after, claiming her and making sure she knew it. But then again, she liked the anticipation, the burning heat of his eyes on her as he watched her. Mia didn't look back, she couldn't, but she was damn excited for whatever the hell happened next if that was just a taste of what she had to look forward to.

Sam walked back to where his truck was parked by the stables and whistled out to his dog. He patted his leg, praising Blue when he ran immediately over and trotted beside him the rest of the way.

Mia had been right, there was only one reason he'd showed up at her place in the morning, and it had everything to do with him wanting to make sure her date wasn't there. Seeing her, alone and wearing her PJ's, had comforted him. Clearly she hadn't stayed at Preppy Guy's place, either.

Two reasons. He was only lying to himself if he didn't acknowledge the fact that he'd thought of little other than kissing Mia at the bar the night before.

His phone buzzed in his pocket and he plucked it out, seeing it was Nate.

"Hey," he answered.

"Hey yourself. Thought I'd check you actually made it home last night and didn't do anything stupid."

Sam laughed, feeling lighter than he had in a long time. "Perhaps I should get you to define stupid?"

Nate's chuckle was deep. "Were there any black eyes, fists flying, woman stealing or . . ." he laughed again. "Hell, I don't know!"

By stealing he wondered if kissing someone who was

taken, at least for the evening, counted. "Nothing happened. I'm working this morning, up bright and early. You?"

"I've been up since the crack of dawn. My lovely ladies were so pleased to see me they decided to wake at four thirty a.m.," he said. "See you tomorrow?"

"Yeah, see you tomorrow," Sam said.

"Oh and Sam? I don't believe your bullshit for a second. Something went down last night, you're just too chicken-shit to tell me."

"Yeah, something like that." Sam said goodbye and put his phone back in his pocket.

In the past he'd always told Nate everything, but times had changed. Hell, he'd changed. He'd gone from bachelor to loved-up without even realizing how quickly he'd made the transition, and it had been him not Nate who'd been ready to settle down. He'd believed he'd found the one, that he wasn't going to repeat the mistakes his parents had made, and yet here he was, single and not knowing what the hell his future held. While Nate was at home being the dutiful husband with two kids to boot. It was more than ironic; it was flat out impossible for Sam to wrap his head around sometimes.

He noticed that Mia hadn't been down to feed her horses yet, so he filled their hay bags and checked their water. He wasn't one for compliments, but he did admire the fact that she didn't have a groom. Sam was almost positive that her father would have happily written the check for another worker, but she was gritty and determined, and clearly liked proving people's perceptions of her wrong.

By the time he'd finished up in the stables, he could feel a glow on his skin, the day heating up and his own temperature rising from doing the work. When he'd risen early to feed out his own ranch, the day had still been new, dewy and cool, but now it was getting hot.

"Come on," he said to Blue, waving a hand and stopping to collect some more hay. He'd made huge progress with the stallion, and he was actually looking forward to working him again today. He'd thought about getting Mia to film him working with the magnificent but troubled horse, rather than getting a crew to come along, but he'd decided against it. This was just he being who he was. He'd become too used to all the work he did, particularly the trickier stuff, being filmed and uploaded for his followers to see.

"How's he doing?"

Sam turned to see Mia standing not far away, arms crossed over her chest. He drank in the sight of her; hair pulled up into a messy ponytail, tight faded jeans with boots, and a smile as big as Texas. She was a knockout, even without all the makeup and sexy-as-hell clothes going on from the night before. Suddenly, he couldn't get enough of her.

"He's good," Sam replied, turning his attention back to Tex as he crossed into his paddock. He might be making a little headway, but he wasn't about to take his eyes off him and give him the chance to lash out. "I think you'll be quietly surprised."

Mia must have moved closer because her voice traveled easily to him. "I honestly didn't think anyone could ever get through to that horse."

He stood patiently, hay on the ground for Tex to walk over to. He did. Slowly, but it was progress, and instead of having his ears pinned back hard or lunging at him with his teeth bared, his ears flickered, more cautious than anything else.

"With this guy," Sam said softly, all his attention focused on the animal in front of him, "it's about reprogramming his brain. We need to show him through our actions that he has nothing to fear, and reward the right type of behavior that we want to see more of."

"The fact he's trusting you enough to eat in front of you like that is incredible," she said. "I can't believe it."

"Well, believe it," he said, reaching out to touch Tex, firmly but slowly touching his neck. "The next step is you taking my place, because if he can't trust you, then everything I do is essentially worthless."

He moved to stand beside Mia, closer than he would have as little as a day ago. He leaned deep into the railings, elbows on the fence. Sam stared at the stallion a moment before turning to look at the woman beside him.

"This isn't a fairy tale, Mia," he said, his voice gruff even to his own ears. "There is no way this has a guaranteed happy ending."

She stared back at him, her gaze unwavering. "Are we talking about the horse here or us?" she asked.

He looked at her mouth, something he was starting to develop a habit of doing. Sam forced his eyes up, locking on the blue aqua that was just as mesmerizing to him.

"We're talking about the horse," he replied.

Her smile was sweet, but she still turned away from him, gazing back toward Tex. "I never thought it was a fairy tale," she said simply. "I know what you think, that I'm no match for a horse like him, but the truth is, I'm all he has. Once you're gone, anyway."

Sam nudged her with his elbow, forcing her to look back at him. "That's not true. I didn't know you when I first came here, but now? I know that you're kind, honest and full of passion and grit about what you do. Not to mention you're actually a hell of a horsewoman."

"Wow," she said, grinning. "I can't believe how good that feels, having you compliment me like that instead of putting me down."

"Don't give me that bullshit," he said, leaning back so he was facing her better. "You must get compliments all the time."

"I do," she said with a nonchalant shrug. "But most of the time they're loaded compliments because of who I am or what someone wants from me. At least with you I know you're being real. There's no bullshit about the way you are with horses. You take it seriously and I appreciate that."

"Well, good. Because I damn well mean what I say, and I don't go giving out compliments unless they're warranted."

"So about that fairy tale," she said, eyebrows arched.

"I need to know if you can do it, or if you feel like you have too much history with him?" Sam asked, knowing the question was loaded for her. "If you're too raw from what happened, if you deep down know that you're not his forever owner, then we'd be better transitioning from me to someone else." He paused. "I'm sorry."

She shook her head, making her long ponytail swish from side to side. "There's nothing to be sorry about. It's a fair question."

"So?" he asked.

"So you're wrong. I am the right person, and I'm not bringing any of my baggage to the table. I want to form a bond with him. No one wants that more than I do." She leaned into him, surprising him, her touch catching him off guard.

They stood, side by side, staring at Tex.

"He's my horse, and I'm going to be his forever home. I need you to be clear on that," she said.

Sam nodded.

"You sure that's not the only fairytale we're talking about?" Mia's voice was lower, softer this time. "Or should I say *non*-fairy tale?"

He stiffened, not liking where their conversation was heading. There were no fairy tales where he was concerned, not ones with him being the nice guy or the prince riding in to save the damsel on a white horse, anyway.

"I don't know where you're going with that," he managed.

She gave him a look that said she didn't buy his lack of understanding. "Look, let's be honest here." He saw that she looked uncomfortable, but he had to give her credit for tackling something uncomfortable head on. His way of dealing with whatever was happening between them had been to turn up on her doorstep like a maniac and kiss her without saying a word in greeting first.

"We kissed and it was good," she said simply, as if explaining something mathematical. "You turned up this morning, clearly wanting to see if I was, I don't know, *otherwise involved*, and then we kissed again."

"Yeah, you're about right with all of that," he said, feeling his face change, unable to stop the hint of a smile as it twisted his mouth sideways. He turned to face her, admiring her, reaching out to touch the end of her ponytail now it was falling over her shoulder. It was like spun gold in the sunlight, silky and soft.

"And now you're trying to figure out a way to tell me why things are too complicated," she finished. "Or something like that. Maybe I'm not your type, or maybe you just don't want . . ."

"Stop," he said, tugging on the end of her ponytail then.

"Ow!" she glared at him, eyes wide.

"You're *exactly* my type," he said, not releasing her from his gaze, wanting her to see how much it pained him to push her away when she should have been his ideal woman. "My problem is that I'm not looking to get involved with *any* woman. It's complicated, but relationships aren't my thing."

"Relationships are always complicated," she said softly, not taking her eyes away from his. She surprised him by reaching for his hand. "But I don't need a relationship, Sam. I'm leaving around the same time you're scheduled to finish here. The show jumping season kicks off properly then and I'll be on the road, and I don't need anything in my life to complicate things."

He felt her thumb rub across his hand, remembered what it was like having her in his arms, having those fingers kneading the back of his neck when he dipped down to kiss her. There was no denying that he wanted her, because he did and his body would only betray him if he tried to pretend otherwise. But she'd never struck him as the love 'em and leave 'em kind of girl. Maybe he'd read her all wrong. Again.

"So let me get this clear," he said, moving closer, forgetting all about the horse he'd intended on giving his attention to. "You definitely don't want a relationship?"

"Does every girl need to be desperate for Prince Charming to sweep her off her feet and keep her for the rest of her life?" Mia asked. "There are times when fun will do."

He hid his surprise. Either he'd read Mia all wrong or she was playing with him.

"No, she doesn't. But I thought you were more of a, how shall I put this, *traditional* girl."

"Oh really?" she asked, doing the cute-as-hell thing where she sucked in her bottom lip beneath her front teeth

Sam moved closer, their bodies only inches apart now. "Yeah, really. I guess I got you all wrong, huh?"

"Yeah, cowboy, you did. Because I've had daddy around trying to take care of me and do everything for me all my life. The last thing I want is to fall into the lap of man wanting to own me like a possession and tell me what to do."

Sam was tired of talking. She was smart and quick with her words, but he was interested in the other things her mouth could do well, like kissing.

"Just over three weeks. That's what we have left, right?"

Mia closed the little gap left between them. "Three weeks," she whispered.

"Three weeks of a no-strings-attached affair before we go our separate ways for work?" he asked, wanting to make it absolutely clear what he was getting himself in for. He'd been called a jerk before, but it hadn't been because he'd misled a woman. That wasn't his style and it never would be.

"Three weeks," she murmured back. "And then maybe a late night catch up or two when we're both back home at the same time."

Sam would have laughed but she didn't give him the chance. Mia grabbed him by the back of his head, gripping his hair and tugging him forward, her mouth closing over his and showing him exactly what she had in mind. He had no idea where this version of Mia had come from, or what exactly he'd done to unleash it, but damn, he liked it.

He scooped her up, grabbing her under her butt and sitting her on the fence. Then he pushed in hard against it as her legs wrapped around him, their mouths still fused, her fingers still locked into his hair. Sam kept his hands on her butt, skimming her hips, but when she started to giggle he pulled back, wondering what the hell was going on.

"What?" he mumbled, getting an eyeful of her ample chest when she stretched back, laughing.

"My dad would have a fit if he looked out now from the house and saw me making out with the hired help."

Sam glanced over his shoulder, suddenly thinking about the fact that the main house had rooms that faced this part of the ranch. "I'm hardly the hired fucking help," he sputtered. "I'll have you know I'm the best goddamn horseman this side of Texas."

"Oooh, and I thought you didn't have a big ego. How wrong I was," she teased.

Sam hauled her down from the fence and smacked her on the ass, grabbing her wrist when she tried to protest and get him back.

"Easy tiger," he whispered, his voice gruff as Mia's eyes flashed with challenge. "Don't go getting cocky without making sure you're up for the fight."

Her arched eyebrows laid down the challenge. He realized she'd glanced at his crotch. "I'm not the one getting cocky, *sweetheart*."

Sam grabbed her again, not caring who the hell was watching. He wasn't afraid of Walter Ford, and his daughter was a grown woman well able to make her own decisions about who she damn well kissed and where.

"You're crazy," he murmured, holding her tight and crushing her mouth to his. He tasted her, inhaled her, felt her. She was intoxicating. At least he had three damn weeks to get her well and truly out of his system.

Mia kissed him back, matched his urgency, proved to him that she was so different from the woman he'd expected to be spending time with on the ranch.

"*Crazy about you*," she whispered, smiling against his mouth and making him do the same.

She finally pushed back, taking a step away from him. He watched as she adjusted her ponytail, still smiling. She looked even prettier when she was smiling.

"But now we've got work to do," she said. "So how about we limit this *affair* to when we're off the clock?"

Sam saluted, shaking his head as he climbed the fence to go back in with the stallion. "Yes, boss."

Chapter 11

MIA watched Sam, admiring the way he had the stallion moving around him. It was impossible to believe that this was the same horse who'd been effectively blacklisted by everyone on the ranch. She glanced skyward, imagining Kimberley looking down and watching, smiling at her beautiful Tex finally finding his way back from the brink. He wasn't perfect, but he was behaving better than she'd seen him since the accident.

"He's doing a damn fine job."

Mia turned, face breaking out into a smile when she saw her brother standing there. "Hey, Tanner," she said, giving him a quick kiss on the cheek. "Good to see you home in one piece."

"Just here for the night," he said, kissing her back. Her brother was big and burly, but to her he was like a big teddy bear. Not so to anyone else who came across him, but he'd always been sweet and protective of her, and she was closer to him than her other siblings. They were the black sheep, the ones who did their own thing instead of what their father wanted.

"You staying here?" she asked.

"Yeah, just the night. I'm riding later today."

Tanner often stayed over at the ranch house, sometimes at her place, when he was traveling close to home. But he had his own place a couple hours' drive away.

"Imagine my surprise when I look out this morning and see the horse whisperer trying to teach my little sister how to kiss?"

His smile was devilish, his eyes glinting. Mia didn't hesitate in punching him, slamming her knuckles into his arm. He tensed, of course he couldn't resist flexing his muscles, but she refused to react to the fact she almost broke her hand when she connected with his rock-hard flesh.

"Shut up," she hissed.

"Hey, I'm not the one making out with the horseman in plain view of the house."

"Hey."

Sam was suddenly calling out, and she was standing between two men who were each probably as prone to bad behavior as the other. She wished the ground would just swallow her.

"Sam, this is my brother, Tanner," she said sweetly. "Tanner, Sam. AKA the famous horseman."

"Nice to meet you," Tanner said. "You've sure got the big guy eating out of your hands. Good work."

Sam nodded and shook his hand. Mia wondered if he'd realized Tanner was her brother straight away. She doubted he was ready to finish working Tex, but he'd quickly made his way over anyway.

"Yeah, we're making some good progress. He's all kinds of messed up, but he's starting to listen to me, and that's a good starting point."

"Looks like you were trying to teach my little sister some tricks this morning, too?" Tanner said, crossing his arms across his broad chest.

Mia looked between her brother and Sam, horrified. "Tanner!" she gasped. "Enough. Get the hell out of here!"

"Hey, you're my little sister. If I'm not looking out for you, who is?"

"Seems to me like your sister's pretty damn capable of looking after herself, at least where I'm concerned," Sam replied, surprising Mia with his calm words. "If there's one thing you'll learn about me, Tanner, it's that I respect animals *and* women. I don't believe in taking advantage, and I sure as hell don't ask anyone, especially a woman, to do anything they don't want to do. We clear?"

Tanner grunted, his smile telling Mia just how much he was enjoying this exchange. "Well, alrighty then. Y'all have a great day."

Mia shoved her brother, making him laugh, but he turned back and kissed her cheek again.

"See you around, sis."

"Be careful today, Tan. One day . . ."

"Whoa, enough with the doom and gloom," he said, holding up his hands and walking backwards. "I'll be just fine. Ain't no bull gonna take me down!"

Mia watched him go, wishing he'd give up the dangerous sport that he seemed to live for, but she knew it was his decision. There was nothing she or anyone else in his life could do to make him change his mind about his career choice.

"Your brother seems like a decent guy," Sam said when she turned back to him.

"My brother seems like a *jerk*," she corrected. "Don't feel you have to hold back where he's concerned, and if you happen to meet my other brother, Cody? He's just as bad, so don't say I didn't warn you. The only difference between them is that one wears suits and the other lives in jeans and plaid."

"Okay, well, he seemed a little overprotective, but that's okay. I can respect that." Sam shrugged. "He has every right to question me."

She considered him, wondering why he was so okay with her brother's interrogation. Tanner had gone way too far, and she wasn't exactly his kid sister anymore, far from it in fact. "You're serious?"

"I've got a little sister. She married Nate King." Sam chuckled. "So I can fully appreciate the whole *protect your sister at all costs* thing. It just about cost me my friendship with him, and my sister was ready to throttle me."

Mia nodded. "Gotcha. Well, now that I know how well you could bond with my brother, can we go back to horse work? Because that's what you're employed here to do."

Sam made a serious face. "Yes, boss lady. Straight back to work it is."

He gave her a look she couldn't decipher. "What?" she asked.

"I was just wondering," he said, his eyes glinting, "when we're off the clock."

She felt a flutter in her stomach, wondered if she'd gotten in too deep with Sam already. Flirting was one thing, *kissing* was one thing, but actually going through with some sort of no-strings-attached affair was another thing entirely, and certainly not something she'd ever done before.

"You just focus on the horse," she said, sounding more confident than she felt. "I don't want anything to distract you."

Sam winked. "Well, sweetheart, you better get your little self a long way from here if you don't want anything to distract me."

Mia knew she was blushing, but she didn't care. She was a woman, she was allowed to blush, and it wasn't like she was exactly used to all this attention.

"Just get back in with the horse," she scolded. "No more flirting, no more comments, and definitely no more winks! I'm the boss in case you'd forgotten."

Sam grinned and started to whistle, going back over to Tex. She stood on the sidelines and watched, wondering how on earth this big, muscular man could be so gentle and kind with horses and so damn intimidating to her. He looked like he should be a bull or bronc rider, the kind of man who used his weight and height to intimidate, and yet here he was before her showing he didn't need to be rough to get results.

And she liked him. More than liked him. She was impressed by him, she was attracted to him, and she wanted to know everything there was to know about Sam Mendes, including why he was so open to a no-strings-attached affair and nothing else.

Her phone vibrated in her pocket and she ignored it. She still hadn't texted Trent back, which meant she needed to take her eyes off Sam and message him, just in case he took her lack of response as a *yes*. The last thing she needed was for him and Sam to have a showdown over her, not now, and not ever. Besides, Kat would never forgive her if she didn't let him down gently, and not responding was all kinds of rude.

She took her phone from her pocket and leaned against the fence to make the call she'd been dreading all day.

After that she was calling Kat, and then she was going to go back to thinking about Sam.

"Are you free for dinner?"

Mia nodded, looking surprised, and he helped to put away her gear, walking beside her into the tack shed.

"Ah, yeah," she said, "sure."

"Good. Do you mind cooking then?"

Mia laughed at him. He knew it wasn't exactly romantic, but then they weren't exactly close to any decent take-out food and his house was an hour away.

"I'd take you out or order in, but I don't have any other clothes with me, and I don't think we'd get anyone to deliver here, right?"

She shook her head. "You're right, and you're also lucky that I like cooking. I'm just not used to making double portions though, so I'm not sure what you'll be getting."

"Can't we raid the main house?" he asked, grinning. "I bet your dad has enough steaks to feed an army up there."

He watched as she put the saddle down she was carrying and gave him a quizzical kind of look. "Actually, that's a great point. I don't eat a lot of meat, so I'm always turning down his offers of Angus beef. Probably why he doesn't bother offering it to me anymore."

"You had me at Angus beef . . ." Sam said. "I'm seriously trying not to drool right now."

"Well, if we do steaks then you can grill them. I'm no good with meat."

Sam tried not to smile, looking at her straight-faced. But then her face fell and she shut her eyes for a beat, shaking her head.

"I don't believe it for a second," he said in a low voice, resisting the urge to tease her.

"How did that end up sounding so . . ."

"Sexual?" he finished for her when she seemed lost for words.

"Exactly."

"Because," he said, moving closer to her, seeing how quickly she reacted to him by the way her cheeks colored, "you expected some kind of booty call, and instead I suggested dinner. Which means you're wondering what's going on, and what's going to happen between us."

She let out a breath, hand resting on the saddle she'd recently placed down. "And just like that you're a mind reader as well as a horse whisperer. Amazing."

"Am I wrong?"

"What, that you thought I only expected sex?" She shrugged, but he knew she was doing a good job of pretending she found it easy to talk like that, rather than actually being comfortable. She was too easy to read.

"Let me start again," he said, moving closer and holding out a hand to her. When she raised her own he clasped it and tugged her into his body. "Would you like to share a meal tonight, so we can discuss our ground rules?" He didn't want her to think this was anything more than it was, but he wasn't about to treat her badly or use her. There was no way he'd ever do to someone else what his ex had done to him. Breaking hearts was not on his agenda, not intentionally anyway.

"Rules?" she asked him, standing on tiptoe. "You have *rules*?"

"Yeah, rules," he replied, pausing before kissing her. "So neither of us ends up thinking the other is a jerk."

Mia was the one who kissed him, her lips whispering

across his, teasing him, drawing him in, and damn if he didn't like the way she took charge. She wrapped her arms around him, and he didn't need any encouragement to walk her backwards, to push her up against the wall in between the saddles and grab her hands. She was full of surprises and driving him wild. He pinned her hands above her, using one of his hands to hold them in place, the other snaking around her, holding her tight to him.

Mia moaned and it spurred him on, the combination of her wet mouth and the way she thrust her hips hard into him making it almost impossible to hold back. But he wasn't about to strip her naked amongst the horse gear, where anyone, including her brother, could find them. He didn't need a black eye or a broken nose from an overprotective big brother for having sex with Mia in a public place.

Sam kissed her one more time, let go of her wrists and skimmed both hands down her body, before pulling back.

"Not here. Come on," he said, tugging her hand.

Mia complied, not fighting his hold. "My place for the night?"

"Not the whole night," he said, slipping an arm around her and liking the feel of her fingers looping through his belt buckle when she did the same. "But yeah, back to your place."

If she was disappointed that he'd said no to the whole night, she didn't say. But that was one of his rules. He didn't stay over. Boyfriends stayed the night. Husbands shared beds with their wives. And he didn't have plans to be any of those any time soon. Or ever.

"I need to check on the other horses first," she said, looking like she wanted to do anything *but* stay behind and do her rounds.

"Mind if I head over to your place and take a shower then?" he asked. "Unless you need help here?"

"Go for it. The door's unlocked and there are towels and everything you need in the bathroom. Use the master one."

He nodded and kissed her again. Her arm was still wrapped around him, and she slowly let go of his belt loop and used one hand to push him away.

"See you soon."

Sam watched her go. If Kelly hadn't happened, if he'd never been through what he had the year before, maybe he'd be standing here wondering if Mia was the one. But nothing could take away what had happened to him, nothing could make him forget the sting of betrayal and the pain of seeing the person he loved treat him as if what they had meant nothing.

He turned and headed for the house, wondering where Blue was. He whistled and waited, knowing his dog wouldn't be far away. When Blue caught up to him he walked to Mia's house, ready to wash off the dust and grit that had attached to his skin from a day out in the hot Texas sun. By the time Mia was done for the day, he'd smell a whole lot better than he did right now, that was for sure.

And this time when he had her pressed up against him, there would be nothing to hold him back.

Chapter 12

MIA pulled her phone out of her pocket when she felt it buzzing and groaned when she saw it was her sister. She clicked to answer, and Angelina's face appeared on the screen. Mia tugged on her braid, cringing when she saw how beautiful her sister looked with her perfect makeup and not a hair out of place.

"You've been holding out on me."

"Hey, Ange," Mia said, smiling at her sister. "Don't tell me, Tanner's been on the phone to you."

"Yup. Something about a rugged horseman feeling you up in plain view of the house. Sound about right?"

Mia laughed. "You guys are terrible! Can't we have any secrets?"

"Honey, you know we can't. Now spill. I've only got a few minutes. And show me the ranch while you're walking, I need my fix."

Mia held the phone out and slowly panned around so her sister could see the stables, some of the big fields and the path leading down to her house. Ange might not have liked horses growing up, but the ranch was in their blood and her sister still loved the place.

"Back to you," Angelina called out.

Mia put the phone back to her face. "I'm kind of busy so can I call you back?"

"Just quickly tell me about him? I want to know everything. I've already Googled him and he looks sexy as hell, and . . ."

"Stop!" Mia protested, her skin on fire just thinking about Sam. "I honestly have to go, I promise I'll call you back later."

"He's there, isn't he?"

Mia sighed. "Good bye, Ange."

Her sister pulled a face and Mia laughed before ending the call. Trust Tanner to have told Angelina. No doubt Cody knew all about it now, too. She looked ahead and started down the path to her place. She was a bundle of nerves, and as she got closer she approached her house as if she was heading into the lion's den, when in fact it was usually one of the places in the world that she felt most comfortable and most true to herself.

She let herself in and went straight into the kitchen to pour a glass of water. She slowly swallowed it, hot and dusty and ready for something stronger. But when she placed it with a clink to the counter, she heard something that she'd missed before. A shower was running. She looked around but saw no evidence of Sam. Mia went back out and noticed his boots were in fact neatly by the door, and she decided to go into her room to see if he was still in her shower or . . .

She stopped, mouth dry, heart racing. His clothes had been discarded on a chair in her room, which meant he'd been in her room naked. It also meant he was most definitely in *her* shower, just as she'd told him to be, only she'd expected him to be well and truly finished up by the time she got back. If only her sister could see her now, hands sweaty, heart pounding and mouth dry. She'd have laughed her head off seeing her in such a state.

Mia pulled herself together and walked closer to the closed door, holding up her hand to knock. She used the back of her knuckles to let out a soft tap-tap, opening the door the barest of cracks to call out to Sam.

"You shaving your legs in there?" she asked, smiling to herself. She was being a whole lot braver than usual, but it felt good to mess around with him.

"My Brazilian, actually. Is that still what girls call it?"

His deep chuckle made her smile even more and she leaned against the door, imagining him in there. The steam would be circling around the walls and dipping down into the glass shower cubicle; he would be dripping wet, his muscles slick from water gliding over them, droplets still clinging to his skin. She was certain even his lashes would have water hugging the ends of them,

"Yeah," she said finally, "we still call it a Brazilian. But if you've dared use my razor for a back, sack and crack . . ."

The door suddenly slid open and she almost fell back into the tiled bathroom.

"For the record, I didn't touch your razor."

She pushed herself back up and scrambled to her knees before getting up properly. Sam was standing with a towel around his waist, tucked so low she could see the most delicious, black arrow of hair pointing down, *all* the way down. His husky voice sent goose pimples across her skin.

Mia swallowed. "Well, good," she muttered. "You just like long hot showers then?"

He turned and disappeared back into the bathroom,

leaving the door open and giving her an impressive view of his shoulders, his damp skin stretched over bulging muscles. His damp, dark hair was curled a little at the ends, and she wanted him to turn again so she could see if the wet hair arrowing down his chest to his groin was the exact same shade.

"Actually it started out hot then ended up cold," he said, running his fingers through his hair to get it back off his forehead and then turning. "I was trying to get my mind off of someone. Funnily enough, you might know her."

If Mia's mouth had been dry before, now it was stuffed full of cotton candy. She could barely swallow.

"Do you want a . . ." she struggled to find the word she was searching for. Why the hell had she made out like she was so confident and witty, that she was experienced enough to get tangled up with a man like him. "Drink?" she managed to ask.

"Come here," he said roughly, holding out his hand.

Mia looked at his naked chest as she reached out to place her fingers against his. Sam's palm met hers and he pulled her in, so slowly she could barely feel herself moving forward.

"Are we going to keep talking around this, or are we actually going to do something?" Sam asked.

She nodded. "I think I was all talk," she confessed. "I don't know what to do."

"You changed your mind?" he asked. "Because this is what it is. If you don't want—"

Mia wriggled forward, dropping contact with his hand and placing her hands firm against his still-damp chest. "I haven't changed my mind." She slowly rose up on her toes, ready to kiss him again, ready to know what it would be like to be Sam's lover. She'd never thought she'd be the kind of girl to want a no-expectations fling, but then, there were plenty of things she hadn't expected when it came to Sam.

Their lips met and she sighed against his mouth, fingers tracing over his skin, feeling how warm he was, how thick his muscles were straining beneath the surface. Mia ran her nails down his back, loving the grunting sound he made when she did it, spurring her on, telling her that it was time to push the boundaries.

Sam clearly wasn't going to sit there and do nothing though. Towel still miraculously tied around his waist, he moved closer into her, holding her hips and nudging her forward. Her stomach tingled, her skin was alive, every little part of her like a magnet trying to connect to Sam, and when she opened her eyes briefly to look at him, she could hardly believe the man who's arms she was in.

He was like he'd stepped straight out of magazine, except Sam looked too tough around the edges to be modeling for underwear or even aftershave. Besides, right now he smelled of her shampoo and her coconut soap, and the look on his face said he meant business.

"Here?" she whispered.

"Anywhere you like, gorgeous," he replied in a deep voice.

Mia's hands slipped around his neck and she leaned into him. "Take me to bed then."

"Just so we're clear," he said, his voice verging on a growl. "This is only sex. It can *only* be sex."

She shook her head, not about to let him call *all* the shots. "No, Sam," she whispered back. "It's not only sex. We can have all kinds of fun, we just can't get attached."

Mia wanted him so badly. Her body was aching for him, her skin flushed, ready for his hands to be touching every single part of her. But she'd always had issues with authority and she didn't like him being the one in charge. This was her decision, too.

"So long as it's no strings attached," he mumbled, not seeming to care. "No expectations."

"Three weeks," she whispered, grinding against him, wanting him. It had been so long since she'd been with a man, and now that she was this close? She wanted Sam, and she wanted him now.

Sam stopped talking then. He wrapped his arms around her and lifted her, clean off her feet, carrying her over to the bed. She gasped when his towel slipped off after less than a few steps, and she felt his erection brush against her butt, the smooth, silkiness of his skin telling her exactly what she was in for.

Sam dropped her onto the bed. He was standing, completely stark naked, and for some reason she couldn't catch her breath. She smiled, her lips slowly tilting up until she couldn't hide it. Oh, she knew she was out of breath, she just didn't want to admit it.

He was incredible to look at. She refused to be shy, boldly looking over his body. His torso and arms were ripped, the muscles big and his skin golden. When he spent most of his life in jeans, she had no idea how his legs were almost as tanned as his upper half, but they were. There was only one section of him that was a much lighter shade of golden, and that was where her eyes had tried their hardest to avoid but were constantly being dragged back to.

Wow. She met his gaze, saw the confidence there and wondered what the hell she was in for.

"Like what you see?" he asked, making her laugh.

"Yeah, actually, I do," she whispered.

He lowered himself down and she thought he was going to kiss her, but instead, before his body skimmed hers, just when she parted her mouth, ready for his kiss, waiting for his lips to melt over hers, he paused. She could feel his hot breath against her skin and she arched up to meet him.

"You have an unfair advantage," he murmured. "*Off.*"

He grabbed her jeans and tried to yank them down, but they were tight and wouldn't budge. She laughed and wriggled, unbuttoning them. He didn't wait, pulling and getting rid of them within what seemed like seconds. Then he got rid of her socks and she held her breath as he made his way back up, trailing a finger across her panties and making her gasp again. She had to give it to him—the guy seriously knew how to get her excited.

"Off," he ordered again.

She decided to resist him, wanted to push his buttons, wanted to see what he'd do. "No," she whispered.

He paused, looking down at her. "Yes."

She fixed her gaze on him, lifted her leg and pushed her toes into him. She wanted to stay in control, at least a little bit. She kept her toes pressed against his torso, knowing exactly what he was thinking when he dropped his eyes down low. Her leg was perfectly arched, and she was giving him a good view of her tiny G-string, which she was certain would be leaving very little to the imagination.

"I never imagined you wearing a G-string under your ranching clothes." His voice was low and deep.

"What, you imagined granny pants?" she laughed. "One thing I always have on is great underwear." It was true; she only liked matching sets, and she liked to feel pretty no matter what she was wearing on the outside or whether she was out for dinner or working horses.

She slowly raised her arms and wriggled out of her shirt, throwing it at Sam. He grinned and tossed it over his head, eyes going straight to her chest.

"Pretty underwear," he said, "but it'd look better off."

She hesitated, not sure, suddenly feeling self-aware with him staring down at her. He was naked already, she knew it was silly, but playing up to Sam was one thing. Going through with pretending to be savvy and sexy in the bedroom was another entirely, especially in daylight with him able to see her every flaw.

"Kiss me," she asked instead, reaching for him and dropping her leg so he could lean over her and cover her body.

He must have seen or heard the hesitation in her tone, because he didn't argue with her or push her further. Instead he lowered himself and met her lips, kissing her softly at first, melting her as she wrapped her arms around him.

Sam's body was warm, hard and lean under her hands, and the unmistakable brush then press of his erection against her was impossible to ignore. His mouth moved softly to start with, his touch harder when she moaned in response to his tongue touching hers, her mouth wider, his kisses pushing away all the doubts.

She arched up into him, extending her neck when he dragged his mouth from hers and started to trail kisses down her jawline then down her neck, not stopping. His movements were slow, so unhurried, and she knew that he had to have been enjoying pleasuring her as much as she was enjoying receiving it.

"Everything okay?" he murmured against her skin as he dipped lower, across her collarbone, down her chest, his tongue circling the top of her breast and then teasing her, moving lower, flicking across her nipple. Even through the lacy fabric it made her moan, felt amazing, igniting licks of want throughout her body.

"Every," she whispered, "thing," she groaned, "*okay.*"

Sam's laughter was warm against her skin, the brush of barely-there stubble across her stomach as he kept moving on his journey south making her want to scream. She squirmed, loving it, wanting it, wishing she could resist so she could pleasure him back but unable to move.

Kat had been right—it had been way too long since she'd had fun. So what if she wasn't supposed to be the type to have one-night stands. What did that even mean anymore? She was enough of a modern feminist to know that there was nothing wrong with enjoying her body, even if she did still feel the whisper of stigma about it.

"Ohhh," Mia's toes clenched the sheets as Sam's mouth closed over her panties, his breath hot as he breathed against her. He looked up, eyes meeting hers, and she knew how much he was liking taking control and making her feel good. It was empowering.

He slid his fingers against the lace, at her hips, still looking at her, waiting, as if asking her permission with his eyes. She was out of breath, unsteady, wishing she was as confident with telling him what she wanted as how she felt.

"I haven't," she croaked out, "I mean . . ."

"Shit, you're not a virgin are you?" he swore, looking alarmed. "I mean that would be fine, that's cool if you are, but . . ."

"Stop!" She laughed, shaking her head. "I'm definitely not a virgin, but it's just been a while. I don't want to, you know, well, I have no damn idea what I'm even trying to say!"

His laugh was deep, humorous but not mocking. And his smile was reassuring.

"Darlin', you know the old saying about never forgetting how to ride a horse?"

Her cheeks were stained red, she could feel them burning, but given the fact that her skin had felt on fire from his touch only seconds earlier, she doubted he'd notice the additional burn.

"So I'm overthinking the whole thing? Damn, complete buzz kill." She flopped back down, wishing the bed would open up and swallow her. Why couldn't she get her shit together and be more confident? Why did she always have to second-guess herself? It happened to her every time she was in the ring competing, and now here she was with one of the most gorgeous men on the planet, naked, and she'd completely killed the mood.

"Do I look like you've killed my buzz?" Sam said, rising and pointing down.

Mia bit down on her bottom lip, eyeing his manhood. "Ah, yeah, well . . ."

"Shut up and kiss me," he muttered, pushing her back and sitting astride her. This time he hauled her up, arms around her when his mouth crushed hers, all softness gone, replaced by a fiercer need that completely matched her own.

This time when Sam slipped his hands behind her back to unhook her bra, she didn't resist. Instead she arched her back, kept her mouth lavishly attached to his, enjoying every touch of his tongue, every caress of his lips. When he dipped his head to her breasts, throwing her bra across the room, she forgot all about being self-conscious or giving a damn about doing the right thing or not. Because Sam was incredibly attentive, and impossible not to be aroused by, and she intended on enjoying every single moment of being the sole object of his attention.

"Holy shit," she muttered, squirming when he left her breasts to move lower. There was no gentle trail of his tongue this time. Instead he went down, grabbed her panties and hauled them off, tugging them over her feet and smiling down at her. She was about to tell him that she wanted to play it safe, that she had condoms in the bedside drawer, but when she opened her mouth his wicked smile made her pause.

"How do you feel?" he asked, lowering himself, moving half off the bed as his gaze dropped to her nether regions.

She managed a nod. "Good," she whispered.

His eyes flashed, every part of her on fire just at the thought of his touch now.

"Only good?" he teased. "Oh, I want much better than *good*. I'd better get to work."

Mia was about to protest, to tell him he was already way better than good, but her words died a fast death in her mouth. She shut her eyes, toes clenched, back arched in ecstasy as Sam's mouth closed over her, his tongue deftly taking charge and making what she was feeling so much better than good.

Sam flipped Mia over, not taking his eyes off her for a second. She was incredible. Her body was driving him wild, her legs tightly gripped against him strong and muscular, her breasts full and high as she sat astride him. She was teasing him, grinding against him, leaning her head back and shaking her long hair out, and if it brushed against him one more time he was going to grab it and yank her down.

But the anticipation was exquisite, and even though he wasn't usually a patient man, sex was his one exception. He didn't like it quick, and he sure as hell didn't like it to be all about him. Seeing the look of pleasure on Mia's face, holding her body and pleasuring her with his mouth as she'd climaxed, that's what excited him. Because now he knew she was slick and ready for him; that she was sated and content, and the evening had only just begun.

"Are you going to keep teasing me like that?" he asked, keeping his voice low.

Her eyes opened, almost feline as she rocked back and forth and stared down at him. "Maybe," she whispered.

"To hell with that," he muttered. "Hop aboard or I'm taking the lead."

Mia smiled down at him, her face relaxed, her body warm and supple as she bent down low, her hair spiraling across his face as she dipped her head. She kissed him, slowly, and as much as he wanted to fist his hand in her hair and pull her down hard, he resisted. Because he liked the buildup, he was already wearing protection, and he wasn't going to hurry her.

She moaned against his mouth as she slid down onto him, taking him inside of her. She moved a little, repositioned herself, and this time her moan was longer, her hands to his chest as she pushed up and rocked back and forth. Her palms were still firm to his chest as Sam locked his fingers against her hips, matching her movements even though he was trying so hard to let her set the pace.

"So good," she moaned, still rocking, not moving anywhere near fast enough for him.

Sam moved, held on to her and forced her to move back and forth faster. When she laughed and tried to slow down, he couldn't be patient any longer. He flipped them, pinning her beneath him and covering her slender body with his, pushing up on his elbows to make sure he wasn't too heavy on her.

Mia protested, laughing at him, making it clear that she

was having as much fun as he was, that she wasn't really concerned that he'd taken over. She bit his shoulder, playfully, and he growled at her and grabbed at one of her hands, pinning it by her side by the wrist. Then he leaned low to bite her breast, using his teeth but making sure not to hurt her.

"Ow!" she muttered.

Sam covered her mouth with his to block out her protest, thrusting deep inside her as he kissed her, moving his lips over and over again against hers, losing himself to the motion of her mouth and the feel of pushing in and out of her. He tried to pull back, but she clamped her legs tight around him, not giving him any room to move.

"Where are you going?" she muttered, her ankles locked behind his butt forcing him forward, making him stay inside. She fought to free her arm and both her fingers locked into his hair, tugging at him, locking his mouth to hers again with no chance of getting away.

He groaned when she thrust up to meet him. Clearly she was used to being in charge as much as he was, and for all her talk about being out of practice, she was doing just fine. Better than fine, she was doing great.

But even so, he wasn't going to let her keep taking the reins from him.

Sam gave her one last, slow kiss, before using his weight to pull up, so he was looking down at her. She didn't have a hope of holding him down now he'd decided not to play that game with her, and he wanted to watch her, wanted to see her face and her body while he was inside of her.

"Sam," she moaned, trying to pull him back down.

"No," he said, hearing the rough edge of his own voice. He admired her full breasts, cupping both of them as he positioned himself, anticipating what they'd looked like when he started thrusting, imaging them bouncing back and forth. Mia gave up resisting and closed her eyes, hands above her head as she gave in to him and let him have his wicked way with her.

Sam lost himself to the feel of Mia, eyes shut as he felt himself building to climax, loving every inch of her body, of the way she felt, of . . .

What the hell?

Sam opened his eyes, his moment over, the delicious sensation taken away from him. He was about to protest, about to complain, until he saw Mia. She'd turned over, the look she was giving him over her shoulder full of naughtiness and telling him exactly what she wanted. She was on her knees, teasing him, her butt in the air. He grabbed hold of her, hands to her hips as he guided himself in.

If it had felt good before, damn it now he was in heaven. Mia's moans filled his ears as he tried hard not to climax, to keep going for her, but it felt too good. When he finally gave in to the feeling, he kept his fingers against her butt, held on to her and enjoyed the sensation of her skin against his, of her smooth, warm body meshed to his when he carefully lowered himself over her. He kept his weight off her as she nestled into the pillow, kissed her neck, using one hand to push her hair out of the way and over to one side. Her neck was arched, her golden skin perfectly soft as he rained kisses across it.

Mia turned, her eyes meeting his, the look in hers a reflection of how lazy and satisfied he was feeling right now.

"Hey," she whispered.

He grinned. "Hey," he whispered back.

She turned and he kissed her mouth, smiling down at

her. "Talk about a way to work up an appetite." Her voice was gravelly, more husky than usual, and she made him laugh. "I'm starving now!"

"Want me to make something?" he asked.

She sighed. "Uh-huh. I'll take a quick shower."

He chuckled. "I made that sound like I'm capable in the kitchen, but I'm not. You'll need to tell me what to do."

Mia burst out laughing, arms around him as she leaned in for another kiss. "You're crazy. I can't believe you tricked me like that. Were you waiting for me to decline your offer and tell you how much I was looking forward to cooking for you?"

He shrugged, his mouth kicking up into a grin even though he was trying so hard to keep a straight face. "Would you think I was an asshole if I said yes?"

She punched his arm. "Yes! But you're just lucky that I happen to love cooking, and I'm not prepared to wait while some novice cook tries to whip something up to impress me. Especially after making me work up an appetite like that."

Mia rose and walked to the bathroom, crossing the room and giving him an eyeful of her pert butt and beautiful, slender body. Her skin was lightly tanned, golden blonde hair long and falling down to the middle of her back.

She turned, as if knowing he'd be watching her, still smiling as she shook her head and disappeared from sight. Sam lay back on the bed, wondering how on earth he'd come to the Ford ranch so reluctantly to work a horse, and had ended up sleeping with an heir to the Ford fortune and crazily entering into a completely different kind of contract. This time, it was his sexual services on offer though, not his horsemanship skills.

"First time for everything," he murmured to himself.

He heard the shower running and imagined Mia in there, water skimming across her skin, hair wet and clinging to her back, naked body shimmering beneath droplets of water. Sam felt himself start to get hard again almost instantly, but he didn't storm in there to go looking for more.

Anticipation was almost as good as the real thing, but Mia was hungry and he wanted her full of sustenance and ready to match his pace. He'd wait until after dinner before going back for round two.

Chapter 13

MIA pinned her wet hair up and put on some light makeup. Usually if she showered late in the day or at night she'd leave her skin bare, but with Sam waiting for her out there, she wanted to go the extra mile.

She'd half expected him to follow her into the bathroom, but he hadn't and when she'd come out he was gone, the only evidence he'd ever been there in the first place was the rumpled bed sheets he'd left behind.

Mia checked her reflection in the mirror, deciding her jeans and tank top looked perfectly acceptable for a Saturday night in. She made her way to the kitchen, surprised to find Sam sitting at her counter, beer in hand.

"I made myself at home," he said, chuckling as she stared at him. She must have looked surprised to find him there like that, because he set the beer down and crossed the room.

Mia smiled when he put his arms around her, melting into him when he kissed her, long and slow, his mouth tasting of beer. She kissed him back, body still tingling from all the wicked things he'd done to her. His stubble teased her skin and her top lip felt grazed from the touch, the whisper of bristles against her skin reminding her of where else she'd felt the very same sensation.

"What did you pick for me to drink?" she asked, stroking one hand down his chest. He had his shirt back on, only now it was only half buttoned up, untucked, and the sleeves were rolled all the way up. He looked so damn sexy she could hardly believe he was in her kitchen with her, or that she'd been brave enough to have sex with the most gorgeous damn man she'd ever crossed paths with.

"Well, I was going to pour you a wine, but there was nothing open. And I didn't think you looked like a beer kind of drinker." He raised a brow. "Or am I wrong? Is there another reason you have beer in the house, like for a boyfriend?"

She felt the corners of her mouth kick up into a smile. "Whiskey. On the rocks," she said, trying to keep as straight-faced as she could. "And yeah, the beer is for my boyfriend."

"You're fucking with me," he swore softly, his eyes catching hers, the look he was giving her making her want to melt.

"Yeah, I am." She laughed when he caught her around the waist, moving swiftly, his hands broad and strong and locking her into place. "I don't have a boyfriend, and the beer is Tanner's. He stays sometimes, and he sure likes to keep my refrigerator well stocked."

"You little she-devil," he muttered as she dipped back, away from him, not letting him kiss her.

She squealed when he hauled her back up, manhandling her, throwing his weight around to make her body comply. He marched her backward, his hard body merged with hers.

"This is going to be a fun few weeks," he murmured as he pressed into her, fingers skimming under her top, teasing her bare skin as he kissed her, his mouth hot and wet.

Yeah, it was. Only she wasn't used to casual or no-strings. She had always been a boyfriend kind of girl, or a not-at-all kind of girl. But she was all grown up now, and she knew better than to go looking for a relationship. Sam was handsome and sexy and fun. He was perfect. And once their time was up, she could focus on her work and not have any distractions. Besides, it was nice to be hanging out with a guy who didn't want or need her money and didn't treat her any differently because of who she was.

Sam's mouth left hers and she raised her hand, wishing his lips were still there, craving the contact. His eyes were stormy as he looked down at her.

"You know I still feel like shit for how I treated you, when I first came here."

"What?" she whispered, leaning back to look up at him. "When you thought I couldn't even ride? When you treated me like some rich princess who didn't know the back of a horse from the front? That what you're talking about?"

His laugh was deep—toe-curling kind of deep. Especially when it was paired with the sexy-as-hell way he was looking at her. "And now I know *exactly* how good you are in the saddle."

A kick of heat flooded Mia's cheeks and she didn't even care. Sam was giving her a look that said he'd seen her naked and loved every minute of it, and she wasn't going to shy away from that.

"Get me that drink, would you?" she muttered. "You're terrible at looking after your boss."

He pretended to tip his hat to her, touching his head. "Yes, ma'am."

"And make it a beer," she told him. Although privately she was wondering if maybe she did need that whiskey after all. Maybe a shot or two of straight liquor was exactly what she needed to make sure she could keep up with the delectable Sam.

Mia sauntered into the kitchen and opened the fridge, relieved to see she did still have some fresh pasta in there. She had a large bottle of tomato pasta sauce she'd only half used, one she'd made weeks ago and pulled out of the freezer when she needed something delicious to eat during the week, so that would have to do.

"Still thirsty?" Mia jumped when something cold touched her back.

"Shit!" she swore, spinning around to see Sam standing there, grinning like mad, holding up a cold beer. "How the hell did you even get that when I've been the one in the fridge?"

He went to press it against her skin again but she slapped at him, grabbing the beer from his hand.

"You staring into the fridge hoping it has all the answers?" he asked wryly.

"Actually, I'm trying to figure out whether you'll care about eating vegetarian."

His brows pulled together. "I thought we were having steaks on the grill?"

She lifted the bottle and took a long, slow sip. "Somebody distracted me," she said. "Seems I was in such a hurry to get back here that I forgot to go get the meat." It had actually been her sister on the phone distracting her from that particular task, but she kept that fact to herself.

Sam touched her shoulder, a gentle, sweet gesture that rattled her more than any sexual innuendo would have. His smile was . . . hard to read. It was genuine and it was warm, but she wasn't sure what it meant or if it was supposed to mean anything at all.

"So what're we eating then?" he asked, hand dropping from her skin.

She sipped her beer again, liking it. He'd been right that she wasn't usually a beer kind of girl, unless it was a burning hot day and she was poolside or something, but she was liking it now. "Pasta and homemade tomato sauce," she said, putting the bottle down and getting out what she needed. "It's good, I promise."

She filled a pot of water from the tap on the back-splash and added some salt. When she turned, Sam was leaning into the counter, propped up on his elbows, beer in his hands.

"Homemade by your housekeeper up at the main house?" he asked, smile kicking out his mouth before he took a pull of beer. "The woman who answers the door?"

"Screw you," she muttered. "I had to fill an entire pot full of tomatoes to make this one jar," she told him. "It took me three hours of slow cooking to reduce it to this delicious sauce, but if you'd rather go up to the main house and see what my father's *housekeeper* is making for dinner, then by all means, go for it. He'll probably enjoy the company."

Sam winked and she could have killed him. "Nah, I think I'll stay put. It's kind of fun watching you."

She shot him a look that was supposed to be fierce, but from the way he was staring back at her, he didn't exactly look scared.

"So, tell me something I don't know about you," she said.

When he didn't reply she looked up at him. His face had changed, the set of his mouth different, his jaw tighter.

"Like what?" he grunted.

She shrugged. "I don't know. Like maybe how you got into training horses. Is that what you've always done?"

Mia emptied out the sauce to heat it, glancing up at Sam. He was staring down at his beer, using his thumbnail to work at the label. She set the jar down. "Did I say something wrong?" She wasn't sure what, but something had changed the mood between them from light banter to something darker. "Sam?" she said after he still hadn't said anything.

When he finally looked up, his smile was forced. "I was a soldier."

Sam saw the look of surprise as it passed over Mia's face. Man, it seemed like a lifetime ago that he was serving, but he hadn't wanted to lie to her. What was the point? It was part of his past, something he was damn proud of doing, but he just didn't like to talk about it. Besides, it wasn't who he was now.

"You were a *soldier*?"

"Yeah, I was." He downed the rest of his beer, needing to drain the entire bottle after telling her. "But it was a long time ago, and I've been working horses pretty much ever since."

She put the sauce on, and tipped the fresh spaghetti into the now boiling water. He watched as she took a wooden spoon out of a drawer to stir the sauce with.

"Were you deployed?" she asked, her voice low, as if she wasn't sure about asking him the details.

"Yeah. Iraq." Sam stood and went to get another beer from the fridge. He glanced over at her. "You want another?"

"Ah, no, I'm good. Thanks."

Sam opened it, went to sit back down but kept walking instead. He moved across the room, looked at her sofa and her trinkets, noticed how many lamps she had and decided to flick them on for her. It was almost completely dark outside now and the lamps cast a warm glow across the living room.

He stopped when he reached the massive glass doors that led out to her patio and pool. It was a small house, but it packed a big punch. The outside was beautiful, and with so much glass around the house, it was like being part of the ranch no matter what room you were in or where you looked out from.

"How did you end up going from soldier to horseman then?" she asked, her voice pulling him from his thoughts and making him turn back to the kitchen. "And why haven't any of the Google hits I've found on you mentioned your past?"

Sam relaxed, the tension falling away from his shoulders, unclenching his fists and letting it go. He liked her even more now. She'd seen how uncomfortable he was, maybe she'd felt it, and she'd moved past the thing he didn't want to talk about. Talking about his horse skills was safe ground. Iraq was not.

"I was pretty fucked up when I got home, and I moved in with Nate for a bit," Sam said, slowly walking back across to Mia. It helped that she was only looking at him every now and again as she finished getting their meal ready; having those aqua eyes fixed on him and showing him pity would have gotten under his skin. He hated pity, and he would have especially hated it from her. "I'd spent half my childhood on that ranch, learned to ride there and had fun, but I wasn't myself when I got back. The only thing that chilled me out was being out with the horses."

"I've read a lot about how horses can help children with their . . ." she paused and he waited for it, wondering what she was about to say, "*problems*. I guess I never really thought about how it could help soldiers with their PTSD."

Sam gulped, his mouth as dry as the desert. He tried not to squeeze the beer bottle too tight. "I don't have PTSD."

Mia visibly paled, and he wished he'd just kept his mouth shut. Usually he would have, but then usually he wouldn't be having this conversation in the first place.

"Sam," she said, setting her spoon down and splaying her hands on the counter in front of her. "I'm not trying to put a label on you. I'm just saying that I can see how horses could help with any sort of trauma."

Once again, he'd been too quick to jump to conclusions where his past was concerned.

"Sorry. Sore spot and all," he mumbled, sipping again. "Some of the guys were affected pretty bad, but mine was more struggling to fit in when I got back. I didn't feel like I had a purpose, I guess."

"So tell me about the horse that tamed you?" she teased. "Or was it the other way around?"

He grinned, liking how easy she was to talk to and how quickly she'd turned the conversation around—again. "You know, I'm pretty careful with my temper now, but I came home kind of bent out of sorts. The smallest thing would set me off, and I was angry a lot of the time. But the second I set foot into the round pen with a horse?" He returned the smile she was giving him, knowing he was talking to someone who knew exactly what it felt like to be around horses and get that buzz from them. "Everything else just melted away. I'd turn into this calm guy and nothing rattled me in there. I've lost my cool a lot in my life, been in more fights than I can count, but I've never lost my cool with a horse. Something about them just brings out the best in me, I guess. It always has."

"And something about you," she said in a husky voice, her eyes dancing over his before pulling away, "brings out the best in every horse."

"I guess it's true what they say, that animals see through to the man beneath whatever façade is in place," he said. "Or woman," Sam corrected.

"I believe that," she said, smiling over at him. Something about her gaze settled him, pulled him back and made him feel more comfortable about opening up to her. There was something about the way she looked at him, the way she spoke, that told him she understood. Or perhaps it was that she didn't look at him with pity because she understood horses and the power they could have over a person.

"Anyway, how did you end up being a show jumper?" he asked, wanting to talk about her before he got pulled too far back into his past. Those months after he'd returned, they were part blur, part nightmare for him; in any case he'd done his best to block them out. "You know, I remember a really cute little girl, in a pretty little dress, arriving in her daddy's big car at the King ranch looking like a real little lady."

He took a pull of beer, the corner of his mouth rising as he saw the look on her face. It was half-scowl, half-disbelief. She planted her hands on the counter and stared at him.

"Me? You remember me there?" she asked. "Is that what you're saying?"

Sam chuckled. "Yeah, I remember you looking like that for all of five minutes, before seeing you sneak down to the horses and come back filthy dirty hours later. But you had a great big grin on your face that made me think it was probably worth getting into trouble for."

She laughed, her cheeks flushing at the memory. He liked seeing her like that, barefoot, smiling in her kitchen, swilling a beer and being so natural. So many of the women he spent time with lately seemed so fake, but then at least it was obvious what they wanted and what they were after. He'd fallen for the woman who seemed like perfect wife material before. He grimaced, staring down at his half-empty bottle. *Look where that had got him.*

"My dad had high hopes for me that involved a corporate career, not a life of being filthy dirty and riding horses."

"Yeah? Well, I can't see you donning a suit and heading off to an air-conditioned office every day," he declared. He'd shudder at the thought himself.

"Funny, my father thinks the exact opposite. He keeps telling me that I don't know what I'm missing out on, or at least he did until we had a big fight about it before my last trip to Europe to ride on the show jumping circuit over there. It hasn't come up again." Her words sounded wistful, and when she turned back to her cooking, he took up his spot at the counter again, watching as she moved about and checked the sauce, tasting it off the spoon and smiling to herself as if she didn't even realize he was watching. Maybe she didn't. It was one of the things he liked about her, that she seemed to have no idea how attractive she was. "He already has two of his offspring working in corporate life, so it's not like that's the problem. Cody and Angelina will be happy to take over the reins of the family business one day."

"It's hard being the black sheep of the family," he said,

rolling his beer bottle between his palms as she tipped out the pasta and steam billowed between them.

"I don't know if I'm the black one, so much as dark grey," she said, making them both laugh. "My brother Tanner, the one you met today, I think he's the black one. Our older siblings perform diligently for daddy, but the bull riding youngest son and another daughter wasting her time riding horses? Not exactly living up to the family name."

Sam watched as she put the spaghetti into bowls and then poured the tomato sauce on top it.

"Yeah, well, having a kid who's the top of her sport? That's something I'd be damn proud of if I was a dad," he said honestly. "It's bullshit to pretend that a corporate job is somehow better than doing what you love every day. I'd put money on it that he's damn proud of you, you just probably surprised him by not following the path he'd always envisaged for you."

"And with that," she said with a grin, "dinner is served."

Sam rose and reached for his plate, hand closing over hers as she went to pick it up at the same time. Mia looked up at him, smiling and wide eyed.

"I'll carry them," he said.

She gulped, the movement in her throat impossible to miss at such close range. Everything had changed between them in an instant, the touch of her skin reminding him exactly how soft and warm she'd been against him in bed.

"I thought we could eat outside," she said, still not moving. "Unless you're scared of getting eaten alive by bugs."

"There's not much that scares me," he said, taking the plate and gesturing for her to walk out ahead of him. *Except getting too close to a woman.*

Chapter 14

MIA wasn't sure how to read Sam. One minute he was sweet and funny, the next he seemed to pull away, a dark cloud settling over his face that she found impossible to decipher.

"Thanks for the spaghetti," Sam said, standing up and stretching. "And the beers."

She smiled. "Glad you liked it." She was also glad about something else they'd done, and was wondering if there was going to be a round two. Her stomach had gone all fluttery, her skin tingling, wondering if he was going to take her by the hand and lead her back to bed. Or to the kitchen counter. Or the sofa. Or . . . she crossed her legs and dug her fingernails into her palms. *Enough.*

"You're leaving?" she asked, trying to hide her disappointment as he collected his car keys from the counter.

"Yeah, I need to get back," he said.

"Right, of course," she said, standing and wondering whether she should kiss him or just awkwardly stand there. What did you do in a no-strings deal? Could she kiss him before he left or was that something you only did in a relationship? The last thing she wanted was to come across as needy.

"Come here," he said, taking the decision out of her hands with his gruff words, his hand claiming her waist as his lips warmed hers and reminded her exactly why she'd hoped he'd be staying over.

Mia kissed him back, mouth moving in time with his, wishing there was more to come instead of it being goodbye.

"See you tomorrow," he said, pulling away and giving her a long, slow smile. "Oh wait, tomorrow's Sunday. I'll catch you Monday then?"

Mia watched him gather his things and go, and she decided not to follow him out and watch him like a puppy that was being left behind. She was a grown woman and she'd entered into an agreement with him knowing full well it was about physical needs above all else.

"Yeah, see you Monday," she replied, walking a few steps and leaning against the wall, trying to act like she didn't give a damn. "And bring your overnight bag next time. This was too short for my liking."

He smiled and nodded, winking as he opened the door and disappeared out into the night. She waited, held her breath, then turned the interior lights off so she could see his silhouette illuminated by the external lighting. When she was certain he'd gone, she slipped down the wall and sank to the floor.

What the hell was she doing? What had she gotten herself into? And how the hell could he leave like that after the evening they'd had? Mia took a deep breath and forced herself back up. She couldn't sit there like a forlorn puddle on the floor all night, and she definitely wasn't about to start feeling sorry for herself. The trouble was, she liked Sam, a lot. And although she knew that he liked her back—he had to—she also knew that it was only about one thing to him; he'd made that abundantly obvious. She needed to be sensible though. He had animals in his care, and he probably needed to get back to them.

Her phone was vibrating, she could hear it chirping away somewhere in the kitchen, so she went off to find it. By the time she did, it had long ceased ringing, but she noticed there were text messages from Kat. A lot of them. She went into the fridge and pulled out a bottle of wine, retrieved a glass and poured herself a generous amount. Then she made her way over to the sofa, tucked her feet up and dialed her friend.

"Oh, it's the heartbreaker," Kat answered.

"Ha-ha, very funny," she replied, taking a sip and sinking back into her cushions. She looked out, wishing she was still sitting poolside with Sam instead of wondering why he'd left so fast, like he was suddenly in a hurry.

"Seriously, I thought you'd get on well together. What was wrong with him?"

Mia went to reply that nothing was wrong with him, when she realized they were talking about different men.

"There's someone else," she admitted. "I've kind of, well, entered into an arrangement." Mia cringed. It sounded terrible calling it that, but she always told Kat everything and she wasn't going to start lying to her now.

"An *arrangement*?" Kat asked. "What the heck does that mean, and who is he?"

Mia blew out a breath and took another sip of wine for courage.

"*Ohmygod*, it's that horse trainer, isn't it?"

Mia sighed. "The one and only."

"I'm coming over. I want to hear everything." Kat's

laugh echoed down the line. "And don't drink all the wine before I get there."

Sam walked up the steps of his sister's home the next day and knocked lightly on the door. He'd been scolded before when he'd knocked too loudly and woken sleeping babies, and after ending up with an infant in his arms crying inconsolably, he wasn't about to make that mistake again.

"Hey!"

Nate opened the door with one of the tiny humans in his arms. Sam knew better than to get too close, or he'd end up having to pretend he knew what he was doing with her. "Something smells good."

"That'd be the meat," Nate quipped. "We have half a cow out there on the grill, seriously."

Sam didn't doubt him. The King family dinners were big, and with three growing families to feed, they always went through a lot of food.

"You know, I think you've forgotten how to knock like a man," Nate teased, leaning close like he was whispering a secret to him. "You're supposed to actually make some noise on the timber. You're lucky I even knew to let you in."

"Fuck you," Sam swore good-naturedly, wishing he could punch Nate, but there was the slight problem of the small child in the way.

"Hey, man, could you . . ."

Sam turned to listen to Nate, groaning when his friend passed him the baby. "Dammit, Nate!" he protested, awkwardly trying to reposition his niece.

"Hey, Sam." Faith came past, with her long dark hair loose, barefoot and wearing jeans and a shirt. She looked like she had every time he'd seen her with Nate: relaxed, happy, barefoot and smiling. He hated to admit it, but Nate had been damn good for his little sister. "See you've got your arms full there."

"Your goddamn husband seems to offload to me every time I'm here." He kissed his sister's cheek. "Why do I always feel like I'm going to break her or something?"

He stared down at the sleeping child in his arms, his blood pressure rising when she stretched and opened her eyes. *Shit.*

"You're not going to break her," Faith said easily, as if she had every confidence in him. "She's way past the tiny limb breakable stage, okay? So long as you don't drop her, you'll be fine."

Great. So all he had to do was not drop her when she started squirming. Easier said than done.

"I hear you've got it bad for one of the Ford girls?" Faith teased, her voice low as they walked outside where the others were. "I don't think I've met her."

Sam took a deep breath, fighting to keep a lid on his feelings. "I'll kill Nate for that," he muttered. "And no, I don't have it bad. She's a nice girl and I'm working there. That's it."

She was also damn beautiful and he'd thought of little else other than getting her back between the sheets since the night before, but he wasn't about to tell his sister that. He also felt like shit for walking out on her so abruptly, but if he'd had to extract himself from her bed even later in the evening, it would have been worse trying to explain himself. He wasn't staying the night with her, not now, not ever.

"So what's she like?" Faith asked. "Come on, tell me!"

"She's nice," Sam said, knowing he had to give his sister something. If he didn't, she'd be like a dog with a bone.

"*And?*"

Faith was staring up at him, and just when he pulled his gaze from hers, a tiny, chubby hand reached up and touched his jaw, little fingers playing across his skin. She had him then. His tiny, cherubic little niece, the one who could be so charming and other times cry her damn eyes out when he held her, was looking up at him with such a sweet expression on her face that it nearly choked him.

"And nothing," he said quietly. "The only members of the opposite sex that I'll be falling for, Faith, are these two girls. They can have me wrapped around their little fingers and I will love them forever, but there's no room for anyone else. You know that."

She shook her head, like she was disappointed in him, but he knew that wasn't what she meant. Faith was happy and she wanted the same for him, she'd already told him as much.

"It doesn't have to be that way forever," she said, leaning into him and putting her head to his arm. "Just because you've been hurt once . . ."

Sam stiffened. "What you and Nate have is one in a million, and I couldn't be happier for you. But it's not going to happen to me, Faith, so stop pushing."

She nodded and when she stood on tiptoe to kiss his cheek he bent to let her and gave her a one-armed hug.

"I'm gonna find a seat in the shade so I can have a good chat with my niece," Sam said, smiling, wishing Faith would stop worrying about him.

"If you ever want to invite her for dinner . . ."

Sam gave Faith a look that he hoped was full of enough fury to get her to back off, but she just laughed at him and disappeared back into the other room. Which left Sam still with a baby in his arms, who seemed to be drifting back off to sleep, and a lineup of King brothers, beer bottles in hand, standing around talking shit and laughing.

Sam nodded when Nate plucked a beer from the ice bucket he had outside, walking closer to take it from him.

"Thanks. Just what I need."

He smiled at Chase and then nodded to Nate's youngest brother Ryder as he sank down into a chair and took a long pull of beer. For a moment he wondered what Mia was doing, whether she was out walking horses or relaxing poolside in the late afternoon sun.

"I hear you're all bent out of shape about Mia Ford," Chase said, grinning with his beer bottle hovering in front of his mouth.

"Oh, been there, done that," Ryder said, shaking his head. "Poor bastard."

Sam's face heated, like a volcano had erupted under his skin as he stared back at Ryder. "What did you say?" he asked, voice so low it was a wonder Ryder even heard him.

"Easy," Nate cautioned, moving closer and putting a firm hand on Sam's shoulder.

"Oh fuck, no I didn't mean I'd been there done *her*." Ryder chuckled. "I meant been there in the all messed up over a woman department." Ryder gestured inside to his wife. "With *her*."

Sam settled, the temperature cooling, no longer feeling like he was going to explode.

"Yeah, well, either way you can all fuck off, because I'm not messed up over her. Nothing's going on."

Nate and his two brothers burst out laughing. "Yeah right," Nate said through his laughter, "and watch the F-bombs around my daughter, would you?"

Sam looked down at the child in his arms. He bet she'd heard a lot worse, but he said a silent apology to his niece and stretched his legs out in front of him. So much for a quiet night with friends to keep his mind off Mia. If it wasn't for his nieces, he'd have told the lot of them to go to hell and stormed off back home.

"Seriously, if you like her? Go for it," Nate said, sounding nothing like his best friend since elementary school. "Life's complicated, but your love life doesn't have to be."

Sam scoffed. He was about to tell him that Nate had had the most complicated love life on the planet before he'd married Faith, but he held his tongue. They didn't need to rehash that conversation.

"You remember you used to have that rule of no women coming back to your place?" Sam asked.

Nate nodded. The other two were already in conversation about something else, so it was just the two of them now.

"Well, rules exist for a reason, and I have the same kind of rule. Whatever happens between me and Mia? It doesn't mean anything." Which was why he wasn't planning on seeing her until Monday. He didn't want to get too close to her, and that meant respecting their boundaries.

Nate swilled his beer and Sam leaned back.

"I get it," Nate finally said. "Trust me, I get it. And so do these other two meatheads here. But sometimes it's worth risking . . ."

Sam shook his head. "This conversation is over. I don't need all the goddamn sensitive, new-age bullshit from you."

Nate shrugged. "Fine. Come watch me turn some steaks. I won't mention her again.

"Good," Sam replied.

Steaks sounded great. He could stand there, stare at the meat and watch Nate. And he could eat it, then he could get the hell away from all the people trying to matchmake him and make a getaway for home.

His phone buzzed in his pocket and he grudgingly retrieved it. Whoever was calling him on Sunday could go to hell; it was probably his agent and . . . *damn*. The one person he was trying not to think about.

Sam cleared his throat, wondering if he should have just let it go to voicemail.

"Hey, Mia," he said, shooting Nate a sharp glare when he turned to face him. Trust him to be listening.

"Sam, I'm sorry, I didn't want to call you but there's been an accident."

Her voice was flat, cold, quiet. The hairs on his arms bristled in response, his throat catching. "What's happened? Are you ok?"

"I'm fine," she said quickly. "It's Tex. He's had an accident and he's behaving terribly. The vet won't treat him."

Sam relaxed, instantly calming when he realized she was fine. The horse he could deal with, but not her.

"I'll drive over now, but it'll take me an hour, maybe just under."

"Thanks, Sam. I really didn't mean to trouble you on a Sunday."

He nodded even though she couldn't see him. "It's fine. I'll see you soon, and just leave him be. He'll be calmest with no one around him."

Sam hung up and turned around, and found Nate standing and staring quizzically at him.

"What?" Sam scowled.

"Nothin'. Just sounded like you were about to leave."

Sam grimaced. "I am. The stallion I've been working, he's . . . Nothing. I just have to go."

"You're leaving already?" Faith appeared in the doorway, her other daughter on her hip, pudgy little legs wrapped around her waist. "We're about to eat."

"Any chance I can take it to go?" he asked, giving his sister what he hoped was an apologetic look as he passed his half-asleep niece to Nate.

She nodded. "Let me grab you a container. Nate, get a couple of steaks off and you can help yourself to the salad and potatoes on the counter inside."

Sam felt bad for leaving, he hadn't seen Nate and Faith a lot since work had exploded for him, but he couldn't leave Mia to deal with an out of control stallion on her own.

He took the container offered, filled it, and stopped to give his sister a hug. "I'm sorry. I'll make it up to you."

"Just be happy," she said with a smile. "So long as you're happy, I'm happy. You don't have anything to apologize for, okay?"

If only everyone was as accepting and kind as his sister. When he'd come home from Iraq, she'd helped to pull him through the worst of it, and it had made him doubly protective of her. But it also meant that he always felt like he'd let her down for not being there more to help her when she'd needed it the most, and he'd never forgiven himself for that.

He pushed thoughts of his sister aside as he jumped in his car. It was time to deal with a stallion and to pretend he wasn't secretly pleased to have an excuse to escape the family dinner and see Mia again.

Chapter 15

"HEY." Sam jogged over to Mia, calling out as he approached. She turned, eyes wide, looking so vulnerable his first instinct was to move closer and wrap his arms around her. *She's not your girlfriend.* He balled his fists and smiled instead, hoping he looked sympathetic.

"It's not looking great," she said, voice so quiet he wouldn't have recognized it as being hers if she hadn't been standing in front of him. "The ranch hands were moving some cattle past, two young bulls had broken through a fence overnight and were close by to Tex. He clearly didn't like them being near him, and he flipped out. He was caught in the fence and thrashing about and no one could help him. They just had to wait until he got himself unstuck, and he really did a job on his legs."

"Hell," he grumbled, moving past Mia to lean on the fence and take a closer look.

Tex was standing, looking miserable, pressed up against the fence and sulking. Sam could see blood dripping from his knee, but it was more matted than flowing freely now, and he had a few other cuts and scrapes from what Sam could see.

"He doesn't look *so* bad," Sam said, turning back to Mia.

"You haven't seen him walk yet."

Shit. Sam sighed, looking from her to the horse. "I'm sorry. I know how much he means to you."

"What do we do?" she asked, her voice husky and full of emotion. "I just don't want to give up on him when you're finally seeing some progress."

Sam folded his arms, refusing to get closer to her. This wasn't his horse, it was hers, and he wasn't supposed to be emotionally invested.

"Has the vet gone?" he asked.

She nodded. "Yup. Pretty much told me he'd come back to euthanize him. I could have asked my friend Kat to come over, but she's not a big animal vet and I didn't want her putting herself in danger."

Sam could have killed the vet right now, but he knew that his hadn't exactly been an unreasonable response. No one should have to risk their life to administer care to an animal.

"I'll go and take a look at him," Sam said, before turning back to her. "No, you know what? Let's both go in."

Mia didn't look convinced. "You're sure?"

"I want to check him over, then leave him for the night. He can sulk and feel sorry for himself, and we can tend to him again in the morning if he'll let us."

He could see Mia's throat move as she gulped, but he didn't pause to offer comfort. Instead Sam slipped through the fence and held out his hand, guiding her through and keeping hold of her a few beats too long, her palm warm and soft against his.

"I'm going to treat him like I always do, act like nothing has happened," he explained. "But I want you as my eyes and ears, okay? No agitating him, just soothe and keep a watch on his face for me, so you can see any change in his temper or pain levels. And stay close."

Sam moved toward the stallion, careful with his eye contact and keeping his movements slow and predictable. He didn't want to do anything to alarm him. He quickly realized that the wounds that looked the worst were in fact ugly but probably superficial. The blood would dry up, the puffing would go down, but it didn't explain his lameness.

Tex moved a few steps then and Sam cringed. "Christ," he swore, before offering comfort to the horse. "You're okay, bud. Just gonna take a little look."

Tex was scowling, his top lip pulled back in a sneer that told Sam he was one step away from having the horse's teeth lodged into his arm. He stood, watching, assessing, thinking.

Holy shit.

Sam backed up a few paces and indicated to Mia to follow him. She looked worried.

"I don't know how I never thought of this," he said. "Damn rocks for brains," he muttered.

Mia stared at him quizzically. "What?"

"He had that huge fall, a fall that he managed to survive, but do we know what treatment he received?" Sam asked. "I mean, how well was he looked after? Who worked on him?"

"I don't understand," Mia answered. "There was a vet on site, he was checked over immediately and treated. He wasn't left with any injuries that I'm aware of, because money wouldn't have been an object."

"Treated for what could be seen," Sam said, "just like we're looking at some gory injuries right now that need attention, but will probably heal just fine on their own."

Mia looked perplexed. "I'm not following."

"He's in pain," Sam said, glancing back at the horse and feeling for him, seeing the look on his face that told him how stupid he'd been not to see it in the first place. "He's turned from happy to grumpy, and he's only gotten worse. I suspect he's dealing with chronic pain that's made him, excuse my language, given him that *fuck you* attitude."

Mia's eyes widened. "How could I not have thought of that?" she murmured.

"Horses have accidents, but we expect more from their bodies than we do from ours. He's possibly lived with pain for years now, and this accident has made everything worse for him. To get him to trust again," Sam said, "we need to treat the root of his problems."

Mia laughed, the noise a cross between happy and hysterical. "So what exactly do you suggest we do, horse whisperer?"

He leaned in, brushing a loose strand of hair from her face. When her eyes met his he smiled, letting himself go with it instead of pulling away. "I say that I call in all the favors I have, and get the best massage and physical therapist there is here to work on him. I think cold laser therapy might help, too."

Mia paled, her eyes shutting for just longer than a blink. "You expect someone else to get near him?"

He shrugged. "I don't care whether he needs sedation before every treatment. If this is his last chance, then we're going to give him a damn good shot of living past the end of the month."

Mia leaned into him, her head to his shoulder as they both looked toward Tex. Sam slung his arm around her, content to stand there and stare. Mia was calming, made him feel that after so long pretending to be someone that didn't come naturally to him, he was finally having the chance to be himself.

"Sorry I had to call you over," she said.

Sam dropped a kiss into her hair. "Trust me, it's fine. I was getting a hard time from my brother-in-law, so it wasn't exactly a hard decision to leave."

"Still," she said, turning to him, tongue darting out to moisten her lips in a move he doubted she even knew was so tantalizing to him. "I feel bad dragging you away."

Sam glanced at his watch, saw that it was almost four now, and he didn't particularly want to call on his contacts and beg for special favors late on a Sunday afternoon.

"You know, there's something you could do to make it up to me," Sam murmured, claiming Mia's mouth before she had time to reply.

"Oh yeah," she mumbled against his lips. "I can't imagine what that would be."

The sun was hot, her lips were pillowy, and her body pressed to his was warm. He couldn't have thought of a better way to spend his evening than with Mia.

"You want to come back to the house with me?" she asked when he pulled back and smiled down at her.

"Sounds like a damn good idea to me."

The next day, Mia stood and watched as Sam edged close to Tex, holding a needle that the vet had decided was much better off in Sam's hand than his own. Tex was calmer today, but it didn't take a trained veterinarian to see that the horse was miserable.

"This the horse I'm here to see?"

Mia turned and came face to face with a middle-aged woman with a big smile, holding a case in one hand, her other extending out.

"Yes. I'm Mia," she said, shaking hands and introducing herself. "And over there is Tex. We're just waiting for the sedation to kick in."

The woman frowned. "Tina. Pleased to meet you. I'm not happy about the sedation, but I trust Sam enough to know that if he says we can't touch a horse without that, he's more than likely right."

Sam appeared then, leaving Tex to relax. "If you want to keep all your limbs and avoid teeth marks, then I'm definitely right," he said with a chuckle, enveloping Tina in a big hug. "I owe you big time, thanks for coming."

Tina's smile was warm. "He tell you that he worked wonders on a young filly of mine? I always told him I owed him anything and everything, so I guess this makes us even, huh?"

Sam laughed. "Yeah, if you manage to help this big guy then we're more than even."

Mia noticed that Tex's bottom lip was droopy, which told them all that he was starting to relax.

"Is there anything we need to do to help you?" Mia asked.

"I'll have both of you in there with me so I can focus on my work and not worry about what he's doing," Tina said. "Sam, you clip his lead rope on and keep hold of it, and Mia, you can be my eyes and ears."

Within minutes they were all in position, and she

watched as Tina started to massage Tex, her movements strong and purposeful. She hadn't doubted for a moment that Sam's friend knew what she was doing, but seeing her in action was impressive.

"Will he feel any relief straight away?" Mia asked quietly, never taking her eyes off the horse.

"Look, it's hard to know," Tina replied as she worked over his hindquarters. "From what I can feel already, we've got something deep going on in his back end, and if he's out in other places and has been for years? It could be that he gets worse before he gets better; then again he might feel relief. I'll do my best today, and follow this up with the cold laser therapy, and that should definitely provide some pain relief. But I'm warning you that he may need treatment over a long period of time if the issues are as deep as I suspect they are."

Mia traded glances with Sam and then watched Tina work. It took an hour for her to finish, and Mia noticed she had a bead of sweat across her forehead from the physical work. Within moments she'd retrieved the case she'd been carrying and was holding a machine, which Mia guessed was the cold laser. It was something she'd read about but not seen used before.

"I'd usually alternate treatments, but given the state of this horse and the fact he's been sedated, I think we're better to do as much as we can today to help him."

Tex had moved a little, less floppy looking than he'd been before, but the moment Tina put the machine on his hindquarters, the area she'd flagged as a potential problem, the horse's bottom lip hung down again, the ultimate sign of relaxation. Mia didn't doubt he was enjoying it.

"I love this treatment because the horses respond so well," Sam told her, voice low as he stroked Tex's neck.

"My old mare just stands there, no need to even head collar her, she's so relaxed having the treatment done. This could be a breakthrough for this one."

"I hope so," she answered, watching still, hoping and praying that this was the miracle they needed. Because time was fast running out.

Once the laser treatment was finished, Mia let Sam walk Tina out and she stood and stared at the stallion. She'd done everything she could, she knew that, but giving up on him would be heartbreaking, and no matter what anyone said, it was a promise she'd made that she didn't ever want to break.

"What are you thinking about?" Sam asked, surprising her, his arms looping around her from behind. She grinned when he rested his chin to the top of her head, making her feel ridiculously short beside him.

"Just about Tex. I really hope it works for him."

"Me too," Sam said, and she knew he meant it. He was already seriously invested in the horse, and she doubted he'd like to admit defeat with any project. "What do you say to dinner tonight? I hear there's this little Tex-Mex place not far from here."

Mia leaned back against him, his face now beside hers as she snuggled into him. "Been doing some research have you?" she asked.

Sam laughed. "Actually I was just thinking it'd be nice to take you out instead of you having to cook. What do you say?"

"I say that sounds fantastic," she said honestly, spinning in his arms. "And if you want to feed my horses for me while I go make myself look beautiful, that'd be even better." Mia gave him a quick kiss then broke free from his hold, walking backwards.

"Hey, isn't that what grooms are for?" he grumbled.

She grinned. "Don't have one. Sorry!"

Sam was grinning straight back at her as she left him to do her chores for her, knowing he wouldn't mind throwing her horses their hay. Especially if it meant not having to sit on her sofa waiting for her to get ready to go out.

Chapter 16

"WOW."

Sam leaned into the doorway as he looked at Mia. She did a little twirl and laughed at him, which made his mouth twitch into a smile. She was nervous, her cheeks flushed and her shoulders slightly rounded, and when her eyes finally met his he wasn't about to stand there and let her blush.

"Gorgeous," he said, gently touching his fingers to her jaw as she lifted her head. Sam paused, looking down at her mouth, lips plump and parted, kissing her slowly and carefully so he didn't ruin her makeup. She'd made a big effort and he wanted her to know he'd noticed.

"You sure know how to make a girl swoon," she teased. When Mia's fingers brushed his he clasped her hand, their palms pressed together as he tugged her toward him and out the door.

"I think I could be a little overdressed for where we're going," she murmured, looking uncertain.

Sam shrugged. "You look great to me." He looked her up and down, her tight faded blue jeans, heels, a cute little top with tiny straps that he was sure could break with one tug, and a leather jacket slung over her arm. "I'll wait if you want to change back into your riding gear though?"

She laughed and leaned into him. "Ha-ha, very funny."

Sam opened his mouth and then shut it, pulling the door closed behind them and walking down the path with Mia to where his vehicle was parked. He was going to tell her that she looked just as beautiful when she had her hair pulled back and her old boots on, but he didn't. This was already feeling too much like a date, too much like something more was happening when it wasn't supposed to feel like that.

"So what's on the menu tonight?" Mia asked.

Her eyes were bright, her smile warm as they reached his car and he opened the door for her.

"Hmm, chili chicken, and maybe some delicious but hard to identify meat?"

Mia laughed and he found himself trying to think of something else witty just to see her look like that again. He closed her door and walked around, getting in beside her.

"Bluey!"

Sam groaned as she threw her arms around his dog. Blue was standing in the middle, separating the driver and passenger seats, and making it impossible to glimpse more than the top of Mia's head now.

She lavished some more love on his canine before Sam muttered and pushed him back. "Stay," he said firmly.

Mia patted her hands on her jeans and he grimaced.

"Sorry, he really needs a bath."

"I don't care," she said simply, wiping her hands and then leaning back into the chair. "Honestly, I don't."

He believed her. Now that he'd seen her so many times, in her element with her horses and out on the ranch, he doubted she cared a bit about a smelly dog, but he'd still have liked to have a vehicle that smelled less old socks and more . . . anything other than that.

"You've never told me all that much about you," Mia said, breaking the silence as he reversed then turned around.

"I've told you plenty," he said, ready to dive head-first away from this particular conversation. "What is it you want to know?" He regretted asking her that the moment the question shot out of his mouth.

"Well," she started, shifting in her seat. He glanced at her and saw she was facing him now, one knee tucked up. "Do you think you'll always live in Texas? *Have* you always lived here?"

He nodded. "Yes, ma'am to both," Sam said, relaxing somewhat. He didn't mind those types of questions.

She reached out and ran her fingers down his arm, the one he had resting between them. Her touch was light as she stroked him.

"Have you been in love before?" she asked.

Sam almost drove clean off the road. "Next question."

Mia laughed, her fingers leaving his arm. "Sam! Come on, it's just us here. Do I take it there's one who got away who you've never stopped loving?"

He gripped the steering wheel, about ready to spin it and turn straight back the way they'd come from.

"Wrong on both counts. Now can we please talk about anything other than me?" he asked, exasperated. He sure as hell wasn't about to start talking to her about all his past screw-ups, especially where his love life was concerned.

Mia went quiet then. He glanced at her, taking his eyes off the road twice to see her side profile, the way she was so obviously deep in thought as she sat there, staring straight ahead. Sam sighed and decided to lighten the hell up. She wasn't asking to be nosey, she'd been trying to make conversation and he'd been an ass about it.

"Mia, I'm not the best at—"

She shook her head when he paused and looked at her again. "It's fine. I shouldn't have asked."

"There's no great love to speak of, but I've had my heart broken before if that's what you were asking. Haven't we all?"

"Yeah, I suppose," she said. "Although I've more had tiny pieces of my heart broken off multiple times than one big break."

He softened, his jaw losing the tight clench he'd been holding it in before. "How so?" he asked.

"Oh, well, I guess I fell for a guy before realizing he was no different than the last. He liked me because of my money, he wanted to meet my father. Did I mention wanting my money? That's kind of been a recurring issue for me."

He liked that she was trying to make light of it, her humor making it sound funny when in reality he knew it would have been so hard for her.

"I suppose it didn't take me long to figure out that I'd somehow been choosing douchebags over and over again, but then it became easier just not having expectations and not dating."

"That's one of the saddest things I've ever heard," he said, finding it hard to believe that someone as smart and beautiful as Mia had found it hard to meet someone decent. "If you couldn't find someone half decent, it doesn't leave much hope for the rest of us."

"Very funny," she chuckled.

"Come on, Mia. You're beautiful and talented and

smart, you're so much more than the money you'll inherit one day."

She went quiet, and he glanced over at her more than once, wondering what she was thinking and whether he'd said the wrong thing.

"Mia?"

Her smile told him she was fine. "That's very sweet of you to say. Thanks, Sam."

Sam kept quiet, not about to tell her that she was welcome because it was true. Mia was way too good for him, and even now he wondered what he thought he was doing, working on her ranch and then sleeping with her in his downtime. At least tonight he was taking her out instead of just being another in a long line of men who only wanted one thing from her. At least his thing wasn't money.

He kept driving, then pulled off the road when he saw the sign. It was a little place in the middle of nowhere, but he'd heard good things about it and he was hoping Mia was open-minded. He'd grown up eating plenty of food like this, in places like this, but he wasn't so sure about her.

"You like hot food?" he asked as he cut the engine.

Mia leaned in and kissed him, expectantly. "I think it's a little late to be asking me that."

He kissed her back, forgetting all about not wanting to upset her makeup, cupping the back of her head, not able to let her escape that quickly. Her hair was soft in his palm, her lips painfully soft against his. One thing he'd never expected was to be necking like high-school kids in a half-empty parking lot with one of the wealthiest heiresses in the state.

Mia dabbed at the corners of her mouth and below her bottom lip, wondering if she had any lipstick on at all, and whether the remnants were smeared across her face. Sam was holding her hand, and when they walked inside she had to wait a moment for her eyes to adjust. The place was dimly lit but had a nice enough feel to it, even though she noticed that she was perhaps the only non-Hispanic person there.

"I'm guessing this is going to be authentic Mexican," Mia said with a grin, leaning into Sam. "Which means our mouths are going to be on fire soon, right?"

"Have you ever been to Mexico?" Sam asked as they took a seat at a rustic timber table, sitting across from one another.

"A few times."

"Ever eaten at street stalls?" he asked.

She shook her head. "I'm not going to say. You'll just think I'm a princess."

"Hey, most people go to Mexico and stay at over-priced resorts, that does not make you a princess," Sam said, leaning closer across the table, fingertips tracing a pattern on her hand. "When I went, I was pretty young. The memories blur together now, but I was there to see relatives on my father's side. My grandfather was Mexican, and we'd go visit sometimes. So when we were there we'd eat all the street food, and it was amazing."

She smiled back at him as a waiter placed a candle on their table that flickered and made shadows dance across Sam's face.

"See, it wasn't so hard to tell me about yourself, was it?"

Sam winked and then rocked back, speaking Spanish and ordering. She caught a few words, but it wasn't a language she knew well.

"You just said I had a big butt and a hairy top lip, didn't you?"

Sam laughed and leaned in, like he was about to share

a big secret with her. "I just ordered us tequilas, and the best dishes this place has on the menu."

"We didn't even see the menu!" she protested.

"Would you believe me if I said there were only three items?"

Mia narrowed her gaze, trying not to laugh at him. She hadn't seen a lot of this side of Sam, the funny, easygoing side to him, away from horses and sex and . . . she smiled to herself. She only knew him with either horses or sex involved, period.

"No."

Sam grinned, waving the waiter over when he saw him carrying their drinks. "I asked him for his own personal favorites, told him we'd trust him."

Mia shrugged, happy to try anything. "To good food," she said, holding up her glass and clinking it to Sam's.

When she took a sip it burned a fiery trail down her throat that warmed her right to her belly. "That's strong," she said, taking another sip. "Strong but good."

Sam drained his as she watched. "Glad we appreciate the same drinks." Mia took another sip, liking the heat that spread through her body as a result of it. "I'm going to be good and drunk before the food hits the table."

"Enjoy the buzz. I'm only having one, to take the edge off."

Of course, he was driving. "Edge off what?" she asked.

"Sitting here with you and being forced to tell my life story."

Mia held up her glass and clinked it to his. "Ah, yes, back to you. What were we up to?"

He grunted. "My mom left us, and for some reason as we got older, Dad pulled away from his family. Maybe he was embarrassed."

"You'd think he'd have wanted to be closer to them since he was raising you on his own."

Sam's laugh was dark. "I wouldn't call what he did *raising* us. In fact, I don't think he can take any credit other than not letting us starve."

Mia nodded, not about to attempt a soothing reply. Sam's face said it all—the husky tone of his voice telling her that whatever had gone on between him and his dad was something he still held deep.

"You're making me feel bad for moaning about my own dad so much," she admitted.

Sam shrugged. "The fact that I had a shitty upbringing doesn't mean you can't feel the way you do. But yeah, if he didn't raise a hand to you or make you feel like a worthless piece of shit, then he's probably not as bad as you think. Hand on my heart, I can honestly say I'm better off now he's dead, and I'm not trying to be an asshole saying that, it's the truth."

They both took another sip then, and Mia studied Sam from across the table. Talking about his father had made his eyebrows knit closer together, his face drawn as he stared down into his drink. Whatever had happened between them, even so long ago, clearly still troubled him now.

Some of their food arrived then and Mia sat back, the aroma heavenly as she looked at the plate between them. Her stomach grumbled and she laughed.

"I forgot to eat lunch, I'm starving," she said.

Sam gestured for her to start, and she obliged, taking some of the meat from the plate.

"Steak fajitas?" she asked, making him smile, changing his face back to the warm, open expression she was used to.

"Ah, and here I was thinking you were a virgin with Mexican food."

"I think everyone knows what a fajita is, you idiot!" Mia laughed and they traded glances, making heat flood her body as she thought about the other meaning of that word. She was definitely no virgin, not where Sam was concerned.

Mia took her first mouthful of the tender steak, putting a piece on her fork before folding the rest of into the tortilla. She nodded. "Mmmm." She took a proper big bite, watching Sam do the same, their mouths too full to say anything other than keep eating. The peppers and steak were divine, the flavors strong and hot.

"So good," she finally managed, licking her fingers just as another plate was put in front of them.

Sam licked his fingers and grinned at her. "It might not be expensive eating, but it's damn good," he said, sitting back and looking from her to the new plate of food placed between them.

"What's this one?" she asked. "Fish?"

"Yep, fish tacos," Sam replied, nudging the plate closer to her. "He said it's spicy so be careful."

She loved how colorful the food was, the fish surrounded by some sort of chili and tomato salsa that she bet was as tasty as it looked.

"I'm going to explode if I keep eating this fast," she said.

"So sit back a bit, relax," he said, as he picked up a taco and grinned at her. "Drink some more tequila."

Mia did exactly that, taking a little sip, finding it refreshing after the hot food. Maybe she was getting a little drunk already, or maybe it was just that she felt relaxed in Sam's company, but she felt good. And he was right, there

was definitely something good about dining somewhere
unpretentious and eating damn good food. After studying
him a bit longer, watching his jaw move, his eyes meeting
hers for a moment and making her feel all fluttery inside,
she picked up her taco for something to do. The flavors
burst in her mouth, the hot chili balanced by lime juice,
but still leaving her mouth pleasantly on fire.

"Good?" he asked as she reached for her drink. She
wasn't sure if it would make her mouth hotter or help to
cool it.

"Uh-huh," she managed, wondering how he seemed so
cool as he raised a brow and finished his tequila.

"Want some water?" he asked her, but he was already
waving the waiter over and saying one of the few words
in Spanish she perfectly understood.

Once the water arrived she drained the glass. "How is
my mouth getting hotter?" she muttered, noticing the way
Sam was looking at her, his grin telling her that he was
clearly finding her amusing.

"The chili does that sometimes," he said. "I'm just
doing a good job of putting on my poker face."

She rolled her eyes at him, doubtful that he was pretending. He was probably well used to food this hot and
just enjoying seeing her squirm. "I actually loved it, the
flavors were amazing."

Sam pushed their empty dishes aside and leaned in
closer, his elbows on the table. With his shirtsleeves rolled
up and his tanned forearms on display, he looked too handsome for words. His smile was wide, his dark eyes warm
as he watched her, and she wondered what he was thinking about.

"So tell me about you," he said. "I think it's about time

you told me why you were so keen for . . ." his mouth kicked up in one corner, "a no-strings affair."

Mia wasn't embarrassed, but she always found her skin flushed when Sam talked to her like that, when his eyes never left hers and made her feel like the only person in the room. It was a feeling that she liked as much as it made her uncomfortable. "There's not a lot to tell."

He laughed. "Why do I not believe you?"

"Honestly, I just . . ." she strummed her fingers along the glass in front of her before looking back up and meeting Sam's gaze again. "I guess I'm sick of my expectations not being met and I don't want to compromise who I am for anyone. I'm never going to be barefoot and pregnant, happy to live off my trust fund or a husband's bank account. But the men I meet that seem impressed by what I do, they always treat it as a hobby, or else they see me as someone to provide *them* with the lifestyle they want. The only guys not like that are the ones I've met through show jumping, but, I don't know, nothing has ever come of those dates."

Sam touched her fingers across the table, his thumb brushing back and forth against her hand. "I don't think you've been looking in the right places. There are plenty of men who would love you for who you are, money aside. And I bet there are guys who see you, hell, maybe even compete against you, who'd love to ask you out but they're probably just intimidated."

She liked his optimism, even though she didn't agree with him. "Intimidated by me?" she asked, watching how his face changed, feeling his thumb stop moving. "So these men, they're not like you, then? Because you haven't seemed even remotely intimidated by me."

"Better men than me," he replied, reaching for her glass and taking a sip of tequila before pushing it back across the table to her. "Trust me."

"I think you're too hard on yourself." The words came out before she'd had time to think about them, the alcohol maybe making her more brazen than she would otherwise have been. "I'd like to know why *you* were so hell bent on not ending up in a relationship. I'm at a stage in my life where I don't want or need to settle down, but you, you give off the vibe that you don't ever want to be in a relationship."

More food arrived, the smell filling Mia's nostrils almost immediately. But she still didn't take her eyes off Sam, watching as his jaw tightened, visible even in the dim light.

"I'm not made for relationships," he said. "Once I was, but not now."

She was about to ask him more, wanting to find out what had changed him, what had made him the way he was, but the waiter appeared and made a fuss of asking them how their meals were. She smiled and nodded and Sam spoke, and when they were alone again he helped himself to the dish in front of them. Mia was so full she doubted she could eat much more, but she put a little on her plate.

"Chili con carne," he said, his plate full. "He said he noticed you flapping your hands around your mouth after the last dish, so they're hoping this one doesn't blow you away."

Mia laughed and looked over to see the chef leaning out of the kitchen, watching her with the waiter craning his neck beside him. She gave them a little wave before taking a mouthful of the hot chili, beef, bean and tomato dish. Like everything else, it was amazing, spicy but so tasty.

She touched her heart and smacked her lips together, making the men across the room laugh. When she turned, laughing herself, back to Sam, she noticed a change in his expression, a sadness there. Or maybe she was just imagining it.

"Pretty good, huh?" he asked.

"Amazing." Mia put more on her plate, eating until her belly was beyond full.

"I think this might become one of my favorite places," he said.

"We should come again next weekend and the one after that," Mia said, "I want this all over again." Sam opened his mouth and then she groaned, holding up her hand. They weren't going to be together then. Sam would be gone then, and what they had would be over.

"Would it be so bad if we saw each other still?" she asked.

"The longer it goes on the harder it becomes to . . ."

She shrugged. "Whatever. It's fine. I was just meaning that the food was so good."

"You could bring preppy guy here," Sam teased. "I'm sure he'd love it."

Mia glared at him. "That date was a favor to my best friend. And you know what? If I hadn't met a certain cowboy who got me all hot under the collar, maybe I'd have had more fun with him. Maybe he stared at his damn phone all night because he could tell I wasn't that into him."

Sam leaned back in his chair, but the way he looked at her made her feel like he was only a breath away. If she shut her eyes, she could feel that hot breath of his on her skin, could feel the weight of his body as it shifted against her, the familiarity of his touch. It was like he was undressing her with his eyes.

"Who made you so damn scared of commitment?" she asked him.

Sam gave her his poker face again. Only she saw through it and then some. "Let's just say that whatever happened to me made me pretty certain I'd never trust anyone with my heart again."

"Sounds like we've both had some pretty good relationships in the past," Mia said, not wanting to push him and deciding to make light of it and move on. "But seriously, why did this one hurt you so bad? She was seriously that nasty?"

"Yeah, something like that," Sam muttered, pushing his chair back. "You want to stay longer or go?" he asked.

Mia pushed her chair back and stood, too. "Let's go."

She watched him walk away and pull his wallet from his pocket. She let him pay; heaven knew they were paying him enough for his few weeks of work that she didn't feel bad letting him cover the bill. Besides, she was pretty sure he would have told her off if she'd offered to pay her share, anyway.

She drank in the sight of him, never tiring of the way his jeans fitted him, the way he moved, the breadth of his shoulders and the glint in his eye when he turned to her.

"Thanks for dinner," she said when he spun around and reached for her hand.

"Hey, you've cooked for me, this was my way of saying thanks," he said, drawing her in for a kiss. She expected his lips to touch her cheek, to brush her lips perhaps, but he stopped moving and kissed her properly, like he was reminding her of what was to come, and she didn't mind one bit.

His mouth was spicy, just like hers, the tequila making her giddy, making her want more even though they were still standing in the middle of a restaurant. Sam had some dignity though, tugging her outside as he raised his hand and waved to the waiter who was no doubt having a laugh watching them.

When they reached Sam's truck he pushed her roughly back against it, claiming her mouth again, only this time no one was watching and he knew it. His hands skimmed beneath her top, pushing it up, connecting with bare skin, and she moaned when he pushed into her, his belt buckle cool against her stomach.

Mia raised a leg, hooked it around him, desperate to feel him even closer. Sam's hand closed around her thigh, fingers digging deep, holding her there, before running his palm around her upper leg to cup her butt.

"I think I should take you home," Sam muttered in her ear when he finally broke their connection, his breath fast, his mouth still inches from hers.

Mia ducked back in for another quick kiss, which turned into her grinding against him and him exploring her mouth like he'd never kissed her before.

"Home," she whispered, running her hands down his chest, loving the feel of his hard muscles beneath it.

Sam gave her a sexy-as-hell wink before walking away from her, shaking his head like she was the naughty one. She laughed. *Maybe she was.*

Sam found it damn hard to concentrate on driving back to the River Ranch. Mia kept running her fingers up and down his thigh, always stopping before connecting with his crotch. She was driving him crazy.

When they finally pulled into her driveway he fought to go slow, aching to thump his foot on the accelerator and get to her place fast. Finally he pulled up by the stables, at the same time as her hand pulled away.

"You're in big trouble," he growled out, reaching for her, but she gently pushed him away.

"Sorry, I . . ."

Sam touched her arm. "You okay?"

She shook her head. "I don't feel so good. My stomach's kind of leaping around."

Sam was about to respond when she pushed open the door and bolted away, the little lights that illuminated the path down to her house the only reprieve from the darkness. He followed, worried about her, but not wanting to crowd her.

He listened to her door open, soon went through it himself and shut it behind him. And then he heard a sound that made his stomach weaken. She was definitely sick.

"Hey, anything I can do?" Sam called out, moving into her bedroom to stand beside the bathroom. He didn't look in, wanting to give her some privacy.

He heard groaning and his heart went out to her. Dinner had tasted so good, but something told him that maybe it hadn't been prepared so well. But then would she be sick so soon from that? He guessed so.

He walked to the kitchen, poured her a glass of water and returned, knocking lightly on the door. "I'm coming in."

"No, don't!" she groaned out.

Sam did anyway, going straight in and setting the glass down on the marble top. Then when she lurched forward, on her knees, hands on the toilet seat, he scooped her hair up and held it off her face.

"Go," she whispered. "Please. Don't . . . want . . . you . . ."

He winced when she was sick again, over and over, but he patiently held her hair and rubbed her back, feeling terrible for taking her to out for dinner only to have her sick so soon after.

"Have some water," Sam said, finding a hair tie in the drawer and managing to twist it around her hair successfully so it didn't fall forward. Then he passed her the glass. "Here."

She took a small sip and passed it back to him, before lying on the cool tile, her cheek pressed to it.

"You can go," she whispered against the floor.

Sam stood and ran the bath instead, knowing she must be feeling terrible. He listened to her vomit again and returned to rub her back, doing what he could.

"I'll fill the bath, then you can get in when you start to feel a little better," he said.

It was almost an hour later when Mia rose from the floor, holding out a hand to him. He pulled her to her feet and slowly undressed her, slipping her camisole off when she raised her arms and then sliding her jeans down over her ankles and off. When she was left in only her lacy panties, he carefully peeled them off too, admiring the curve of her ass and the softness of her golden skin as he did so, even though he never touched her sexually while he helped her. She was sick and he didn't touch women who weren't in the mood.

"Here you go," he said, taking her arm and helping her in.

She sunk down, her hair still in the rough ponytail he'd formed for her.

"Thanks," she murmured.

"Warm enough?" he asked.

She looked at him and gave him a barely-there smile, but he saw it.

"You don't have to stay and look after me," Mia said quietly.

"I know." Sam checked she had towels on the heated rail and moved the water glass closer in case she wanted some. "I'll just sit out here a while."

He went back out to the kitchen, pulled the drapes and blinds and checked that her cat had food. The feline soon heard him and wound around his legs, and he tipped out some kibble and gave him a stroke. Then he went back into her bedroom, turned on her bedside lamp, and pulled the drapes in there, too.

"You're still here?"

Mia's soft voice made him turn. She was wrapped in a big fluffy white towel, her face scrubbed and pink, her hair twisted up on top of her head now.

"How are you feeling?"

"Embarrassed that you saw me like that," she said. "And on the cusp of it starting all over again."

He frowned and pulled the covers back, beckoning for her to come over. When she did he waited for her to lie down then pulled the covers up to her chin, bending to kiss her cheek.

"I take it we won't be going back for fish tacos next weekend?" he teased.

"Sam!" she groaned.

He stroked her face then stood back. "You're even beautiful bent over a toilet, Mia. Any man who hasn't been able to see that before has rocks in his head."

"I'm sorry tonight ended like this," she whispered.

"Yeah, me too."

He quietly slipped out then, so tempted to stay to make sure she was okay. But he didn't. Couldn't. Nothing had changed, and he'd looked after her as best he could. Their date had been fun, sexy, enjoyable as hell, but he didn't stay over, period, and her being sick didn't change that.

Chapter 17

MIA waved out to Sam when she saw him. It had been two days since she'd seen him; the day before she'd stayed in bed late feeling sorry for herself and her tender stomach. And with Tex receiving his treatments instead of being worked, Sam hadn't been hanging around for long. Although he'd texted her and told her he'd been making some slow progress, she was looking forward to seeing how the treatment and training had been going.

And looking forward to seeing Sam.

After the way he'd looked after her, she'd started to think about him differently. She shuddered thinking about the way he'd seen her, the way he'd had to strip her out of her clothes and hold her hair back while she was sick. But the flipside to how mortified she felt was the tingle she felt thinking about how caring he'd been, how unflappable he'd been even when everything good about their night had turned to crap.

"Hey, gorgeous."

Mia spun around and was face to face with the man she was thinking about. Damn, he looked good. Every time she thought about him, she wondered if she'd imagined how handsome he was, until she saw him and realized he was every bit as good as she remembered.

"Have I missed you already?" she asked, flushing as his eyes swept over her, up then down.

"Sorry, early session today. And he's not having another treatment until tomorrow."

She smiled, hopeful. "How's he doing?" Mia was ready for some good news.

Sam's grin said it all. "He's good. *Real* good."

She let out a breath she didn't even know she'd been holding. "That's the best news I've heard all day."

Sam moved closer to her, his lips twisting into a smile. "Want to go have some tacos or chili to celebrate?" he teased.

Mia groaned. She'd been hoping he wasn't going to bring that up. "I'm so sorry," she murmured. "I don't even know what to say except . . ."

"I'm just messing with you," he said, touching her arm, his fingers teasing her skin even more than his words had. "And trust me when I say there's nothing you have to apologize for."

Mia sucked in a breath when his fingers tickled higher, moving up her bare arm. He stopped at her shoulder, watching her, staring into her eyes and making her think wicked thoughts. Missing out on three nights of fun with Sam had been unfair, and she wanted him. Now, tonight, tomorrow . . . she didn't care when so long as it was soon.

"Do you have plans for the rest of the day?" she asked, waiting for him to kiss her, *wanting* him to kiss her. She decided not to wait for him to make the move and stepped into his space.

"I do," he said. "But plans are made to be changed."

Her lips parted to accommodate his, and she was reminded of exactly why she liked him so much. His mouth played across hers and she sighed when he pulled away. "But I'll be back tomorrow."

Mia shook her head and grabbed his collar, tugging him back a little, not ready to let him get away just yet. "Will you be passing this way later?"

He smiled. "Maybe."

"Then come by tonight. I'll cook and we can . . ." she shrugged. "Let's just say that I'm sure we'll find something to do."

Sam's warm laughter made her crack, unable to keep the come-hither expression on her face she'd been trying to perfect. "See you later then," he said, winking and pulling away from her.

Mia stood, one hand on her hip, the other shielding her eyes from the sun. It was good to be feeling like herself again, to be flirting with Sam and enjoying the fresh air. Now she needed to forget about him for a while, ride her horses, get all her work done, then figure out what to cook for Sam. Or maybe she wouldn't bother cooking, she thought wickedly. Maybe she would just open a good bottle of wine, slip into her bikini, and wait poolside for her lover to swing by.

She laughed to herself as she crossed over to the stables, calling out to her horses and loving the sound of them nickering in response. This was her happy place, the one place in the world that made her heart skip a beat, but Sam was quickly becoming the one person in the world she looked forward to seeing, the only person who'd ever made her feel an unfamiliar mix of excitement, anticipation and contentment. And it scared her.

"He'll be gone soon," she muttered to her mare as she

let herself into her stall. She'd had the ranch hands feed her horses and care for them for the past two days, and Indi was especially pleased to see her again. "He'll be gone and then I'll wish I never let him get under my skin, won't I?"

Her horse snuffled her pockets and Mia stroked her neck affectionately, pressing a kiss to her warm, hairy cheek. Deep down, she wondered if maybe Sam would want to see her again, after their time was up, but she was smart enough not to get her hopes up. She'd agreed to his terms, *wanted* the same terms he had, and it wasn't his fault he'd made her feelings leap all over the place.

Sam rounded the corner and found Mia stretched out, lying on a pool recliner beneath a big umbrella, eyes shut. He was about to alert her, then realized she was sleeping, or at least it looked that way. Her pool was like something out of a resort—a perfect long rectangle of the deepest blue, with four perfect sun loungers and umbrellas between them lined up on one side.

He took off his hat and set it down beside her drink on the side table, drinking in the sight of her lying there in her bikini, hair wet and fanned out around her, one knee raised. Her mouth was parted and he smiled down at her, not wanting to give her a fright but wanting to surprise her nonetheless.

Sam carefully positioned himself above her, trying not to make a sound, bending low, his mouth hovering over hers. He kissed her so softly, wanting to wake her with a smile on her face, his lips barely brushing hers, caressing her.

"Mmmm."

Her low moan, still half-asleep, spurred him on. He kissed her again, stroking her hair, gently rousing her.

When her eyes finally opened, lazy and half-lidded, he pulled back to look down at her properly.

"Hey," she whispered, catching her bottom lip between her teeth.

"I was going for the *she's expecting me* vibe rather than the being molested in your own yard kind of vibe," he said, suddenly wondering if he'd pushed things too far now that she was beneath him and looking vulnerable in her string bikini and he was fully clothed.

"Shut up and kiss me again," she mumbled, grabbing the back of his head and forcing him back down again.

Sam didn't need to be told twice. He braced himself with his hands above her head, pushing down on his elbows. She squealed when his belt buckle touched her bare stomach, wriggling beneath him, fingers at his shoulders, legs wrapping around his back.

"You're trouble," he muttered as she fought to unbutton his shirt.

"Just trying to get my money's worth," she said, laughing, breathless as she tried to flip them around, only the lounger was too small.

"Shit!" Sam swore as he felt the furniture go beneath them, the chair tipping as he fell to the concrete, instinctively keeping his arms wrapped around Mia so she didn't hit the ground. Instead she landed tight against his chest, rolling slightly once they'd landed.

Her eyes were wide, her hand fluttering to his face.

"Are you okay?" she asked, and he could tell that she was trying not to giggle even though she did look worried.

"I'm just pleased I have my clothes on," he grumbled, pushing up. "Otherwise I'd have a skinned ass right about now."

Mia stood, her long limbs almost close enough for him

to touch. "I think you should take them off now," she said, grinning at him and beckoning with her finger. Then she turned, ran the few steps to the edge of the pool, and dove in.

Sam laughed as she disappeared beneath the sparkling, perfect blue water. She was one hell of a woman, and she was driving him crazy. He stripped off, meeting her gaze when her head popped up out of the water, her mouth blowing little bubbles, teasing him. When she scooped a handful of water and splashed it at him, he growled and paused at the edge.

"You asked for it," he yelled, naked and diving into the pool after her.

"No!" Mia shrieked when he made a grab for her, fingers around her wrist, capturing her and forcing her to turn. She laughed as she struggled, until he had both her wrists in his one hand, behind her back, pressed hard against her.

"I've been thinking about you all afternoon," he told her, slowly releasing her wrists and smiling when those same wrists looped around his neck. Mia folded her legs around his waist, holding on to him, and he walked them both over to the steps at the other end.

"Thinking about what?" she asked, nipping at his earlobe.

Sam caught her chin and kissed her, slowly, forcing himself to enjoy every moment of her mouth against his. Mia ran hands through his wet hair, down his arms and back up his back and over his shoulders. Her touch drove him wild, and he kept his lips locked to hers as he slowly pulled the strings on her bikini. First her top, and then the ties at each hip.

Mia didn't resist, but she did moan against his mouth,

pressing into him. The water lapping against them caused her top to fall down and float away, and Sam waded into shallower water so he could trace down Mia's chest, mouth dragging across her wet skin, taking her nipple into his mouth and sucking, first softly and then hard.

Mia yanked him back up, one hand fisted in his hair, moving against him, grinding against his erection, the soft fabric of her bikini bottom slowly drifting down and then away. She slipped down on to him as his mouth met hers again, stifling her moan, taking her in the water and loving the feel of her nails against his skin, her wet mouth gliding against his.

Of all the things, he'd never had sex in a pool before, and he doubted he'd ever be able to dive into sparkling blue water without thinking about Mia again.

Mia lay back against the concrete, the hard surface still warm from the hot day, even though the sun had long started to fall, the sky darkening above her, now a dark pink. Her stomach rumbled and Sam's palm pressed to her skin, softly rubbing.

"I think you need sustenance," he joked.

"After that work out?" she teased. "I'd say so!"

They'd been lying beside the pool for a while, but she didn't care. No one usually came by her place unannounced, other than her siblings, and they were all away. Anyone else would go to the front door rather than making their way around the side, and the back part of her property wasn't visible from the ranch, other than down the path. She'd been careful when she had her landscaping plan done to ensure her pool and patio was entirely private from the main part of the ranch. Besides, nothing had ever felt so good as her skin being warmed by the concrete and a naked Sam by her side, and right now she couldn't give a damn if someone *could* see them.

Reluctantly she sat up, seeing Blue sitting by the house. "I really hope he wasn't watching us before," she said, smiling down at Sam. She held out her hand and he took it, sitting up beside her.

"I don't think he'll care."

She pushed at him, laughing, and stood up. She looked at her bikini floating in the middle of the pool now, surprised when Sam seemed to read her mind and effortlessly dove in to get it for her. He tossed the bikini out then shook his head, water droplets flying, before hauling himself out. The water dripping over his tanned, muscled body made her heart skip a beat all over again.

"Don't look at me like that," he warned, walking closer, not slowing down.

"Like what?" she asked.

"Like you want something all over again."

Mia grinned and kissed him, squealing when his wet arms surrounded her, his wet chest cold against her warm skin. She noticed he had something else ready and waiting for her, too.

"Food first," she warned. "Then we can play."

Sam slapped her on the backside, and she took the wet bikini from him, watching him shake like a dog. One moment he was a gentleman, the next he was as uncouth as the next guy.

Mia was dry so she patted Blue on her way past and walked straight in. She'd left a towel for herself just inside the door though, and she threw that to Sam. Then she went into the kitchen, turned the oven on and took out everything she needed to make pizza. She had bases in the fridge, and she quickly brushed some olive oil on them, taking out a wine glass and pouring herself a drink, and then opening a beer for Sam.

"I like this kind of cooking," he said, brows arched as he joined her. He had the towel wrapped around his waist as he sat and rested his elbows on the counter. "I could get used to this."

Mia wanted to ask him if he was serious, but she didn't. He was teasing her, and she didn't want to ruin the mood. She glanced at the oven and decided it would be ready enough, slipping the thin pizza bases on to the tray and then putting them in the oven.

"Sorry, show's over. I'll be back soon."

In her bedroom, she slipped into a silky robe, knotting the waist, and checked her reflection in the mirror. Her hair was nearly dry, slightly tangled and messy, and her cheeks were pink. But instead of putting any makeup on, she decided to stay as she was. Sam hadn't seemed to mind the way she looked in the pool, so there was no need to change anything now.

She found him sitting where she'd left him, and Mia reached for her wine glass, taking a long sip before placing it back down and getting out everything she needed. She started with chopping peppers, and when Sam silently joined her around the other side of the counter, she slid a board and the chorizo sausage down his way for him to slice. Mia took the tray out of the oven and spread tomato sauce across each pizza base, followed by peppers, mushrooms, chorizo and some ham, then she sprinkled some cheese across the top and an extra drizzle of sauce.

"You make it look so easy," Sam said.

She put the tray back in the oven and turned to him. "That's because it is."

He stared at her, their eyes locked, Mia's breath rough.

Sam walked into her then, scooping her up and sitting her on the edge of the counter. She crossed her arms behind his neck but kept her hands in the air as he kissed her, pushing her robe aside, nudging at her thighs, trailing his mouth over every inch of her as she moaned at being pleasured in her own kitchen. When he finally stopped, when he looked up at her with such intensity in his eyes, she moved forward and let him tug her down, taking her, pushing inside of her and making her bite down on his shoulder.

Sam took all of her weight then, pulling her against him, walking her backwards against the door of her pantry as she bucked against him. Mia cried out when Sam slowly sunk to the ground, taking them both down, pushing so deep inside her as she found herself sitting astride him, on the floor, as they both reached climax.

Buzzzzzz.

Mia burst out laughing and buried her face in Sam's neck as the oven timer sounded out.

"We couldn't have timed that better if we'd tried," Sam joked.

Mia laughed. "Come on, help me up. I don't want to burn them!"

Sam smiled down at Mia, tucked up in his arms. His stomach was still full, he was so sleepy he could have passed out on the sofa, and Mia's long hair was spilled around him like woven silk. He ran his fingers through it and smiled when she turned to look up at him.

"If I don't move I'm going to fall asleep," she said, groaning and stretching, sitting up so she was still tucked against him.

"I think it's time for me to head home," he said reluctantly, sorely tempted this time to give in and just curl up in her bed. They'd eaten and talked, then watched a movie . . . it was all so normal, so nice. But he knew how easily he could get caught up with being around Mia, and he was already starting to feel like he was in too deep. Tonight had been too good, too relaxing and way too easy to get used to.

"You really want to drive all that way in the dark?" she asked, looking disappointed.

He nodded, kissing the top of her head and forcing himself to stand. "Yeah, I'd better get going."

She smiled, but he could see it wasn't the response she'd been hoping for. Mia reached for a blanket and he watched as she snuggled into it, looking like she was too comfortable on the sofa to bother moving.

"I'll let myself out. Thanks for tonight."

He bent to kiss her one last time, and not for the first time he wondered if he was being stupid, if he needed to lighten up and let whatever happened, happen. Her mouth touched to his in a slow, warm kiss, and Sam eventually straightened.

No. Staying over would be too easy, falling for her would be too easy. What they had was fun, and he needed it to stay that way.

"I'll see you tomorrow," he said.

Mia blew him another kiss. "Until tomorrow, cowboy."

Sam whistled and Blue jumped up and followed him. Tonight had been fun, but the only person he'd be sharing a bed with tonight was his dog. The one constant in his life who had never, ever let him down.

Chapter 18

MIA couldn't believe it. A week after his first treatment, she watched as Tex moved around Sam, his movements extended, his body supple. It was like the horse knew that his trainer had been the one to help him, and when he was asked to stop, he tossed his head and turned in toward Sam, eyes bright, ears forward.

"It's like he's a different horse," Mia said, incredulous as she swapped glances with her father. He was standing by the railing, watching, and she hoped he realized that Sam had been worth every penny and then some. If he hadn't figured out what was wrong, there wasn't a person who would have supported her to save Tex's life.

"Impressive," Walter called out. "Good work."

Mia crossed over to her dad, surprised by the genuine smile on his face as he watched Tex.

"Sam's worked wonders with him," she told him. "Seems like he's been in a lot of pain for a very long time, and once that was solved . . ."

"He's got that horse eating out of his hands now, hasn't

he?" Her father chuckled. "Seems he was worth the gold I had to pay him."

"I need to say thank you," Mia said, reaching out to her dad and touching his arm. He looked surprised and she took it even further, giving him a long, warm hug. "If you hadn't been so generous, he'd be dead by now. I don't even know what to say other than thank you so, so much."

Tears filled her eyes when her dad held her at arm's length. "You know, you're my only child who's never asked me for a penny, Mia. The others think they haven't, but when they were younger there was always something they wanted. You were different."

"You know how I feel about making my own way," she said, her voice husky with emotion. It wasn't often she had moments like this with her father—he'd never been big on talking about their feelings.

"When you came to me as good as begging for help with this horse, I knew it meant something to you. And it seems you were right." He kissed her cheek. "You made a good decision here, Mia. I'm proud of you."

She felt like a little girl beaming back at her father after receiving praise. "Thanks, Daddy."

"Just don't go asking me to pour money into any other horses. You hear me?" he asked, sounding gruff.

He was probably as surprised as she was at their little heart to heart.

She watched him go, smiling as she thought about what he'd just said. Maybe it was just because she was getting older, or maybe her father was slowly seeing how much she enjoyed what she did for a job, that she was good at working horses. Either way, it was nice to be getting along so well with him.

Once he was gone, Mia ducked between the rails and

went over to Sam. He was stroking the stallion's neck now, his movements slow and deliberate. When she touched his back he turned.

"That horse owes you his life," she whispered, standing on tiptoes to press a kiss to his cheek. "Even my father agrees that you've been worth every exorbitant penny we've had to pay you."

"Hey, the horse had a bad few years," Sam said simply. "And I'm not the one who's been working magic on him. Although you've definitely been getting your money's worth from me, huh?"

She ignored his sexual innuendo. "You're the one who figured out what was wrong, Sam, and that counts for everything," she reminded him, letting him unclip the horse before slipping her arms around his waist.

Sam chuckled and wound the rope around her, hauling her gently towards him until she bumped into his body. Mia tipped her head back, looked into eyes that seemed to be smiling at her, twinkling as he brought his face closer, the rope still loosely swayed around her.

His lips were warm as they brushed hers, sending the familiar tingle through her body, the rush of excitement that touched all the way to her belly as she kissed him back. For a man who'd started out by driving her crazy for all the wrong reasons, he'd certainly redeemed himself.

When she pulled back and gazed up at him, Mia knew she was playing a dangerous game. She'd agreed to something that was fully physical and non-emotional, but the way she felt about Sam, it wasn't just about the sex and the fun for her. She felt something real for him; for the first time in her life she wanted more, she'd met someone who challenged her and thrilled her, someone who saw her for who she truly was.

Mia swallowed, wondering what to say, wishing she knew the right way to tell Sam how she felt.

"As much as I'd like to kiss you some more, I'm feeling like we're being watched."

He nodded behind her and Mia turned, laughing at the way Tex was staring at them. Even though he was no longer attached to a rope he was still standing where they'd left him.

"Don't worry, I don't think he minds," she teased.

"Hey, I'm the one he loves. I'm just worried that he might see you as a threat and take a chunk out of your shoulder with those big teeth of his."

Mia knew he was only being silly, but it wasn't so long ago that Tex had tried to do exactly that to her. "Fine," she replied, stealing one more kiss before pushing away from him as he laughed and unspun her from the rope. "I'll see you back at the house."

Before she walked away, she turned back to him, holding her hand high to shield her face from the late afternoon sun. "Why don't you stay tonight?" she asked, nervous as she asked the question. If he stayed, it would be the first time, and it felt strange asking him when he'd never said yes before. "We can open champagne and celebrate, and—"

"Darlin', I can't," he said, throwing her a smile even though he was saying no. "But that doesn't mean we can't celebrate."

She kept her smile fixed, didn't want him to see through the façade to how disappointed she was. "No problem," she said, ducking back through the fence and heading to the stables. She couldn't lie to herself, but she wasn't going to let Sam see how much he'd started to mean to her, if he didn't even want to stay the night. She was a big girl, and she needed to put on her big girl panties and deal with the fact she was getting exactly what they'd agreed on. It wasn't his fault if she suddenly wanted more.

Sam watched Mia as she sipped her champagne. She was tipsy but not drunk, and she was smiling as she set her glass down on the counter. When she looked up, seeing his eyes on her, she sauntered forward and made them both laugh.

She was so beautiful she took his breath away sometimes. He opened his arms, smiling as she stepped in against him, her sigh against his lips as she claimed a kiss, making him grin. His lips kicked up before he kissed her back. *She's not yours.* He folded her in his arms, her hair brushing against him as she tipped back a little and looked up at him.

It was hard to hold back sometimes, to remind himself that what they had wasn't for keeps. She was so easy to be around, and he was starting to like the way she called him out and stood up for herself. And when they were like this, just the two of them, it was tough to remember they only had another week before everything came to an end. He'd done his job with the stallion, but that was the only part of being at River Ranch that felt like it should be ending.

"Want to go to bed?" Mia asked.

He didn't reply. Instead he bent and scooped her up, carrying her to the bedroom without saying a word. Her head was against his chest, her arms slung around his neck, as he strode through the house.

"Where's Blue?" she suddenly asked.

"Stalking your cat I'd guess," Sam replied with a chuckle.

"Do you think we should check on them?" Mia asked, twisting in his arms.

He held her tighter, looked down at her and stood at the foot of the bed. "No," he grumbled. "There's only one thing we're doing right now, and checking that the dog and cat have become friends isn't it."

Sam set Mia down, hand on her arm, the other rising to stroke down her hair as she stood before him. They were only inches apart, but the air between them made it feel like more, and he stepped up into her, tucking a finger beneath her chin to tilt her face up. Mia's lips were parted ever-so-slightly, her eyes wide and warm as she stared back at him, never breaking their gaze. He drank in the sight of her standing there, her long hair grazing her shoulders and falling down her back, before burying his fist in that long mane and tugging her head back a little.

Mia gasped, her mouth opening more, and he crushed his lips to hers, kissing her with everything he had. If he weren't so damn scared, if he could find it within himself to open up to her, then he would have, but for now this was all he had to give and he wanted her to know how much she meant to him.

Still kissing her, pausing only to trace his lips down her neck when she tipped back further, exploring his way to the top of her breast before making his way back up to her mouth again, he started to unbutton her shirt. Mia's hands started to work on his buttons as he finished hers and gently slipped the shirt from her shoulders, exposing bare skin that made his breath catch. It didn't matter how many times he saw her naked, she always had the same effect on him.

He dropped lower, kissing his way down, slowly unzipping her jeans and pulling them down. He ran his tongue over her panties, grinning when she groaned, and reached for her wrists to hold her in place. He pushed out a hot breath against her skin which made her squirm, kissed her lightly all around, tongue tracing against skin as soft as butter. When she fought against his hold on her and pushed her fingers through his hair, gripping on to it, he resumed taking her jeans off, slipping them all the way down and tugging them off when she lifted each foot in turn. Undressing her had become one of his favorite things to do.

When he glanced back up to see her standing in only her underwear, he slowly stood and shrugged his own shirt off, then his jeans. Mia was looking at him expectantly, her tongue darting out to moisten her lips. Sam pushed her, his hand to her chest, gently, listening to her laugh as she fell back onto the bed. Then he climbed on top of her, elbows on either side of her head as he kissed her. He was happy to go slow tonight, to let her decide how fast she wanted to go, and from what he could tell, she was enjoying the pace.

Mia's hands circled his shoulders, her nails digging in as she ran her fingers down his back, kissing him, tongue laced with his, their movements unhurried. When she pulled back and pressed a kiss to his jaw, and then his neck, Sam moaned, holding his weight above her still, not wanting to crush her as she wriggled beneath him. Her teeth grazed his neck and then her lips plucked at his collarbone, sucking, teasing him as she moved. It wasn't until she went to tug at his boxers that he realized she'd already taken her own panties off.

Sam helped her, using one hand to tug his down so he didn't drop down onto her, and the moment he turned back she was pressing on the back of his head, pulling him down, forcing his mouth back to hers. *So much for slow.* Mia kissed him like she'd never been kissed before, urgent now, the unhurried, slow pace of moments earlier long gone now.

"Sam," she murmured against his mouth as fingers closed around him, feeling his erection, guiding him in.

He was about to protest, to tell her he hadn't had enough time to pleasure her first, to . . .

Oh hell. Mia was already wet for him as he slid down into her, her fingers digging into his butt as she showed him exactly what she wanted, wriggling beneath him.

"You're wicked," he whispered in her ear, giving her what she was asking for, pushing deeper inside of her.

Mia clenched herself around him, moaning and arching her back, her breasts coming up to meet him, as he closed his mouth over one of her erect nipples, sucking hard and liking the way she bucked in response beneath him.

It just so happened he was fine with wicked, especially when it came to Mia.

Mia draped herself over Sam, unable to get enough of him and trying to give him a reason not to go. She wanted him to herself, selfishly, all night. She wanted to wake up next to him and then snuggle back into him; have him make love to her on rumpled, warm sheets before she rose for the day. Every night they spent together left her satiated in one way, but when he left, all she felt was emptiness. How could she have been so sure she wasn't going to want more from him, so certain that a few weeks of fun were going to be enough? She groaned inwardly; that had been *before* he'd shown his true self to her, when he'd been arrogant and so unlike the type of man she'd expected to ever fall for.

Dammit, she wanted more!

"Sam," she whispered, kissing his chest and tucking tighter against him. He responded, lips to her hair, warm body pressing in to hers. She loved the way he reacted to her, the way he touched her. Mia took a big breath and slowly let it out. "Stay," she said.

His arm tightened around her and she wondered if he actually would this time. She hadn't realized how much it annoyed her, but they only had a few days left and she wanted to make the most of it. Why was he so damn insistent that he couldn't ever stay over? Would it be so bad to wake up beside her, to roll over, bodies warm, sheets rumpled, and have morning sex before eating breakfast together?

Sam didn't say anything. She wondered if he was asleep and listened to the steady rise and fall of his chest. His breathing was relaxed, deep and strong, but she glanced at his face and saw that he was looking at her now, his head propped up just enough by the pillow.

Mia wriggled, tucked her chin to his chest and gazed at him. She couldn't believe how much had changed between them. When she'd first met him, she'd been full of anticipation and he'd ended up coming across as a too-confident asshole, but now? She'd seen a different side to him, a warmer, more loving side. The same side that she guessed all of the animals he worked with got to experience.

"What are you thinking about?" he asked, stroking her face, his fingers skimming her skin.

Mia sighed, lost in his dark brown gaze, more content than she'd ever felt. "That I love you," she said simply, before realizing the words had come out of her mouth.

Sam stiffened and he pushed up, sitting up in bed now, eyes still locked on hers. She reached for the sheet, pulling it over her breasts and staring at him. Shit. Why had she said that? Why had those three little words spilled from her like they were the most natural thing in the world to say? But they were true, she knew in her heart they were probably the truest words she'd ever said, even if she was regretting ever letting them spill out now that she could see the horrified look on Sam's face.

"Mia," Sam started, but she shook her head, refused to let him continue.

"Is it that big of a deal?" she asked, knowing that it was because she'd never said it before to a man. "Maybe I shouldn't have said it, but it's how I feel."

"The problem is that we *had* a deal," he said, voice so low it was more like a whisper. "Mia, this wasn't supposed to happen."

"So?" she said, not seeing what the problem was, her face heating up, embarrassment rising. "We had a deal, but what we have, it's so much more than that. Tell me I haven't been imagining it? Tell me that you still feel the same about me as you did when we first slept together?"

Sam pushed the covers off his legs and stood, looking at her like she was . . . she groaned. She didn't even know what. He looked like she'd just told him that she had a sexually transmitted infection, not that she loved him!

"The problem is we're not supposed to be doing this!" he said, running a hand through his hair, standing naked and staring at her. "This was supposed to be—"

"*Fuck* you, Sam," she swore, clutching the sheet tightly to herself. "I just said what I was feeling. I'm sorry you find my honesty so hard to accept."

He gave her a long look before grabbing his boxers and jeans and starting to get dressed. He didn't look at her again, just methodically got dressed and located his things like he needed to escape in a hurry.

"So you're leaving, just like that?" she asked. "You're walking out on me like I'm not good enough for you? This is what I get for opening up to the man I've been sharing my bed with?"

He barely looked at her, a quick glance before staring at the wall behind her, and she felt the hot sting of tears piercing her eyes. She felt used and dirty and unloved, and now she knew why she was supposed to hold that part of herself back, why she should never have let herself fall so hard for Sam. He'd wanted her for a good time, not a long time, and she'd been so caught up in how she was feeling that she'd forgotten how damn clear he'd been about it.

"Yeah, I think I need to go," he said quickly. "It'd be better to make this a clean break."

"Why won't you ever stay over? Is because I asked you again, or is it because I told you I loved you?" she asked, furious that he wouldn't even make eye contact with her. She was on her knees on the bed, sheet still covering her, palm itching to slap into his cheek. "Tell me Sam! I deserve to know, goddamn it!"

"What we had was just sex, Mia," he said coldly, finally meeting her gaze. "If you thought it was more than something physical, then I'm sorry, but I'm pretty sure we set out clear ground rules from the start, and it was never my intention to lead you on."

She gulped, wondering who the hell the stranger of a man before her even was. His voice was so flat, so unemotional, so unlike the man she'd just spent the past three weeks with. "Maybe I thought that was okay, at the start, but you can't help the way you feel." The words were hard to push out but she forced them, needing to hurt him, wanting to elicit some kind of response from him. "Is it so wrong that I was honest with you?"

He didn't reply, and she shouted at him, so angry she wanted to hurt him.

"Tell me you don't feel the same, or are you just a god-damn coward?" Mia didn't believe him, didn't believe that this side of him was the true Sam. She'd lain in his arms, been loved by him, caressed by him, cared for by him. The Sam she knew was not this heartless asshole of a man! What the hell was going on with him?

His smile was cold and never reached his eyes. "I just don't feel the same," he said simply, before collecting his shirt and turning to walk out of the room. "I'm sorry Mia, but it's true."

Mia stuffed her fist to her mouth, a sob stammering in her throat, choking her as she refused to let it out. She waited, quivering, in silence until she heard the click of her front door. She slowly pulled her hand from her face, the sobs guttural, the sound of her pain howling around her as she sunk down into her covers. The bed was warm from their bodies, it still smelled like Sam, the sheets on his side rumpled, the pillows still bunched from where he'd been pressed against them.

She cried like she'd never cried before, her face wet as she buried herself into the feather pillow, curling her body tight as she fought wave after wave of fresh pain. Sam had changed her. Sam had made her finally open herself to another human being, made her show her vulnerabilities and trust in someone else.

She wanted to hate him, but all she could see was his smile, all she could feel was his warm breath against her skin, his hard body pressed to hers as he scooped against her in bed.

But Sam was gone.

She sobbed, more quietly now, her body no longer

heaving like it had only moments earlier. She clutched the covers tight and shut her eyes. *Now she could see him.* Now she could see the ice-cold gaze, could conjure the image of him standing there, about to leave.

He was no better than any other guy who'd wanted her for her money, in fact he might even be worse. Because Sam had pretended to care, pretended that he didn't want anything from her, then he'd lured her in, made her fall in love with him, and made her think he was falling, too. She'd known the ground rules, but the way he'd been with her had made her think they'd both been falling, pushing the boundaries at the same time.

Mia refused to open her eyes. She didn't even bother flicking the bedside lamp off or going to lock her door. When her cat leapt onto the bed, she felt him snuggle against her legs but she didn't greet him or emerge from where she was hiding. The covers were over her head, the pain inside of her was only getting worse, like a knife slowly being inched deeper into her heart, and she wasn't going to move until morning.

She was never going to let herself be hurt like that again, not by Sam or any other man. She'd learnt her lesson, and the only person she could ever rely on was herself. He might have seen the real her, might have seen her for who she was and what she stood for, but in the end, it hadn't made him any different than any of the jerks she'd been with in the past. They might have wanted her money, but Sam had only wanted her for sex; not one man had ever wanted her just for her and it hurt like a motherfucker.

Fuck!

Sam slammed his fist into the side of his vehicle, wincing in pain as his knuckles ricocheted off metal. But it didn't dampen his fury, didn't dent the pain and anger erupting inside of him like a tornado of emotion.

Goddamn her!

He hauled his door open, stepping back and hearing a yelp erupt from behind him. *Shit!* He bent to touch Blue, pissed that the dog was cowering like he was about to hit him, too. He'd never purposely hurt an animal in his life, and angry or not, he wasn't about to start now.

"Sorry," he muttered, apologizing and hating that even his own animal was scared of him. He'd almost forgotten Blue was with him, would have probably roared off down the drive without him if he hadn't stepped on him by mistake. Sam pointed for him to get in, seeing the way his dog got in the back and curled into a tight ball, clearly not wanting to ride shotgun with his master in this kind of mood.

Even my goddamn dog thinks I'm an asshole.

Sam shut the door and drove, forcing himself to go slow even though he wanted to rev the hell out of the engine. It was late, there were no lights on in the main house as he glanced in the rearview mirror, and he wasn't about to cause a scene.

He gripped the steering wheel tightly, anger rippling through him, twisting and torturing him as he fought the urge to lash out again. In front of Mia he'd put on a façade as strong as steel; in reality, he wanted to bellow from the pain he'd inflicted on her, from the agony he'd seen reflected in her gaze.

He knew because he'd felt it before. He'd been the one facing a cruel, heartless partner; he'd been the one in love and with his heart ripped to shreds. And now he'd done it to Mia, and worst of all he'd made it sound like he'd never, ever cared about her in the first place, which was a blatant lie.

"Uggggh!" he bellowed, sounding like a monster even to his own ears. He pushed down on the accelerator, driving too fast now but not giving a damn.

If he didn't care about Mia, if he truly didn't feel strongly about her, then why the hell did it feel like someone had a hand clutching his heart, cruelly twisting it, hurting him, inflicting pain on him? But he didn't, he couldn't. He'd kept part of himself back, he'd refused to get too close to her, it had just been about the sex. Hadn't it? *Who the hell was he kidding?*

He should have pulled over, knew it was the logical thing to do instead of driving like a maniac, but he kept on driving through the night to get home. He needed to be in his own place. He needed to hide away from the world and figure his shit out.

Kelly's face flashed before him, her innocent shrug hitting him like a fist to the gut as he saw the scene that haunted him playing through his mind again. When he'd found his ex in bed with another guy, in his home, in his own goddamn bed, she'd shrugged and smiled, not even concerned about being caught out. He'd noticed her engagement ring first, glinting on her finger as she demurely reached for the sheet to cover herself, her smile fake. He'd been fooled be her, had loved her and treated her with the utmost respect, and she'd been sleeping around on him the entire time.

"Come on, Sam. What did you expect, leaving me here all day alone? I thought you were traveling for a few more days."

He'd seen red then, had yelled and hurled himself at the

naked guy grabbing for his jeans, and slammed his fist into him, connecting with his jaw. The adrenalin had hit then, the pain ripping through him as he'd fought the poor bastard who'd been unlucky enough to be caught. And then he'd turned on Kelly, snarling at her, scaring her. She'd called the police when Sam had rammed his fist through the wall, claimed he'd threatened her, tried to pretend like she was the innocent victim.

He'd yelled at her, *sure*. He'd demanded to know what the bloody hell she thought she was doing, *definitely*. He'd stood there with his fists balled and his body on the verge of exploding, listening to her bullshit words once her lover had disappeared, too, but he'd never, ever laid a hand on her.

The one thing he had done was storm over to her and snake his fingers around her wrist, holding her in place as he'd tugged the diamond from her finger as she screamed. There was no goddamn way he was going to let her keep the ring he'd bought for her, promising to love her and care for her, pinning his heart to his sleeve.

The one woman he'd ever fallen for, the one woman he'd promised to love, had crushed him.

He saw Mia's face in his mind, wanted to shut his eyes to push her away, but he kept them trained on the road ahead, forced them to stay open. Mia hadn't deserved to get hurt, he never should have gone near her in the first place, but he'd made it so clear, hadn't he?

Mia was everything Kelly wasn't. She was open and honest, kind and loving. She was the woman he should have trusted. But he couldn't. No matter how much he tried to tell himself otherwise, he couldn't ever open himself up to pain like that again.

I love you.

Her words cut deep. He should have held her, should

have kissed her and let her down softly. He should have explained to her what had happened in his past, but there was only one person he'd ever confessed the whole truth to, and that was Nate.

Instead of dragging it out through court, Nate had told him to settle. His career had been taking off in a big way, and Kelly had claimed assault, had gone for half of everything he owned, and claimed emotional distress. Sam had sat across from her, first clenched beneath the table so damn tight he'd almost pulled a muscle, and under duress eventually agreed on paying her out just to move on and keep her quiet.

It had broken him and torn apart something inside of him at the same time. And it had ripped away his ability to love, to trust anyone other than himself and his family, and with it any chance of ever being the man he'd been before he'd caught Kelly cheating on him.

Sam eventually pulled into his driveway, cut the engine and sat in the dark outside his house. Silence engulfed him. The moon was covered with cloud, the darkness absolute, and it wasn't until Blue nudged his arm, his cold, wet nose forcing him to surrender from his own silence that he got out of the vehicle.

"Hey," he muttered, hand kneading through his dog's fur. "You're all I've got, buddy. It's just you and me now."

He needed to keep a lid on his anger. He needed to do something to contain it rather than explode, couldn't afford to go back to the place full of hurt and darkness that he'd lived in when he'd returned from active duty. After Kelly, he'd been swept up into the bitterness and hurt that spiraled from a nasty separation, but he'd found his own way back, hadn't become as far gone as when he'd come home from serving. He hadn't been the same man, he'd emerged with wounds so deep that he knew they'd be buried within him forever, but he'd done it and he'd just vowed never to let it happen to him again.

"Come on," he said to Blue, touching his leg when he stepped out of the car for the dog to follow him. "Let's go."

Sam used the torch on his phone to light the way to his stable block, knowing that his ranch hand would have stabled his best horses for the evening hours earlier. He'd let Mia think he needed to get home each night to feed his own horses, but it had been a façade. He'd always had a ranch hand and he'd never had to get home, he'd just been too terrified of getting too close, of either of them getting hurt.

He'd left because staying over was for boyfriends. For fiancées. For husbands.

He'd never held her all night in his arms—even though getting up from her bed, Mia's warm, naked body was so hard—because he hadn't wanted to get close to her or start thinking about how nice it would be to have her in his bed every night.

He'd left because he hadn't wanted to hurt her, and in the end he'd done exactly what he'd always feared.

Sam entered, let himself quietly into the big stable block, taking a few steps before leaning against a timber stall door and slowly, silently shuddering his back down until his butt hit the cold concrete.

He'd fucked everything up. He'd tried so damn hard, and it was all his fault.

A sob erupted from him, a noise Sam had never let out before, the emotions of everything he'd been through catching in his throat for the first time in his adult life. He'd been angrier than a bull seeing red, full of so much fury that he'd scared himself, but he'd never, ever let himself cry.

Tears slipped down his cheeks as he tipped his head back and closed his eyes tight.

He was damaged goods. He wasn't good enough for Mia, didn't have enough of himself to give her, and she deserved better. He was fifty shades of fucked-up, and there was no way he was going to hurt Mia any more than he already had.

Blue whined and leaned against him, and he buried his face into his fur, holding him as he cried, alone except for his dog on the cold, damp floor of his barn.

Chapter 19

Three weeks later . . .

MIA thrummed her fingers across her steering wheel. She could do this. She could *so* do this. She forced herself to open the door, took a big breath and stepped out of the car. She took a look around and smiled, imagining Sam here. The ranch was beautiful; nothing over the top, but the home was beautiful and everything was in good condition. Not to mention he had some pretty amazing-looking horses grazing in the fields closest to the house.

She drank in the timber fences and big oak trees, the recently mown grass that stretched along the length of the driveway. It was strange to think she'd spent so much time with Sam, but she'd never seen where he lived and he'd never talked all that much about it. She wondered if he had any other stock, or whether it was just horses, and she strained to see a field in the distance and wondered where his boundary fence was and how much land he had.

Mia forced herself to look back at the house. What she had to do now was stop gawking at his ranch and get up to the front door, except that her boots felt like they were filled with lead and her hands were so sweaty she had to keep rubbing them down her jeans.

She had this. Mia walked up the steps to the two-story, cream, timber house and bravely raised her hand to knock. What she'd had with Sam, it wasn't just physical. He could pretend all he liked, but she knew that he felt the same. If he didn't then he was a damn fine actor, but she wasn't letting him get away with walking out on her without a proper explanation. He was either an unfeeling bastard, or he couldn't deal with his feelings, and she was hoping it was the latter. It had been almost three quarters of a month now. Three weeks of mourning him and trying to hate him, of moaning to Kat and trying to keep her heartache from her family. Of working Tex without him and trying to emulate everything she'd learned from him. Of expecting him to call and hearing nothing, and deciding that her fate rested in her own hands. It was time she gave him a second chance to see if he regretted the way things had ended between them. She knew how stubborn a person could be, because she was as stubborn as a mule sometimes, so this was Mia stepping up and putting her heart on her sleeve—again.

Mia heard footsteps and stood back. Her heart was pounding as she waited, hoping she didn't crumble when she saw him. She wanted to stand there and tell him how she felt and demand to know if he felt the same.

The door swung open and Mia held her breath, tingles running up and down her body, her mouth opening to . . .

Ohmygod.

"Hi. Can I help you?"

"I, I . . ." Mia stared at the beautiful woman who'd opened the door. She had long dark hair and even darker eyes, and she had the cutest baby on her hip who was smiling straight back at her. A noise from inside signaled that there was another child, too.

"I think I have the wrong place," Mia finally managed, standing back and looking around. She must have remembered it wrong, or maybe she'd turned down the wrong drive. "I was looking for Sam."

"You've got the right place. Can I let him know who came by while he was out? Or do you want an iced tea? I've just made a jug." The woman laughed when her daughter waved her pudgy little hand. "I could do with some adult company here!"

Mia wished she could hate her, but she didn't. This woman, this beautiful, kind woman who was standing there inviting her in without any idea of who she was to Sam, wasn't the one to hate. A big diamond glinted on her ring finger, a wedding band resting below it. Mia's stomach turned. How could she have been such a fool to let Sam play her the way he had?

"Thanks, but I'll keep going."

Mia turned, hands shaking, legs trembling so badly she wondered how she'd even make it to the car. But the woman took a few steps, moved closer, her smile haunting Mia.

"You sure you don't want me to tell Sam you stopped by?"

Mia turned back in time for the baby girl to hold her chubby little hand up. She waved back to her, acting on autopilot, trying not to lose it.

"We're missing him so bad while he's away, aren't we pumpkin?"

The words were like a fist into Mia's gut, winding her, felling her, making her want to scream.

"It's fine. I'll catch him another time."

Blue came bounding around the corner then, and Mia

dropped to pat him, unable to resist the dog. It wasn't his fault his owner was a lying dirt bag.

"Hey," she cooed, bending low, her face touching his fur. Tears fell and wet his coat, but she only gave herself a moment before pushing up and walking to her car. She kept her head held high, ignored Blue when he ran back to her, sending him away with a point of her finger as she'd seen Sam do.

When she was in the car she numbly clipped her seatbelt and started the engine, forcing herself to drive slowly as she glanced in the rearview mirror and saw the woman standing, still watching.

Sam had told her he wanted a no-strings-attached relationship. He'd always refused to stay over. He'd made it clear that he wasn't interested in anything serious or committed. He'd been horrified when she'd told him she loved him and questioned how he didn't feel the same.

He'd just forgotten to tell her that he had a wife and child at home waiting for him. That he couldn't love her because he was already too busy loving someone else.

Tears started to fall steadily down her cheeks, blurring her vision. How could this have happened to her? How could the man she trusted so much, a man she believed was so much better than that, have used her in that way? Even when he'd hurt her, when he'd refused to acknowledge his feelings for her, refused to acknowledge the way she felt for him, she'd never hated him.

But this was so much worse than what she'd thought. She'd slept with another woman's husband, and she was going to have to live with that forever. She would never, ever hurt another woman like that intentionally, and she sure as hell wouldn't have accepted being the other woman for Sam if she'd known. Growing up, she'd seen the pain her mother had been through, watched her silent misery as her father had cheated on multiple occasions right up until she'd passed away. People talked, and even kids whispered, especially when she'd been a teenager and Mia had always known that for all her father's good traits, fidelity had not been one of them. It had been awful knowing her father had a mistress when her mom was so sick.

And now she could cause someone else's heartbreak. If Sam's wife found out? She'd be the one biting back tears, trying to decide if she was strong enough to leave a man she loved, just as Mia's mother had. That beautiful, sweet woman back there had been so kind, not having any idea why Mia had turned up on her doorstep, what she'd done with her *husband*.

Mia gasped, the noise catching in her throat and bringing another big sob. *It wasn't fair.* She pulled over, stopping her car on the side of the road and slamming it into park. She let the tears fall, sobbed silently, slumped against her steering wheel as she cursed Sam with every bone in her body. Except for her heart. Her heart was too busy despairing, the pain inside of her so deep. How could she have let this happen? Had she been so intent on having fun, on playing along with a no-strings affair, that she'd somehow missed the warning signs?

She cried a few minutes longer, let herself wallow and hate and be miserable, and then she reached to open her glove box and pull out some tissues. She was better than this. She was strong and she wasn't going to let a man break her. Sam was a lying bastard, and she couldn't let herself cry over him or mourn him, because he'd never truly been hers in the first place.

Mia dried her eyes, glanced up to check how puffy and red they were in her mirror, and decided she didn't give a damn. She had a long drive home, then she needed to prepare to hit the road. She had her next out of town competition in two days' time, and she was more determined than ever to win now. Nothing was going to stop her proving herself and making it to the top. Nothing and no one.

He'd already ripped her heart out when he'd walked away from her. The stone-cold look of his gaze, the downturn of his mouth as he backed away like he was edging away from a fire; they should have been clues enough that he wasn't interested in her the same way she was in him. Instead she'd shown up, hat in hand, wanting to see if she was wrong, to give him another chance. Wanting to see if she'd been wrong, if something else had been hurting him, trusting her instincts, instincts that had been so, so wrong. She would never make that mistake again. *Never.*

Sam waved to the crowd as he left the ring, knowing they were all there for him and that they deserved everything he could give them. But he just wasn't feeling it today, and his performance had showed that. He was tired of doing the same thing, he was tired of answering the same questions and smiling at people who wanted more from him than he could give. And he was tired of feeling like a jerk.

When he'd walked out on Mia, he'd thought it was his only option. He'd panicked. She'd said the one word that terrified him, that he refused to accept or say in return, and she'd gone back on everything they'd agreed on. But what she'd said as he'd walked out had haunted him, every day and every damn night when he was lying awake desperately wanting to fall asleep. Her words still curled around him when he was least expecting it, washing over him, making him feel like the biggest asshole on the planet, even three weeks later.

"Are you telling me you don't have any feelings for me?"

He forced a smile as some young fans came racing up to him, ducking beneath the ropes that kept him from the public as he left the venue. Sam stopped and bent to sign their books, ruffling heads and winking. He wasn't hanging around for long after this one, but he wasn't so much of a jerk that he wouldn't stop to sign a book for some kids.

He grimaced as he returned to the stables to get his things, words echoing in his head, Mia's face, her big eyes and downturned mouth, telling her just how much he'd hurt her. He was an A-grade jerk where she was concerned, and he fucking hated himself for it.

"I love you."

Sam suppressed the bear's bellow that was buried inside of him and stalked off to his horse truck. He'd brought two of his own horses for this exhibition, and he needed to load them and get back on the road again. He wasn't overnighting, not here and not anywhere.

He owed Mia an apology, a damn big one, but he wasn't going to give it to her. She was better off without him, and the more she hated him, then the easier it would make it for him to stay away. There were so many things unsaid between them, so many things he wished he could explain.

But there were reasons he didn't get close to anyone, multiple reasons. He'd done the right thing, it just didn't feel that way. *Yet.*

Sam stretched, smiling at the sensation of something warm against his face. He turned, slowly opening his eyes, ready to kiss . . . dammit! He pushed Blue away, wiping at his cheek and grimacing.

"How many times do I have to tell you not to lick me when I'm sleeping?" Sam muttered. "And off the bed!"

Blue obliged, disappearing from his room and leaving him to lie on his own. He'd been dreaming about Mia. Of course he'd been dreaming about Mia. Now that he wasn't with her, she was the only thing he couldn't stop thinking about.

"Morning!"

Sam groaned and pushed the covers back, deciding he might as well rise. His sister had been staying over while he was gone, and he was fairly certain there was no chance of sleeping in. The girls would either be awake or ready to wake, and he could do with a coffee before morphing into uncle mode for the day.

"Morning," he called back through the open door, guessing Faith was in the kitchen. He pulled on jeans and a t-shirt and ran a hand through his hair.

"How was it?" she asked.

He shrugged, walking barefoot over to the coffee machine to see if it had any water in it. One of the first expensive purchases he'd made for the house was a coffee machine; he'd always joked that he needed an intravenous line with coffee in it, and he'd worked the thing to death since the day it arrived.

"Fine. How about you? What's new?"

Sam held up a coffee cup and Faith nodded, so he made her one before doing his own. He passed hers over and nudged the sugar bowl in her direction.

"I'm looking forward to Nate coming home," she said. "It's tough looking after the girls without him, and he's never been away from us this long."

Sam sat down at the counter, toes curled against the cool metal of the barstools. "He's still arriving home this afternoon?"

"Sure is. He's coming to get us on his way through." She

laughed and leaned across the counter, resting on her elbows, cup between her palms. "It was nice staying here though. I think I'd make a good pet-sitter."

Sam chuckled. "Yeah, I'll keep you on." Faith was usually great at coming by while he was away for longer periods, making sure the ranch hands were doing their jobs, but this time she'd asked him if she could stay and keep an eye on the mare who was due to foal. He'd promised Faith the foal for herself, since it was from one of his favorite mares, and he'd never seen his sister so excited about a horse before.

Faith usually spent her time at his place bugging him about his lack of an art collection, always pushing her personal passion on him, but today she was giving him a look he couldn't decipher. He wasn't even aware any of those existed, given how good he'd become at reading her over the years.

"What's up?" he asked. "Shoot."

"A woman came by yesterday," she said, sipping her coffee and clearly pretending it wasn't a big deal. "She didn't want to leave a message but—"

Sam sat up straighter. "What?" he asked. "Who was it? What did she look like?"

Faith shrugged. "I thought it might have been Mia," she said. "Long blonde hair, blue eyes that looked wide as saucers when she saw me, and she drove a new-looking Mercedes. The 4×4 kind."

Sam slumped down again, staring into his coffee. What had Mia been doing here? It could have been someone else but the description was bang on and he doubted another woman would have come looking for him.

"So was it her?"

He nodded. "She fits the bill." He knew without a doubt

that it was Mia, but he wasn't going into details with his sister. Faith had already done her best to get information out of him, but he wasn't going there, not even with her.

"What happened with Mia? I mean, she looked kind of sad. I thought you liked her?" Faith sighed. "Come on, Sam, you can't keep blocking me when I ask you about her. Nate thought you were really into her."

"I was." He wasn't going to bother lying, not to Faith. Besides, if he answered her it stopped her talking.

"So why the sad face? What happened between you two?"

He sighed, swallowing the rest of his coffee before answering. "How about none of your business?"

She glared at him, hand on hip as she stood up. "Give me a break," Faith snapped. "You're all kinds of my business. I don't take that kind of bullshit from Nate and I'm not taking it from you."

Sam glared straight back at her, but he knew she was right. She was his sister, and if anyone deserved to know why he'd been walking around like some kind of cartoon character with a permanent grey cloud hanging over him, it was her. "We were casual, it was nothing serious. And before you say anything, we both agreed on those terms before anything happened, so don't go thinking I'm a jerk."

She gave him a look. A fierce one at that. "Why?"

"For Pete's sake, Faith. I don't want to talk about it. How many ways can I say that to you? Give me a goddamn break!"

She threw her hands up in the air. "How about *you* give it a break. You're the one holding on to the past and letting what happened choke you from ever being happy. And don't you *ever* speak to me like that." She was furious, her eyes flashing. "And before you say it, I was there for you,

I've seen you at your worst, so don't go thinking you have to be some big strong, macho guy all the time for me to respect you. You should know better than that."

He stayed calm, clenched his jaw and stared at his sister before answering. "I'm happy," he said through gritted teeth, trying not to flare up. "I'm not on some mission to be miserable."

"If you're comparing yourself to the Grinch, then sure, you're happy," she said, her tone laced with sarcasm. "But seriously, you need to get over the past and give yourself a chance to be happy. *Truly happy,* Sam."

Sam bit his tongue. He wasn't going to fight with his sister, not over this, especially when he'd never even told her all the details about his ex. Maybe Nate had told her, but he doubted his friend would share his secrets, even with his wife. "It just wasn't meant to be. Now can we move on and talk about something else, or are we going to be stuck on this all day?"

She gave him a long, serious look, before shrugging and turning back around to whatever she'd been doing before he'd come into the kitchen. "Fine. But if I see you looking like a lovesick puppy next week still? I'll be like a dog with a bone."

Sam gave her a wink and walked his cup back to the coffee machine. He was desperately in need of more before he went out to feed the horses.

"Uh-uh," she said, whisking the cup away. "Too much caffeine is bad for you. You'll never get a decent sleep if you keep drinking that much."

He let her go, reaching for another cup from the overhead cupboard. "First of all, it's morning so I'm not worried about bedtime right now, and second, I drink it *because* I don't sleep. I'd be a dead man walking otherwise." He grimaced. "And you're not my mother, so lay off."

One of his nieces cried out then and Sam took his chance to make himself another quick coffee and head outside while Faith was distracted. He loved spending time with his sister, but she needed to back off. He wasn't a child, he wasn't going to fall for anyone, and he sure as hell wasn't going to change his mind about Mia. He couldn't. She had so much to give, and he had nothing. Not anymore.

And maybe not ever.

Blue walked at his heel, and he pulled on his boots and walked out into the fresh morning air. He was greeted by a chorus of neighs, his equine friends all noticing him the moment he moved near them.

For a brief moment, he wondered what Mia was doing. Whether she was feeding out in her stable block, saddling up already for her first ride of the day, or stretching out in bed after a sleep in. That was the mental picture he'd never been able to erase, her lying in bed, soft cotton sheets all rumpled around her, hair mussed up and tousled around her face, and that beautiful body that always seemed to hum for him.

"Come on, Blue," he murmured.

Blue whined, like he knew what he was thinking about.

"You saw her the other day, didn't you? Bet you miss her like crazy too." Sam dropped a hand to his dog's head for a second then strode on down to the hay shed. He was glad he hadn't seen her, because keeping his distance was one thing, but looking her in the eye and lying again was a whole other skill set entirely, one he didn't think he had. Or ever would.

In a few days he would be off on tour again. Part of him

wanted to stay at home and do nothing, wallow, spend time with his own horses. But the other part of him wanted to get away, to stop overthinking everything and questioning his decisions. Besides, the money was good. Once he did this, he wouldn't have to work again for the rest of the year. Perhaps even the next year.

Blue whined and he looked down at his dog, sitting faithfully beside him, head cocked, eyes so intense like he was trying to tell him something.

"You think I'm a dumb idiot, don't you?" he asked.

Blue made a whining noise again and Sam nodded. "Yeah, I know. And I'm a jerk for leaving you again. But Faith will take good care of you."

His sister would be gone soon, back home with Nate, and he needed to touch base with the house sitter he used when he was gone for longer periods. She was good with the horses and she'd be the one in charge of monitoring the foal alarm fitted to his mares. This time of year was always the hardest to leave the ranch, even though he had good people working for him.

His thoughts turned to Mia again even though he was trying so hard to keep her out of his head. Maybe he should have been to see her, to explain himself, but would it have made her hurt any less? Would it have made what happened between them any easier? He doubted it. And his gut told him to leave her the hell alone. She didn't need to deal with him and the shit storm of pain that came with him.

Chapter 20

MIA pulled her mare up, checked her and stopped her from racing forward.

"Whoa girl, nice and steady," she murmured, holding the reins tight then releasing as Indi lifted up, hooves tucked up neatly as she soared through the air. They landed with a soft thud, clearing the jump easily. They were half way through the course now and they were making great time.

Mia swallowed hard as they turned sharply and raced toward the next fence. Her stomach was churning, nausea making it hard to concentrate, but she refused to give in. She was here to win, and nothing was going to stop her. *Nothing.*

Indi was going too fast and she slowed her for the last two strides before letting her do her thing without interfering. They cleared the next one easily, and then the next, until there were only three to go. Mia gagged, bile rising in her throat.

"Dammit," she swore, riding hard, focusing on her horse, only wanting to think about the stretch and pull of horse muscle beneath her, the power of Indi as she pushed off from the grass. Mia cringed, hearing a knock, but when she glanced back she saw the rail had only rattled and hadn't fallen.

"Two more to go," she whispered. "We can do this!"

She pushed her on, cantering fast, soaring over one and then the other. But instead of fist pumping the air and letting her mare enjoy the applause and show off, snorting with her tail in the air, Mia rode straight for the exit. She slowed to a trot and her stomach settled a little, but she didn't feel great. Where was Tanner? She knew he'd been here, he'd come to see her earlier and help her get her team ready, but . . . there he was. Talking up a pretty brunette, leaning in, all charming as usual.

"Tanner!" she called out, riding toward him, dismounting when she reached the crowd and pushing through. "Tanner!"

He looked up, smiling until he saw the look on her face and strode toward her. "What is it?" he asked, concern etched on his face.

"Take her," Mia managed, thrusting the reins at him and undoing her helmet strap. She tucked her whip under her arm and ran, sprinting for her horse truck. She could see it, the big black horse design on the side. She reached it and ran around the back, bending over just in time, out of sight from prying eyes as she retched and retched, her stomach heaving.

Mia finally stood up, leaning against the truck, hand on her stomach. What had she eaten? What was going on?

"Mia?"

She heard Tanner's deep voice and she wiped at her mouth, stomach still tender. "Hey, I'm just around here."

"What happened?" he asked. "Everything okay?"

"It's just my stomach. I don't know what's going on." She leaned back against the truck again as Tanner stood with her horse. She was feeling light-headed now, like she could faint. "Must have been dinner last night. I wonder if anyone else is sick?"

He frowned. "You sure that's all it is? You haven't seemed yourself lately."

"That why you decided to come watch me today? You felt sorry for me?"

Tanner gave her a steely stare. "I'm your brother. I might be a dick a lot of the time, but I know when my little sister needs some company. Besides, you looked like shit yesterday. Maybe you're coming down with something?"

She rolled her eyes then laughed at herself. She was behaving like a child and Tanner was only trying to be nice. "Thanks for the compliment. Nothing better than someone noticing the dark rings under your eyes."

"Seriously, is everything okay, or is there something going on?"

"Asks the guy who's probably broken more hearts than I can count." She wished she'd kept the thought to herself, because when her brother leveled his gaze on her, she knew he was going into overprotective mode. She'd kept her family in the dark for weeks but now that she'd been to Sam's house, she wasn't interested in protecting him or lying to her family about what had happened.

"Some asshole hurt you?" he glowered. "Who? That horse guy?"

She shrugged. "Not his fault entirely. He told me he didn't want anything serious, that it was no strings, and I stupidly thought it had turned into something more."

Tanner looked pissed. His jaw was clenched tight and there was a weird vein standing out from his forehead. "He ended it?"

"More like he walked out my door and went back to his wife's bed. But yeah, I guess you could say he ended it."

"Motherfucker," Tanner swore, looking like a kettle about to boil over. "I see him, I'll kill him."

She took a tentative step forward, waiting to see how dizzy she felt, but the wave of nausea seemed to have passed. She took the reins, happy to deal with her own horse. They had another round coming up after the clear round, and later in the day she'd be competing on one of her young horses. She lay one hand to her brother's broad chest, smiling up at him.

"No, you won't," she said. "Look, I thought what we had was something more, I was the stupid one. It's not something you haven't done to countless women before, so don't go pretending like he's the only villain in the world, okay?"

"Yeah, well, we're talking about you," he grunted. "And for the record, I've never been married and if I did ever make a commitment like that? I'd never cheat."

Tanner pushed her away and kept hold of the reins and she let him, feeling a little queasy again. If she was going to keep to her schedule for the day, she was going to have to admit that she needed her brother's help.

"Thanks for today," she said.

He shrugged. "Just get better so we can go out for beer and pizza tonight. If I'm your groom for the day, you'll damn well owe me."

Mia laughed and ducked back into the truck to get a bottle of water. She walked into the kitchen area and opened the fridge. And then she froze. It had been just over three weeks since she'd last seen Sam, and they'd been together for a few weeks. When had she last had her period? Mia set down the water she was holding, reaching for the table and slowly sitting down.

She had to have it wrong. They'd been careful, there hadn't been . . . *ohmygod*. She'd been sick. There had been that one night when she'd been sick. Had it made her pill ineffective? Had it . . . *holy shit*. Shit. Shit. *Shit*. She'd missed it that night, and the next when she'd still been feeling sick. When she'd still been running to the toilet and not holding any food down.

Mia instinctively looked down at her stomach. Could she be pregnant?

"You coming?" Tanner called out.

She took a deep, shuddering breath and picked up her water bottle again. On second thought she grabbed one for her brother too, and a protein bar they could share. Perhaps she wouldn't be having beer with her pizza tonight.

"You alright?" Tanner asked, no doubt noticing the fact all color had drained from her cheeks.

"Yep, great," she lied, passing him the water, feeling her hands shaking, butterflies coming to life in her stomach.

If she was pregnant, she'd deal with it. She loved kids and she had plenty of money. She was in a better position financially than so many single women who might find themselves in the same position. She gulped, palms sweaty. If she was pregnant, everything would be okay. But it sure as hell wasn't going to stop her from riding or jumping or doing what she loved. And as far as she was concerned, Sam would never find out. He didn't need to.

"You sure you're up for the next round?" he asked, eyebrows pulled together.

She smiled wryly at him, going to touch her stomach again but resisting.

"Fords don't quit," she said. "Isn't that why there's never been a bull you haven't said yes to riding?" There was no way she was about to confess her worries to her brother though, which meant putting any pregnancy fears aside until she was on her own.

Tanner grinned. "Damn right. Now get your ass up in the saddle then and don't go turning green again."

She was glad Tanner was with her. He could be a jack-ass sometimes, but most of the time he was the perfect mix of over-protective big brother and whip cracker, never letting her get away with anything.

Baby on board or not, she was going to win today, and no one and nothing was going to stop her.

Mia's hand was shaking when she reached for the stick. She'd peed on it and carefully put the little cover back over the end of it, and for the past two minutes she'd been fidgeting and pacing around the bathroom. She even had her door locked, despite the fact that there was no chance of anyone walking in on her.

Pregnant. The word may as well have jumped out and smacked her in the face, it hit her with so much force.

Mia stared at it, unbelieving, and quickly dropped it into the garbage bin. She took a deep breath and ripped the other test from the packet. She forced herself to go again, doing the same thing with this stick, only this time when she put the little cover back on it she fled the scene.

Her kitchen was bathed in sunshine and she quickly poured herself a glass of water, hand shaking as she lifted it to her lips and took a slow, steady sip.

"Hey, gorgeous!"

The glass slipped from Mia's hand, shattering on the bench, water cascading to the floor.

"Tanner!"

She'd just about jumped out of her skin, his voice taking her by surprise. She'd been in a complete, silent, world of her own.

"What's got you all jumpy?"

Mia didn't answer, just quietly bent to collect the larger shards of glass. One cut her palm, but she didn't care. Tanner appeared with a plastic bag and bent beside her, nudging her, laughing, until she raised her face to him and he saw her tears. "Mia, what's wrong?"

She just shook her head, wishing he hadn't come over, wishing she wasn't faced with telling her brother what was going on.

"Mia?" he set the bag down and took the glass from her hands, eyes full of concern. Tanner wasn't usually the sensitive one in the family, hell, he was a brute most of the time, but right now, she could see he was feeling her pain and it cut her up even more inside.

She went to open her mouth, went to say something, but nothing came out and all she could think about was the test that she'd left in the bathroom. She walked past the glass and padded back, retracing her steps. It had been minutes, and if it was positive again . . .

She was pregnant. Mia was smart enough to know that two tests weren't going to be wrong.

She heard a noise, turned and walked out, her fingers clenched tightly around the plastic stick.

"Mia, what's going on with you?" Tanner asked, standing in her hallway.

Mia held up the test, moving toward him, waiting for

his eyes to drop from hers to the result. The moment he read it and clicked, his eyes returned to hers.

"*Mia*," he said, shaking his head. "Oh hell," he muttered, stepping forward and opening his arms.

She ran into them, crying softly against her brother's chest, holding him tight. She wanted to be happy. She didn't want the tiny baby growing inside of her to feel her pain and think he or she wasn't wanted. And the last thing she wanted was for Tanner to feel sorry for her. But damn, it felt good to share it and let him hold her instead of shouldering it alone.

When she finally pulled back, Tanner couldn't have been further from pitying her, she could tell from the look he gave her.

"I'd say let's have a beer, but maybe we should try something else," he said with a chuckle.

Tanner put his arm around her shoulders and they walked back out to the kitchen. He'd cleaned up the glass and when he made a move to the fridge, she gratefully sank down into a chair at the table.

"I don't want to be insensitive here, but have you thought about what you want to do?" he asked.

She nodded. "Yeah," Mia touched her stomach, already feeling protective. "I can't do anything other than love what's been given to me."

Tanner smiled. "I figured as much. Is it—"

"Sam's," she said for him. "Yup, the one and only."

They stood, staring at one another, Tanner looking like he didn't want to open his mouth and say the wrong thing, and her trying to figure the whole thing out in her head.

"You want to keep this to yourself for a while?" Tanner asked.

Mia let go the breath she was holding. "Yeah. I think so."

Tanner nodded. "I know I haven't had the best track record keeping your secrets, but this," he said, his smile kind, "*this* is a secret you can trust me with. This is yours to share. I'm not going to be picking up the phone to Ange or Cody, you have my word."

Mia stepped into her brother and hugged him, laughing when he wrapped his arms around her and bear hugged her, swinging her around.

"You're going to be one hell of an uncle," she said with a giggle.

"Don't I know it!"

Any other time she'd have slapped him for being so damn arrogant, but today it was kind of comforting.

"Want me to make you an iced tea?" he asked.

Mia went to laugh then bit the inside of her lip, deciding not to make fun of him. Tanner had never, *ever* offered to make her anything in her life, let alone tea. She didn't even know he was capable of making iced tea. "That'd be nice, thanks."

She went and curled up on the sofa, tucking her legs up as she stared out the window. It was raining, the soft pitter-patter on the roof making her smile. It was the perfect type of day to be holed up inside, and it wasn't often she lazed a day away instead of keeping busy outside.

Since Sam had walked out, she'd tried to keep herself busy, working Tex and slowly gaining his trust. But it was progress, and her father hadn't said anything about putting him down. He'd mumbled about the exorbitant amount of money the stallion now owed them, but he hadn't said anything else and she was certain he was proud of how she was dealing with the previously untameable horse, even if she couldn't take credit for the transformation.

Sam could. It was Sam who deserved all the credit for

Tex, and as much as she hated him, despised everything he'd done to her, she had two things to be grateful for now. Saving a stallion destined for death, and the baby she suddenly couldn't stop thinking about.

A shudder tickled down her spine, made her cringe. A baby who was never going to know her father. A baby who was one day going to ask her why all the other children had daddies and he or she didn't.

She'd be lying if she didn't wish that it had happened differently, that the Sam she'd known and fallen for had felt the same, that no one else had been involved, that he'd been with her when she realized that something wasn't right, that there was a life growing inside of her.

"Everything's gonna be fine, sis," Tanner said, passing her the tea. She didn't tell him that he'd put it in the wrong glass, just smiled back at him, not so sure but hoping he was right.

"I know. Everything happens for a reason, I need to keep telling myself that."

"Just because this asshole—"

"Stop," she said, shaking her head. "Don't, Tan. I want to hate him so bad, but . . ." she sighed. "I'd rather just try to forget he ever existed." Mia knew how silly that sounded, given the huge reminder she was going to have in her life, but she didn't want to become bitter and twisted.

"Fine," he said, grunting. "But don't you expect me to throw my arms around him and sing Kumbaya."

Mia laughed. "Hey, I said I didn't want to hate him, I didn't say you couldn't."

Chapter 21

"LET me get this straight," Nate said, brows furrowed as he gave Sam a hard stare. "You walked out on her and yet you're the one all fucked up over it? What the hell did she do to you?"

Sam glowered. He didn't want to be having this conversation. Faith had been at him, unrelenting, and now she'd officially released her attack dog on him. Nate was going to be like a dog with a goddamn bone.

"I've told Faith and now I'll tell you, I don't want to talk about it. What's with you two tag-teaming me to try to get me to open up?"

Nate had the nerve to laugh. "No one likes admitting they're a dickhead, but sometimes it has to be done. That's why I'm here."

Sam got up and walked away, not about to listen to Nate carrying on like he could walk the moral high ground.

"Hey, wait up!"

Sam didn't. He walked fast, storming away from Nate, knowing he was so close to exploding and losing his temper, and his friend didn't need to be on the other side of that.

"Sam!" He heard Nate breathing heavily, knew that even if he started to run he'd never manage to get away from him.

"Look," Sam said, spinning around. "Do you have a horse you need me to look at, or was it all a ruse to get me here?"

He could tell from the way Nate hesitated that he was right, and of all the things Nate had done to him over the years, lying wasn't one of them. He knew why his friend was staying silent.

"I goddamn knew it."

"Hey, hold up," Nate said, hand landing on his shoulder, his grip firm. Sam lashed out when Nate's fingers dug into him, slamming his arm away and backing up a step. He didn't want to fight him, but he'd goddamn punch him if he had to.

"Let me go, Nate," Sam growled.

"You haven't seen your sister since she stayed over, and the girls are missing you," Nate said, holding up his hands, showing that he didn't want to fight. Sam felt some of his tension drain away, the moment his sister and nieces were mentioned. "We just wanted to see you."

"They're not old enough to miss me and you know it," Sam shot back.

Nate shrugged. "So what. Hell, *I* miss you, and if I have to pretend like there's an out of control mustang on the property just to get you here, then I'll do it."

Sam stared back at Nate, knew that he was just trying to help him. He was starting to get good at pushing away people that cared about him.

"I don't want to talk about her, Nate. I can't," Sam said, forcing the words out. "So stop asking me, alright?"

Nate indicated with his head and started to walk, and Sam followed, falling into step beside him.

"Something I never told you, hell, I can't even believe I am now, but," Nate said, his voice low and gravelly as he paused, "when I was falling for Faith, the hardest part was knowing I couldn't talk to you about it, that I had to deal with it on my own."

Sam grunted. "Yeah, I just about ripped your head off for looking at her, huh?" He'd never meant to be so protective of his sister, but he'd also never believed Nate could change so much, had been so certain that he'd hurt her and leave her crushed.

"My brothers gave me so much shit about her, but you wouldn't have, not if it had been any other girl I'd fallen for," Nate said. "You would have listened to me and made me see reason."

"You're telling me I need to talk to you?" Sam asked. "Because you haven't exactly convinced me with your sob story."

"Look, I was there, Sam. I was there for you when you came back from Iraq, I lived under the same roof as you and listened to the nights you woke up howling in your sleep from whatever the hell you were still dealing with," Nate said, stopping, hands shoved into his pockets as he leveled his gaze on him. Sam stood tall, stared straight back at his friend. "And I was there for you when Kelly ripped your damn heart out and you know it."

Sam felt his jaw tighten, the familiar tick plaguing him when he clenched his teeth together.

"Look, she did something terrible to you, and I get that. But I did terrible things, too. I slept with married women and I broke hearts, but when I met Faith?"

Sam hated talking about his sister like that with Nate,

but he was right. He had changed. "Yeah, I know, you changed," Sam admitted. "But I can't forget what she did to me," he said, talking about his ex.

"You can and you will," Nate insisted.

Sam stared into the distance, wished to hell he wasn't about to say what he had to say. "Kelly was pregnant." He spoke so low he wondered if Nate even heard him. "We'd talked about kids, and we found out she was pregnant. I was going to tell you, but she wanted to wait until three months or something, and then I found her in bed with him."

He looked at Nate, saw the unflinching look on his face. "Hold up, she was . . ."

Sam swallowed as Nate's words trailed off. "She had an abortion without telling me. I was all excited about becoming a dad, and she'd already terminated it, pretended like she'd lost the baby until my lawyer pressed for information and she laughed at the mediation and told us she'd gotten rid of it. Like it didn't mean a fucking thing to her."

This time when Nate's hand closed over his shoulder, he didn't move.

"I'm sorry," Nate said.

"Yeah, well, so am I." Sam breathed deep, knowing he'd done the right thing in finally sharing what had happened instead of holding it deep inside and letting it fester. "It hurt like hell back then and it still does now. I'll never forget her laughing like it was *nothing*."

"Come on, let's get a beer."

Sam walked alongside Nate and when they finally reached his place, he settled into an outside chair and waited for Nate to bring out their drinks. He knew Faith was out and he was grateful for some time to process before having to pretend like everything was fine.

"You want to know what I think?" Nate asked, passing him a beer and settling across from him, legs stretched out in front of him.

"I get the feeling you're gonna tell me anyway," Sam muttered, taking a long pull of the ice-cold beer.

"If you can't see that Mia is different from Kelly, then you've got rocks for brains. What that girl did was low, but I don't believe Mia is cut from the same cloth, not for a second."

Sam laughed. "I bare my soul to you and you straight out tell me *I've* got rocks for brains?"

Nate shrugged. "You need to let it go, or you're going to end up a miserable old bastard still holding on to the past when everyone else moved on."

"Easy for you to say." But Nate had a point. He knew he needed to let go, but it wasn't something he found easy. "It's like I've tried so hard to be the opposite man my father was, and I've ended up in the same position, with a woman screwing me over and turning me into a bitter bastard."

"You're nothing like your father." Nate's voice was deep, his eyes glowering. "Don't you dare say that."

Sam leaned back, sipping his beer, staring at his boots. "So what do you suggest?"

"I suggest you stay here and get good and drunk tonight, lick your wounds and think about how miserable you are," Nate said with a smile. "Then you pick yourself up and have a good hard think about what you've walked away from. It's better to plead for forgiveness and you know it."

Sam nodded. It wasn't that Nate was wrong, Sam just wasn't convinced he was capable of moving on, of ever licking his wounds enough that they'd heal.

They sat longer, moving on to another beer as the sun

started to disappear. As the bang of a car door signaled that Faith and the girls hard arrived home, Nate stood, but not before pausing and looking down at him, a curious look on his face.

"What did she do to scare you off anyway? Was it that bad?"

Sam took a long, slow sip of beer. "She told me she loved me."

Nate shook his head. "You fucking idiot. Change of plan: stop drinking and get your ass over to her place, now."

Sam ducked to avoid the play-fight fist coming in his direction, watching Nate jog off to meet his girls. Maybe he was right, but it was easy for him to say. But Sam was the one who'd seen the look in Mia's eyes, heard the soft words as they'd passed her lips. And they'd been the scariest goddamn words he'd ever heard in his life.

Sam parked his vehicle near the stable block at the Ford ranch, where he had every day when he'd been working there. Out of habit he glanced down to where Tex was usually kept, but he didn't see the stallion. Depending on how things went with Mia, he might ask if he could head down and see him.

He walked past the stables and down the path toward Mia's place, wondering what the hell he was even doing. Was Nate right? Was he stupid to turn his back on someone like her and not at least try to move past what had happened? Or had he been right that he didn't have enough to give her, that he'd never be able to trust her and commit to her after what he'd been through? Maybe he'd left it too long to plead forgiveness anyway, she might have already moved on.

He'd been staring at his feet as he walked but he looked up then, smiling when he saw the familiar glass house ahead of him, feeling a pull toward it that he'd tried to ignore for too long. The thought of seeing Mia again, of trying to open up to her and explain himself, it terrified him, but he owed it to himself and her to try.

"You've got a goddamn nerve."

Sam stopped walking and found himself face to face with Mia's brother.

"Tanner," he said, nodding and looking past him, wondering where Mia was.

"I'm gonna give you five minutes to get off this property before I shoot you for trespassing," Tanner snarled, his fists bunched at his sides, face like thunder.

"I just came to see Mia," Sam said, backing up and holding his hands up in surrender.

"Yeah? Well, you mess with my sister, you have me to deal with." Tanner edged closer. "I'm counting," he said.

Sam looked at Tanner and nodded. "I get it. I have a sister and I'd protect her with my life. But—"

"What part of me wanting to kill you don't you get?" Tanner demanded, stepping in and moving so fast that Sam didn't have time to fully evade the knuckles skimming past his jaw. The blow sent him staggering but he didn't swing back, wasn't about to have a fistfight with the guy.

"Tanner!" Mia's scream was piercing as she ran from the house, barefoot in jeans and a t-shirt, her eyes wide as she stared at them.

"Mia, please, I just want to talk to you," Sam said, ignoring the fact her brother looked even more enraged now. But she had her hand on his arm, and Sam was certain he wasn't about to pull anything violent again with Mia looking on.

He could have fought back, it wasn't that he was a coward, he'd learned more than his fair share of physical hand-to-hand combat skills when he'd been serving, but he wasn't about to get into a fight with Tanner. The guy was protecting his sister, and that was one of the few things in life Sam understood implicitly.

"Move," Tanner said. "She doesn't want to see you, she's not talking to you, she wants you the hell away from her. We both do."

Mia stepped forward and Sam took his chance, deciding to say what he'd come to say before following orders and leaving.

"Mia, if we can just go inside and talk for a few minutes," Sam said, staring into eyes that had always reminded him of the ocean. He'd almost forgotten how beautiful she was, how effortless she was with her hair in a ponytail and her lack of airs and graces. What the hell had he been thinking running out on her like that? The hurt in her gaze right now told him that she was nothing like Kelly; there was no possible way she could deceive him, no way a woman as sweet and kind as Mia could have ever done to him what his ex-girlfriend had.

"No," she said, moving closer to her brother, like she was scared. "Anything you have to say, you can say in front of Tanner."

Sam nodded. He deserved that. "What I did to you, it was wrong. You scared me and instead of leaving you that night, I should have been honest with you," he said, struggling to explain how he was feeling. "I never meant to deceive you, but, damn it, I fell for you, Mia. I fell for you even though I tried to pretend like I hadn't, and when you said that I . . ."

"That's enough," Mia said, cutting him off before he'd

even finished. She had tears in her eyes and she was clutching her brother's arm. "I will never forgive you, Sam. What you did? I don't even know where to begin. Have you even been honest with your wife or did you just want to come here to make yourself feel better?"

"My wife?" Sam asked, perplexed. "I don't know . . ."

"Don't act stupid, *Romeo*," Tanner interjected. "She knows all about it, there's no point sticking to a story now."

Sam went to answer but Mia spoke before he could. "I came face to face with her, Sam," she hissed. "How could you do that?"

"Mia, I don't know what you've heard, but I don't have a wife."

"Sam, I saw her with my own eyes! I went to your house and . . ."

He relaxed a little, relief pulsing through him. "You met Faith," he said, realizing what had happened. "Faith's my sister," he explained, "she was staying at my place while I was away."

Mia was ghostly white, like all the blood had drained from her face. "So you don't have a child either?" she asked.

"No, Mia, I don't have a wife or a child. All I have is a seriously screwed up past and a lot of shit to work through," he said, wishing they weren't standing outside, and that Tanner wasn't there between them like a guard dog. "I would never intentionally hurt you like that, it was why I insisted on our *arrangement* in the first place, but it didn't work, did it? Because I care for you, and I want to ask you for a second chance. I miss you and it's taken all this time apart and me acting like a stubborn jackass for me to realize how wrong I was."

Mia shook her head. "I need you to leave, Sam. It was

good of you to come by, but things have changed," she said, giving him a sad smile. "I'll be forever thankful that you came into our lives to help Tex, but what we had is over."

She turned and walked away, and Sam tracked her with his eyes all the way into the house. When she disappeared from sight, he turned to Tanner.

"It's time for you to go," he said, but this time he was less aggressive. Sam got it; up until a few moments ago Tanner had thought he'd been a married man deceptively sleeping with his sister. Now he was just a regular kind of jerk.

"Yeah, I'm going," Sam said, backing away then stopping, forcing himself to get out of his comfort zone and admit his damn feelings for once. "I fell for her, Tanner. I want you to know that I never meant to hurt her and if there was anything I could do to change the way I reacted that night, I'd do it."

Tanner nodded. It was barely noticeable but he did and Sam turned and walked away. He'd been a fool. He'd already had to leave his past behind once, when he'd returned from active duty, and he needed to put it behind him again now or he was going to end up miserable for the rest of his life, too fearful of being hurt to ever learn to love and trust again.

Trouble was, he'd left it too late to apologize to Mia. The damage was already done, the hurt was already inflicted. The fact she'd thought Faith was his wife? That was the icing on the cake. But he deserved it. All of it. He knew Mia had been to visit and he'd been too pig-headed to man up and admit his mistake then, to call her the moment he'd known she'd come looking for him. If he had? Then she at least wouldn't have had to spend the last four weeks thinking he was an even bigger jackass than he was.

Mia sat on the edge of the pool, toes dipped in, jeans rolled up to mid-calf so they didn't get wet. She'd known that one day she'd end up crossing paths with Sam, but after a while she hadn't expected him to just turn up on her doorstep ready to apologize.

He wasn't married. The words kept circling her mind, torturing her, making her question everything. She'd spent all this time despising what he'd done, determined not to tell him about the baby, but if he wasn't married, if it wasn't going to cause hurt and pain to anyone else . . . she placed her palm flat to her stomach. She knew the right thing to do, she just wasn't ready to tell her secret to anyone else, not yet.

"I feel really bad for leaving you." Tanner appeared, crouching beside her, blocking the sun from her eyes.

"It's fine," she said, smiling over at him. "You've been my rock, Tan."

He made a grunting noise. "Yeah, well, someone has to look after you."

Tanner kissed the top of her head and rose, looking worried.

"I'll be fine. Go ride bulls and forget all about me, okay?"

He nodded. "Okay. But you call me if you need me."

"I won't," she assured him. It had been nice having him stay a few days, but she was ready to have her house back to herself and she bet he was ready to break free, no matter how much he cared about her. "And anyway, Kat's coming over soon. She's back from her conference and I told her I needed to see her." She wasn't looking forward to telling her because actually telling someone other than Tanner was making it real, but she needed to talk to her. And then once she'd told Kat, she was going to FaceTime her sister. She slowly needed to let her entire family know that the youngest Ford had officially gotten herself knocked up.

"Guess it's just you and me," she whispered to her stomach, pulling her feet up and wriggling her toes to shake off the droplets of water clinging to her skin. Mia walked inside, flicked on the television and sunk down into the sofa. She'd already fed all the horses, and she was exhausted from her rides earlier in the day, so some time flopped in front of the TV was exactly what she needed until Kat arrived. And perhaps some brainless reality shows would stop her second-guessing herself or wondering what else Sam might have said if she'd been brave enough to ask him in.

What if. That was the question circling her mind over and over. What if she'd talked to him? What if she'd told him? What if he'd changed his mind and wanted to be with her, wanted something real instead of the stupid agreement they'd had at the start? What if she'd been wrong not to let him say whatever he'd wanted to say to her in private?

What if. It was a dangerous question and she knew it, but it was one she couldn't have put out of her mind even if she'd wanted to.

A knock echoed out and made her jump. She quickly stood and by the time she reached her door, Kat was already standing in the hall.

"Hey!" Kat said, leaning in for a hug and holding a bottle of wine in her other hand. "Hope you're ready for a drink because after the week from hell that I've had . . ."

Mia burst into tears and couldn't stop. A big sob erupted from deep inside of her and she fought to catch her breath.

"Hey, what's wrong? Did I buy the wrong kind of wine? I can go back for something else?"

Mia laughed through her tears. Trust Kat to make a joke when she was in the middle of a breakdown.

"I'm pregnant," she managed to blurt out, wiping her cheeks and slowly catching her breath.

"Pregnant?" Kat whispered back, her eyes wide as she stared back at her. "By who?"

"Sam, you idiot!" She shook her head. "Your cousin was way too interested in work to even get me to first base, if that's what you're worried about."

Kat slung an arm around her and walked them both into the kitchen. "Come on, let's get you a lemonade and me a big glass of wine. I think I need it."

Mia got out a glass while Kat opened the bottle and she found herself a soda. Then she tucked up on the sofa and watched as Kat settled across from her.

"So Sam's the daddy," Kat said.

Mia nodded. "Yup. Only he doesn't know it yet."

"So let me get this straight, you haven't told him yet because you don't want to ruin his marriage, or because you don't want him to know period?" Kat asked. "Because I'm guessing that termination isn't an option."

Mia shuddered just hearing the word and placed a hand on her stomach. "Just so happens he's not married. It was his sister and her kids." She felt stupid about even confessing how wrong she'd been.

Kat took a big gulp of wine. "So does that change the way you feel about him?"

Mia sighed. "Honestly? I don't know. I mean, deep down I can't shut off my feelings for him, but the way he ended things . . ." She met Kat's warm gaze. "He came by today but Tanner was ready to shoot him and there were some things left unsaid."

"Can I touch your stomach?" Kat asked, setting down her glass and coming over to sit beside Mia.

Mia nodded. "Of course. There's nothing to feel though."

"I know that," Kat said, her palm warm through the thin fabric of Mia's shirt. "Hey, little baby," she whispered, "this is Auntie Kat here."

They both laughed and Mia felt tears prickle her eyes again.

"You don't need a daddy around to be loved, because you've got a whole team of aunties and uncles who'll spoil you rotten. Isn't that right, Momma?"

Mia grinned. *Momma*. She'd expected that title to be a long way off in her future.

"Yeah, that's right," she replied.

Kat tucked up tight to her and gave her a big hug, and Mia shut her eyes. Her baby didn't need a father, but she sure would have done anything for things to be different between her and Sam.

Chapter 22

"PULL over by the mailbox up there," Sam said, pointing further down the road. "I'll just be a minute."

He was in a cab heading for the airport, and the envelope in his jacket pocket was burning a hole in there. It had been a few days since he'd seen Mia, but all it had taken was that one moment of seeing her standing before him, seeing how real her pain was, and knowing he'd been the one to cause it. And seeing her, it had made him see how stupid he'd been. Nate and Faith had both been right; he couldn't keep letting his past control his future.

"Thanks," he muttered, pushing the door open and jogging the few paces. He pulled the envelope out, re-read Mia's name and address for the hundredth time, and then slipped it into the box. There. He'd done it.

Now he just had to wait and see. He had an event in L.A. again, then he was back in his home state for the last part of his Texas mini-tour. And more than a sell-out crowd, all he wanted was Mia there watching him.

* * *

Mia walked in, hot and starving hungry from working her horses, and noticed a handful of envelopes on the counter. Her father's housekeeper usually brought over any mail or deliveries for her, and she'd obviously let herself in while she was out.

She kicked off her boots and pulled her socks off, balling them up and stuffing them inside her boots. She grabbed a banana, peeling it and starting to eat it as she rifled through the mail. One thing caught her eye, a cream envelope with her details scrawled by hand across the front. She laughed. Who sent letters these days?

She set the banana skin down and ran her nail beneath the seal, pulling out a card and seeing it was an invitation.

You are invited to a VIP afternoon with legendary Texas Horse Whisperer Sam Mendes! Learn from the master of horsemanship himself and enjoy the best seats in the house!

Mia gulped. Re-reading the invitation, then scanning lower and seeing when it was scheduled for. *Ten days.* She glanced down at her belly, her tight t-shirt showing a hint of a bump. By then she might actually look pregnant, or perhaps she'd just keep looking like she'd eaten too many cherry pies; she was usually so slender that her bump would make itself obvious.

She went to set the invitation down and noticed there was handwriting on the back. Mia turned it over, her eyes roving quickly across the words.

I miss you. Sam xx

Mia's eyes stung, tears escaping and starting to slowly slip down her lashes onto her cheeks. *I miss you, too*, she thought, clutching the invitation, her fingers tight around the card. After everything, she still missed him, and as much as she wanted to stay away, to protect herself from being hurt again, she knew the pull to go and see him would be too great to resist.

Mia finally put it down and decided to go take a shower. She needed time to think. She'd jumped to conclusions were Sam was concerned, hated him for something he hadn't done, but the only thing she truly regretted was not hearing him out the day he'd come to see her.

Mia turned the faucet on and started to strip, dumping her clothes in a pile on the tiled floor and stepping into the shower. As she let the water run over her, she shut her eyes and saw Sam. Not the Sam with the cold eyes telling her he didn't have feelings for her, but the Sam who'd stroked her back and smiled down at her in bed, the Sam who'd held her hair back when she was sick, the Sam who'd kissed her so tenderly she'd wondered if it was possible to melt in his arms.

And if there was even a possibility of having that Sam back? Then she'd be stupid not to go and see that for herself, no matter how much the thought terrified her.

Chapter 23

SAM stared into the crowd, hoping to see Mia, but it was the third time he'd looked for her since coming out and he hadn't caught sight of her yet. He talked to the crowd, laughed and asked them questions. He even called a spectator from the crowd and let him assist, enjoying his work the most when he was showing and doing rather than just talking, letting him work with the horse alongside. But eventually he was given the signal that it was time to wrap the show up, and he'd become so involved he'd almost forgotten what he wanted to do.

The camera had been panning across the audience, but when it came back to rest on him, Sam cleared his throat and asked for silence.

"As many of you know, this is my last scheduled show of the year," he said, smiling when everyone clapped. "It's been an absolute honor to meet so many horsemen and women on this tour, and without the support of you all, I wouldn't be standing here tonight. It's been a pleasure sharing my horse training skills with you, and I truly want to thank everyone who's attended an event, bought a book and visited my website."

He waited until everyone was silent, clearing his throat again, feeling a weight on his chest that he thought might be anxiety, even though he'd never experienced anything like it before.

"I invited a very special woman here tonight, although I don't believe she decided to come," he continued. "This woman not only gave me the opportunity to work one of the most difficult horses I've been privileged enough to work with, but she made me realize how important it is, for horses and humans, to move on from the pain we've experienced in the past and start afresh."

There was a murmuring, a low level noise in the crowd, and Sam strained his eyes to see what was going on. He was about to continue, until he saw what the commotion was about.

Mia was standing there, her hair soft and windswept around her shoulders, wearing a pretty sundress and cowboy boots, and looking as uncertain as a brand new foal about to test out their legs for the first time.

"Mia?" he asked, forgetting he was on microphone.

She walked slowly towards him and he faltered before quickly moving to her, closing the distance between them. He took her hands, reaching out for her, but his boots scuffed to a halt in the dirt. She was . . . Sam looked from her face to her stomach, the tight waist of the dress making her look bigger, as if she'd put on weight but just in her . . .

Holy shit.

"You're?" he questioned not even able to get the words out.

"Yeah I am, *Daddy*," she murmured.

Sam couldn't think of a time he'd ever cried in public, and definitely not with every eye from a crowd trained on him, but when Mia's shy, sweet gaze met his, her lips tipping up into the slightest smile he'd ever seen, his eyes filled with tears that were almost impossible to contain. His throat caught when he tried to speak, the words there but not coming out.

"Mia," he said finally, "I don't deserve a second chance, hell, I don't think I deserve any kind of chance, but you once asked me how I felt about you, and I lied. I let my past stop me from, well, treating you right, and just like that horse that everyone thought was a son-of-a-bitch, I was too hurt from the past to move forward."

Her cheeks were flushed, and he couldn't stop glancing down at her stomach, but he forced himself to continue.

"I love you, Mia. I think I have from the moment you put me in my place and showed me you weren't afraid to stand up for what you believed in," he said. "I also know that I'll never, ever meet another woman like you in my lifetime, and I want to ask you if you'll do the honor of becoming my wife?"

The crowd was silent. Sam could feel the rapid beat of his heart. And when Mia tipped her head back to look up at him, he held his breath.

"No," she murmured, her smile still sweet, her eyes still so wide and full of expression.

"No?" he asked, as the crowd sighed and someone standing with the cameraman signaled to cut in the background.

"You're going to have to make it up to me before I say yes, Sam," she said with a laugh. "One apology in front of a crowd who already loves you isn't going to make me fall for you just like that. You have to earn it."

Sam laughed and grabbed her, yanking his mic from his ear and holding her tight as he lifted her off her feet. He dipped his head to kiss her, touching his lips to hers and loving the way she sighed into his mouth, the way her body responded to his, her arms around his neck, her fingers against his hair. Finally he felt happy, that he'd found his way home.

It had taken him way too long to figure out how much he loved Mia, or maybe it had just taken him that long to admit that it was possible for a girl like her to love a messed up son-of-a-bitch like him.

"I love you," he whispered, his nose touching hers as he spoke words just for her for the first time.

"I love you, too," she whispered back. "We both do."

Sam grinned as she moved, tucking against his side as he fist pumped for the crowd before sliding his hand across her stomach and gently resting it there as they walked out.

"You've got some explaining to do," he insisted.

Mia glanced up at him, looking worried. "It's not just me now, it's two of us," she said.

"I can see that," he replied with a wink. "And two is even better than one." He cleared his throat, unable to believe that she was with him, that he hadn't screwed up so bad that he was never going to see her again. "My ex, she hurt me, but I couldn't see how different you were from her, and I will be apologizing to you for that for the rest of my life."

"Okay," she whispered as a lone tear slid down her cheek.

The relief in Mia's gaze told him she felt as vulnerable

as he did, and he stopped to hold her, to wrap her in his arms and stand there for as long as she needed. Because for the first time in a long, long while, Sam suddenly knew that everything was going to be okay.

He had Mia. He had a baby on the way. And he was finally ready to leave his demons in the past where they belonged, instead of letting them haunt his every decision every damn day of his life.

Chapter 24

MIA stretched out beside Sam, smiling when his hand settled over her stomach. It was only slightly rounded, but when she'd pushed her arms up her pajama top had ridden up and exposed her bare skin.

She smiled when he pulled her back against him, nestling into his body. She'd been so tired when they'd arrived home, exhausted from the events of the day, that they'd collapsed into bed and with Sam beside her, she'd fallen fast asleep. Now, she was more than aware of the fact they were in bed together, that he'd spent an entire night with her, yet they both still had their clothes on.

Sam moved down the bed and bent low, pressing a slow, warm kiss to her stomach.

"I can't believe we have a baby growing in here," he murmured, kissing her again.

Mia pushed into him, toes flexed against his leg, arms circling around him. "I know."

He held her, stroking her face, his fingers crossing her cheek. "Were you ever going to tell me?" he asked.

She nodded. "Eventually. I never would have kept your child from you, but until the other day, until I knew . . ."

"Shhh," he whispered, moving closer, his thumb brushing her lips. "I know. I sent us both to hell and back, you don't need to explain anything."

She ran her hands down his back, liking the fact that he was at least bare-chested.

"I'm sorry, for everything," he said, mouth close to hers as he spoke. "You opened up to me and instead of listening to you and admitting how I felt, I screwed up."

"Yeah, you did," she said as the sun slithered across them, the blinds still open from the day before. "You have a lot of making up to do."

He laughed, softly, making her smile. "Yesterday I asked you a question, one you gave the wrong answer to."

"Uh-huh," she answered, leaning in, nose touching his.

"I need to know what I have to do to get you to change your answer," he said.

She laughed, touching her lips to his. "I'm not marrying you just because you knocked me up."

Sam kissed her back, took his time, mouth slow before finally pulling back. "Yeah, that's the only reason I asked you, guess you figured that one out," he said dryly.

She giggled when his fingers slipped down her flesh and dipped into the waistband of her pajama bottoms. "Sam!"

"What, don't tell me we can't mess around until—"

Mia slipped her hand into his boxers, making him groan, laughing when he cupped her butt. "Oh, we can do *plenty* of messing around," she whispered.

She smiled against his lips when he kissed her, loving his touch, happy to be back in his arms again.

"I missed you," she whispered. "I really, really missed you."

His eyes glinted, the first time she'd ever seen him look so vulnerable. "I missed you too," he whispered back. "And you will never, ever have to ask me to stay over with you again. I'm here, for good."

"Good," she replied. "Because I might just never let you go."

Epilogue

SAM leaned back in his chair, beer in hand, daughter tucked into the crook of his arm. He watched Mia as she chatted with Faith, the two of them standing by the table, and wondered what they were laughing about. The two of them got along so well, and he was used to them ganging up on him big time—not that he minded all that much.

"You ever get the feeling that they're talking about us?" Nate asked, pulling Sam from his thoughts.

"Don't go thinking you're that important," Sam joked, "They're probably *never* talking about us."

Nate grinned and held up his beer, clinking it to Sam's before sitting down across from him.

"How's the little lady?" Nate asked, shaking his head. "I still can't believe you're a dad."

"Yeah, that makes two of us," he replied, gazing down at his daughter. She was so beautiful, her little mouth parted in sleep as she snuggled into him, wrapped in a pink blanket as he held her. He'd never felt so protective or in love his entire life—falling for Mia had been one thing, but falling for this little girl was something else.

"You know they have these beds for babies, right? They're called cribs, and you can put them in them to sleep on their own?" Nate teased. "They don't actually have to be attached to you twenty-four seven."

"Whatever," Sam glared at him. "This girl can sleep on her daddy whenever she likes."

Sam looked up when a hand came to rest on his shoulder, followed by long hair brushing his face as Mia bent to look at their daughter. He smiled at her when she turned, kissed her mouth before she had time to pull away.

"What was that for?" she murmured.

"Do I need a reason to kiss the best mama in the world?"

Mia laughed and squeezed into the chair beside him, arm slung around his neck, head dropping to rest on his shoulders.

"I wish I wasn't so tired," she muttered, cuddling tighter into him. "How can one tiny human use up every ounce of my energy? I feel like I haven't slept in days."

He set his beer down so he could scoop Mia against him, holding both of his girls. Sam knew fatherhood had changed him; it had made him fiercely protective and he was always thinking about his daughter, wanting to do anything and everything he could for her. But Mia had changed him, too. She'd made him a better man. She'd made him want to fight, to open up and be the man she needed him to be, the man he wanted to be for her.

Sophia wriggled in his arms and he looked down at her as one fist pushed out from the blanket and stretched up, her little mouth open as she wriggled. In just three months, he'd become so besotted with her that he couldn't ever imagine life without her.

"You two lovebirds ready to have dinner yet?" Nate asked with a laugh. "Or are you just going to stare at your offspring all night and make cute baby faces back at her?"

Sam look up and saw Faith sitting on Nate's knee, his hand on her thigh as she leaned back into him. The twins were inside playing, and the food was all set out on the table outside, and his sister and brother-in-law were laughing. Nate could tease him all he liked, but he'd seen the way he was with his girls and he was just as besotted.

"Yeah, we're ready," Sam said, nodding to Mia. "Would you get mine, darlin'? I don't want to disturb Sophia."

Mia smiled, kissing him before pushing off. She was wearing a sundress and boots, like she had the day he'd called her into the ring and declared his feelings for her, only this time she was wearing a diamond on her finger and a smile on her face as big as Texas. It had been their little secret for a couple of days, but keeping his mouth shut about it since they'd arrived today had been almost impossible.

"I'm liking this trade-off," Mia said with a wink. "Me serving you in exchange for daddy daycare duty."

"Mia!" Faith suddenly gasped, making them all look up. "What?"

"How did I not notice that huge rock before? Mia, it's huge! When did this happen?"

Sam grinned when Nate made a face at him. He mouthed something but Sam had no idea what he was saying and just shrugged.

"We wanted to tell you tonight," Mia said, sporting the cutest pink blush on her cheeks that Sam had ever seen. "In person, rather than over the phone."

"She finally said yes," Sam joked, standing with little Sophia still tucked in his arm. "We came over tonight so my sister and best man would be the first in the know."

"Best man?" Nate asked, one eyebrow arched as he stared back at him.

"The one and only," Sam said.

Faith squealed and threw her arms around Mia, and both women laughed and talked and giggled like little girls. Nate waited until Mia and Faith had moved away, before coming over and holding out his hand. Sam clasped it and then Nate pulled him in for a one-armed hug.

"I'm so damn proud of you," Nate said, stepping back and shaking his head. "Man, what happened to the bachelors, huh?"

"Hey, it's when we both start driving minivans that we have to worry," Sam joked.

But he saw the look on Nate's face, knew him well enough to see how genuinely happy he was for him. They'd been through a lot together, and being with Mia and seeing Faith with his best friend, it all made sense now. The universe had thrown a lot at him, but everything had worked out well in the end.

Sophia cried then and he smiled down at her, knowing Mia would be at his side within seconds as he rocked her in his arms and tried his best to comfort her.

"Shhh," he soothed, jiggling her and passing her over to Mia when she appeared beside him and held out her arms. He watched them both, the mother of his child and his little girl. He'd been so close to walking away from Mia forever, and he was so damn pleased he'd come to his senses. He had Nate to thank for that, and his sister. They'd been hard on him but he'd deserved it.

Sam went and got their diaper bag, knowing Sophia would be hungry and probably wet. Mia settled into the chair he'd been in earlier and he stood for a minute, wondering how he'd gotten so lucky as he watched her feed their daughter, watched a little hand rest on her mother's breast, and Mia whisper down to her as she nursed.

"It feels good, doesn't it?" Nate asked.

Sam grinned. "Does it ever." He'd experienced highs in his career, he'd listened to applause from crowds of people who'd traveled from all over to see him work, but it wasn't a patch on the way he felt right now.

Coming soon. . .

Look for the next River Ranch novel
by Soraya Lane

All Night
With the Cowboy

Available in June 2018 from
St. Martin's Paperbacks